SEVEN HOUSES IN FRANCE

Also by Bernardo Atxaga

OBABAKOAK
THE LONE MAN
THE LONE WOMAN
TWO BROTHERS
THE ACCORDIONIST'S SON

Bernardo Atxaga

SEVEN HOUSES IN FRANCE

Translated from the Spanish by
Margaret Jull Costa

HARVILL SECKER

LONDON

Published by Harvill Secker 2011

2 4 6 8 10 9 7 5 3 1

First published in Basque with the title *Zazpi etxe Frantzian*
in 2009 by Pamiela, Navarra

First published in Spanish with the title *Siete Casas en Francia*
(translated by Asun Garikano and Bernardo Atxaga)
in 2009 by Alfaguara, Madrid

First published in Great Britain in 2011 by
HARVILL SECKER
Random House
20 Vauxhall Bridge Road
London SW1V 2SA
www.randomhouse.co.uk

Addresses for companies within The Random House Group Limited can be found at:
www.randomhouse.co.uk/offices.htm

The Random House Group Limited Reg. No. 954009

A CIP catalogue record for this book is available from the British Library

ISBN 9781846554476

The publication of this work has been made possible through a subsidy received from the
Directorate General for Books, Archives and Libraries of the Spanish Ministry of Culture.

The Random House Group Limited supports The Forest Stewardship Council (FSC®),
the leading international forest certification organisation. Our books carrying the FSC
label are printed on FSC® certified paper. FSC is the only forest certification scheme
endorsed by the leading environmental organisations, including Greenpeace. Our paper
procurement policy can be found at www.randomhouse.co.uk/environment

Typeset in Perpetua by Palimpsest Book Production Limited, Falkirk, Stirlingshire
Printed and bound in Great Britain by Clays Ltd, St Ives PLC

SEVEN HOUSES IN FRANCE

I

CHRYSOSTOME LIÈGE SIGNED A CONTRACT TO SERVE IN KING Léopold's Force Publique at the beginning of 1903 and reached his posting in the Congo in August of the same year, having travelled by packet-boat from Antwerp to Matadi, by train as far as Léopoldville, and then, finally, on a small steamship, the *Princesse Clémentine*, to the garrison of Yangambi. It was not exactly the last outpost of civilisation because, as they said in the Force Publique, that honour belonged to Kisangani, some one hundred and twenty miles further upstream, but it was certainly a very long way from anywhere anyone had heard of.

The *Princesse Clémentine* docked at a wooden platform on the beach that served as a jetty. Chrysostome was met by a soldier, who advanced very slowly towards him. He was a young man and, at about six foot five, almost a head taller than him.

'Chrysostome Liège?' he asked.

The new arrival replied tersely: 'Yes.'

'I'm Donatien, Captain Lalande Biran's orderly,' said the officer. Then he pointed to the half-empty canvas bag

Chrysostome was carrying and asked in a more relaxed tone: 'Is that all your luggage?'

Chrysostome replied equally tersely, this time in the negative.

Together they walked back towards the village, and Donatien gave him a brief rundown on the garrison. In Yangambi there was a total of seventeen white officers, twenty black non-commissioned officers, and one hundred and fifty *askaris* – volunteer black soldiers – all of whom were under the command of Captain Lalande Biran, a highly cultivated man, well known in Belgium as a poet, an excellent soldier, and the most gifted of all the officers who had passed through Yangambi.

'The Captain likes things done properly,' said Donatien. 'That's why he's prepared a reception committee for you on the firing range. Don't worry, Chrysostome, you'll soon feel at home in Yangambi, and the days will fly by.'

Donatien spoke very quickly, in bursts, running his words together. He said '*tutrouveratrebienci*' when he should have said '*tu te trouveras très bien ici*'. Sometimes, his Adam's apple moved up and down as if his salivary glands were working overtime and producing too much saliva for him to swallow.

'It's a shame they didn't build the village a bit closer to the river, though!' he said when they had gone some two hundred yards. 'Not the Captain's idea, of course. That was decided by the first officers who came to the region. The Captain has only been here for five years, same as me. I've been his orderly from the start. He really values me. He wouldn't want anyone else.'

They walked up the slope, stepping on the planks laid across the path to keep them from muddying their boots.

When they reached the top of the hill, Donatien paused to get his breath back, and Chrysostome, like an explorer trying to orient himself, shaded his eyes with one hand and gazed around him. Ahead lay the first huts and a few European-style houses, all of which were surrounded by a palisade; lush palm trees grew on either side, and beyond was the imposing sight of the River Congo and a seemingly endless expanse of jungle.

The Congo was a powerful river. It cut straight through the jungle, although the vegetation, as if it continued to grow beneath the water, sprouted up again in the middle of the river in the form of small islands thick with trees and undergrowth. The *Princesse Clémentine*, the steamship that had brought Chrysostome, was still moored at the jetty. Two men were unloading the luggage and another two were carrying it to a building situated on the beach itself.

'That's the Club Royal, the officers' mess,' said Donatien. 'It is, in my opinion, the best place in Yangambi. I'm in charge of the storeroom there. My biggest worry are the mice. It's the same in every storeroom in the Congo, but they don't get their way in Yangambi. I finish them off before they can so much as take one bite of the sugar or the biscuits.'

Chrysostome appeared to have heard none of this and was still gazing down on the jungle. Several columns of smoke rose up here and there among the trees. The inhabitants of the villages or *mugini* were doubtless preparing their meal.

'How many savages live there?' he asked.

'Oh, thousands and thousands of them, all belonging to different tribes. But they don't often attack. Not, at least, at the moment,' answered Donatien.

'Do all those trees produce rubber?' asked Chrysostome.

'Not all of them, but many do. Around the Lomami, though, it's more mahogany than rubber.'

He pointed to the right. About half a mile away, you could see the line of another river – the Lomami. Its waters joined those of the Congo, slowing the latter's flow and creating the pool that served as a harbour opposite the beach.

'The rebels control the whole of this part of the Lomami. But, like I say, lately, they've been pretty quiet. Of course, as soon as they show any signs of activity, Lieutenant Van Thiegel is quick to put them down. He's not as intelligent as Captain Lalande Biran, but he's completely fearless. They say that even the lions shit themselves when they see him.'

Donatien set off again, laughing loudly to show that his words had been intended as a joke. His remark drew no response from Chrysostome, however, and so as they went through the palisade to the square – the Place du Grand Palmier – Donatien decided to say nothing more and to refrain from explaining which of the buildings were the residences of Lalande Biran and Van Thiegel and which was Yangambi's Government House; nor did he indicate the area or hut where Chrysostome would be living from then on. It was tedious trying to strike up a conversation with a tongue-tied novice.

Leaving the palisade behind them, they walked another five hundred or so yards to the firing range. When they arrived, they found the whole garrison waiting for them: the white officers in the front row, smiling, hands behind their backs; the black non-commissioned officers in the second row, also smiling, but with hands folded over their chests; and a little way behind them, divided into five companies, stood the *askaris*, the soldiers recruited from Zanzibar and from among the cannibals in northern Congo; they were standing to attention, left arms rigidly by their sides and right arms holding rifles. Opposite them, next to a dais, at the top of a flagstaff, fluttered the blue flag of the Force Publique with its single yellow star.

One of the white officers in the front row stepped forward.

'That's Captain Lalande Biran,' whispered Donatien.

He was a very handsome man, with blue eyes flecked with gold. He saluted Chrysostome, then ordered him to step onto the dais so that everyone could see him.

It was a ceremony in which military humour prevailed. Captain Lalande Biran began by presenting Chrysostome with the blue uniform and red fez of the *askaris* instead of an officer's pale brown uniform and white hat, a joke which caused everyone present on the firing range to titter, particularly his soon-to-be comrades. Frowning and resisting the desire of the Captain, the other officers and the NCOs to have their bit of fun, Chrysostome solemnly stuffed the trousers and shirt into his canvas bag and donned the red fez.

Large storm clouds were gathering. From one small clear patch of sky the sun was beating down.

'And here is your rifle!' said the Captain, handing him an eighteenth-century, barrel-loading musket, a hulking great thing, weighing at least twenty pounds. More tittering. 'It's loaded. The target's over there. Let's see what you can do.'

At the far end of the firing range, high up in a tree, a monkey appeared to be watching the ceremony with great interest. It was straight ahead, about a hundred yards away. That was the target.

The shot startled all the birds round about. The monkey fell to the ground like a stone.

'Well, if you can hit the target with that great thing, I can't wait to see what you'll do with a really good rifle!' exclaimed the Captain, his eyes still fixed on the place where the monkey had been.

Above the trees, the birds frightened by the shot were still wheeling around looking for somewhere else to perch. Any clear patches of sky were growing ever fewer, and clouds were covering the sun. A heavy rain shower was imminent. It was best not to prolong matters.

'The new soldier deserves a prize, Cocó,' said the Captain, addressing the man at the far end of the line of white officers.

Cocó was a robust, broad-shouldered fellow. He took a few long strides and planted himself in front of Chrysostome.

'I'm Lieutenant Richard Van Thiegel, but everyone calls me Cocó,' he said, handing him a rifle. Compared with the musket, it seemed positively delicate. 'For you, *légionnaire*,' he added. He had belonged to the French Foreign Legion before enlisting in the Force Publique, and, to use a common metaphor, his heart was still there. As far as he was concerned, all his comrades were legionnaires.

Chrysostome continued to frown, as if he found the jokes and the ceremony disagreeable. This wasn't because he was annoyed, however, but because he was studying every detail of the weapon he had been given. It was a real marvel. A twelve-shot, breech-loading Albini-Braendlin. When he held it in the firing position, the butt fitted snugly into his shoulder.

'There are twelve cartridges inside. You can check, if you like,' said Van Thiegel.

Chrysostome removed the chamber and counted the cartridges one by one.

'There are only eleven,' he said, replacing the chamber. The sounds the rifle made were equally marvellous. Clean and precise.

Lalande Biran was watching him intently. This new arrival was clearly no ordinary soldier. He had never known any other 'novice' at a welcome ceremony to check the number of cartridges. Even veterans, who had served in other armies, would never dare to doubt a superior officer's word.

'When are you going to give us a smile?' asked Van Thiegel reproachfully, handing him the missing cartridge. Chrysostome's expression remained unchanged as he weighed the cartridge in his hand as though trying to determine its calibre.

Lalande Biran noticed a strip of blue ribbon round the soldier's neck.

'What's that?' he asked.

'A medal of Our Lady, sir,' replied Chrysostome, raising his eyes for a moment to glance at the Captain, before turning his attention back to the rifle and the cartridges.

'Are you from a village in the provinces?' asked the Captain. He didn't run his words together like Donatien, but pronounced them precisely, modulating his voice: '*Vous venez d'une ville de province?*'

'I was born in the village of Britancourt, sir,' replied Chrysostome. He had a country accent.

'We would be much better Catholics if we had been born

in Britancourt, Cocó,' Lalande Biran said to Van Thiegel. He was from Brussels and the Lieutenant from Antwerp.

Chrysostome pulled back the bolt and removed the chamber. He inserted the twelfth cartridge, closed the chamber, put the rifle to his shoulder, and pointed at a monkey about two hundred yards away, then at the leaf of a tree further off, then he lowered the rifle and asked: 'How far can the bullet travel?'

'About three thousand yards or more,' said Van Thiegel.

On the horizon, the sky had turned black and was falling like a curtain over the jungle; closer to, the rounded clouds resembled the scattered beads of a necklace. Over Yangambi, the sky was still blue, but it was only a matter of time. Another quarter of an hour and it would start to rain.

'Come on, Cocó, let's go and have a drink. I don't want to get wet,' said Lalande Biran.

The Lieutenant gestured to the chief of the black NCOs, who, in turn, gestured to an *askari*. The blue flag of the Force Publique with its single yellow star was immediately lowered. The welcome ceremony was over.

Beyond the firing range lay an untidy collection of huts, cabins, chicken runs, vegetable patches and grain stores; and suddenly, noisy groups of *askaris* and black NCOs set off in that direction, laughing and joking, as if the lowering of the flag had lifted their hearts, prompting them to go and join their wives and children. In many of the huts, fires had been lit and meat and fish were being cooked. The smoke from those fires and, above all, from the bonfires lit to keep off the insects bothering the cattle, drifted over the whole area and added to the festive atmosphere.

In the European zone, however, such good cheer was notable by its absence. The white officers who had walked over to the Place du Grand Palmier – seventeen of them, not counting the new arrival, Chrysostome – looked as serious and tongue-tied as him, and as though they had nothing better to do than wait for the rain to start.

Opposite Government House, African servants were moving about among the different groups, serving glasses of Veuve Clicquot champagne. The officers accepted them carelessly and, just as carelessly, raised them to their lips, not even bothering to say 'Good health'. It was clear that the military humour Lalande Biran had attempted to inject into the welcome ceremony had cheered no one. This was due entirely to Chrysostome's refusal to collaborate.

Richardson was the third highest-ranking officer and, at over sixty, the oldest member of the Yangambi garrison. Seated in a rocking chair at the door of Government House, he reminded Lalande Biran and Van Thiegel of the various welcome ceremonies he had attended throughout his long career. There had been many amusing incidents; for example, it still made him laugh to think of young Lopes' antics with the musket before he eventually fired it. But no two people were alike, and some had no sense of humour at all.

'Today's ceremony was the most boring ever. This Chrysostome fellow is as miserable as a mandrill,' he declared.

The man in question was approaching, holding his rifle in one hand and his canvas bag in the other. Everyone fell silent. Lieutenant Van Thiegel strode over to him.

'Biran,' he reported, after a brief exchange with Chrysostome, 'our new colleague wishes to retire to his hut to rest. I don't know whether I should allow him to do so or not. Traditionally, he should come down to the club and buy a round of drinks for all the officers.'

'Tell me, Chrysostome, are you in the habit of drinking?' asked the Captain.

Chrysostome replied in the negative.

'And what about gambling, do you like that?'

Chrysostome again said 'No'.

Lalande Biran turned to his two colleagues:

'I thought as much, gentlemen. Our new comrade is something of a *rara avis*.'

Van Thiegel grabbed Chrysostome's arm.

'Did you understand what the Captain said? He means that you're a rare bird and that we're going to have to do all your drinking for you.'

Richardson laughed loudly, but no one else joined in. Lalande Biran pointed to Chrysostome's rifle.

'Even if it gets wet, it will still fire, you know. It's not like a musket.'

'Yes, Captain.'

As the name of the square would suggest, an enormous palm tree stood in the centre of the Place du Grand Palmier, and scattered around it were a few white benches that would not have looked out of place in a Paris park. Donatien, Lopes and a few other young officers were standing chatting near one of them.

'Ask Donatien to show you to your hut,' said Lalande Biran, looking at Chrysostome with his gold-flecked blue eyes — *d'or et d'azur*. 'If you want to stay there, do so, but tomorrow morning I want to see you in the jungle. We have work to do in the rubber plantation. Is that clear, Chrysostome? Reveille is at seven.'

This time Chrysostome replied vehemently: 'Yes, Captain!'

Lalande Biran remained silent until Chrysostome and Donatien had left the square. Then he took a glass of Veuve Clicquot from a tray proffered by a servant and set out his views on the new arrival to Van Thiegel and Richardson.

'He'll be a good soldier, possibly an excellent one. You saw what he did with the musket. He shot a monkey from a hundred yards off. He'll make a good guard for the rubber-tappers.'

It started to rain, and the three men went into Government House to finish their drinks in the vestibule.

'Well, if he does turn out to be a good soldier, that will be wonderful. We'll all be very pleased indeed,' said Richardson.

He did not mean what he said. His long years in the Congo had taught him to value cheerful companions, friends who enjoyed drinking and gambling. He didn't care if they made mediocre soldiers.

From the window, Richardson could see the rain, the heavy sky, the blackened trunks of mahogany and teak, the water pouring from the leaves of the palm trees, and the mud forming in the square. His heart told him he was right. Better a happy soldier than a disciplined one.

The officers in the Place du Grand Palmier ran for shelter. A few headed towards the beach and the Club Royal, the cosiest place to be in the rainy season.

Van Thiegel put his empty glass down on a table and walked towards the door, intending to join the other officers at the club.

'He may be a good soldier,' he said, 'but time will tell. As you know, Biran, it's one thing to shoot a monkey and quite another to track down one of those rebels hiding in the jungle. You need more than good marksmanship for that.'

Lalande Biran's gold-flecked eyes smiled. 'He'll be a good soldier, Cocó, I'm sure of it. Do you want to bet on it?'

'Ten francs, Captain. As you know, that's the maximum permitted in Yangambi.'

Van Thiegel had been campaigning for some time for the gambling rules at the garrison to be relaxed to allow them to place bets larger than ten francs. He was convinced that the atmosphere in the Club Royal would be much improved if the limit was raised to one hundred francs, a move that would please both losers and winners. Like drink, gambling – real gambling – helped you forget.

'I've no idea whether he'll be a good soldier or a bad one, but he'll certainly be a miserable one. As miserable as a mandrill. I'll bet you ten francs on that!'

And the three men all laughed with military good humour.

II

THE TASK ASSIGNED TO CHRYSOSTOME OF GUARDING THE
workers was not an easy one, because the rubber-tappers,
all native to the area, wandered about in the jungle at will
and often made use of their superior knowledge of the
terrain to escape. Nevertheless, to use the words of Captain
Lalande Biran, the new arrival immediately proved himself
to be another Chiron – the centaur who loved hunting
– or perhaps an improved version of Chiron, given that
Chrysostome was armed not with a bow and arrow, but
with an Albini-Braendlin rifle. Very few workers tried to
escape on his watch, and those who did never got very far.
With his agility, youth and slight physique, Chrysostome
could make his way through even the densest jungle and his
aim never faltered. Lalande Biran had more than enough
reason to be pleased that such a remarkable officer should
have been posted to Yangambi.

'What he did with the musket on that first day was no
fluke,' he told the other officers during an after-dinner
conversation. 'He's an excellent shot, a real champion. I
doubt there's a better shot in the whole Upper Congo, or

indeed in the whole country. He has, I have to say, exceeded all my hopes.'

There were other notable marksmen in Yangambi, among them young Lopes and Lieutenant Van Thiegel, but Chrysostome achieved with one bullet what they could only have achieved with three or more.

Chrysostome's reputation soon reached the *mugini* in the region, as if a hundred drums had spread the news of his marksmanship throughout the dark jungle and along the damp shores of the river Congo and the river Lomami, and from then on, the workers under his supervision lost all desire to escape and devoted themselves to the collection of rubber with a determination and a will that made them run from tree to tree and from liana to liana even when they had already fulfilled the minimum quota set for each group by King Léopold. Two months passed, and Captain Lalande Biran – reminded once more of Chiron the centaur huntsman and of how he had taught the other demigods and heroes to hunt – appointed Chrysostome shooting instructor, encouraging the *askaris* and the black NCOs to go to Chrysostome in order to learn how to get the best out of their rifles.

One Sunday morning, Biran repeated this advice in a speech intended for the white officers:

'A soldier, my friends, must not only be brave in the face of the enemy, he must be equally brave when facing up to himself. After all, it's not so very hard to shout "Attack!" when confronted by the enemy, it's far harder to struggle with one's own pride. Even Napoleon, having triumphed at the battle of Borodino, which cost the lives of 50,000 Russian and 30,000 French soldiers, was capable of recognising his mistake, saying: "I cannot be that good a general, for if I were, the sacrifice of a mere 20,000 heroes should have been enough to gain victory." It was this humility that made Napoleon great, as well, of course, as his many victories at Borodino, Marengo and elsewhere. Today, I want to encourage you to act in the same spirit. I know it wounds your pride to ask a mere novice for advice on how to handle the Albini-Braendlin, but fight against that feeling!'

On each of the following days, before sunset and once the work in the rubber plantation and the marches through the jungle were over, the firing range at Yangambi was the scene of some unusual activity. The *askaris* in their red fezes, the black NCOs, and the white officers all gathered round Chrysostome, who advised each of his pupils, one by one, on the correct position of arm, neck and foot. Lalande Biran, Van Thiegel and Richardson, the chiefs of Yangambi, watched the classes from a platform in the firing range. Presiding over the scene was the blue flag of the Force Publique with its single yellow star.

These were days of rare intensity and harmony, worthy, almost, of the age of Napoleon, but, after a week, the number of pupils had dwindled by half, then there were only fifty, then twenty. After a month, there was no one left. The shooting classes had come to an end.

'It's not your fault,' said Donatien, looking over Chrysostome's head at the empty firing range. 'The Captain wants us all to be like Napoleon, but that's not easy. If we had a woman like Josephine waiting for us in bed, we might manage it, but we, alas, live in Yangambi.'

This was Donatien's third or fourth attempt to get a smile out of Chrysostome – in vain. He received only this laconic reply:

'It doesn't matter. Some are born good marksmen and some aren't. Like everything else, it's in God's hands.'

Carrying his rifle, Chrysostome set off briskly towards the Place du Grand Palmier. Donatien caught up with him and, deciding to change the subject, began instead to talk about Christmas. He couldn't wait, he said. Captain Lalande Biran spared no effort in ensuring that his men were happy at such a special time of year. He laid on veritable banquets at which one could eat one's fill of goat's meat and the finest fish from the river, and in the card games at the Club, you could even lay bets of up to one hundred francs, rather than the usual ten. The best thing, though, was that, from then on, it rained much less and there was almost no mud. That's why he liked Christmas and New Year. Plus it was the only time he ever received a letter.

They entered the palisade and the Place du Grand Palmier. Donatien pointed to Government House: 'The Captain receives letters from Paris or Brussels almost every week. I don't. I only get them at Christmas. Although Richardson has it worse. No one ever writes to Richardson, not even at Christmas.'

There was a set of pigeon-holes for the officers' correspondence at the entrance to the Club Royal, and on some weeks, Donatien had seen a letter for Chrysostome there, always from Britancourt and always, to judge by the writing, from the same person. The problem was that the person only put the name of the village in the return address and so there was no way of knowing who had sent it, his mother, his girlfriend, a friend. Donatien wanted to know.

Chrysostome failed to take the bait, saying: 'Christmas Day is a great day. A celebration of the birth of Jesus, who was conceived by Our Lady, the Virgin Mary and born in Bethlehem.'

He showed Donatien the medal on its blue ribbon, but said nothing about the family or friends he had left behind in Britancourt.

It was evening, and the palm trees lining the road that led down to the river were like drawings made in India ink; the sky was a sheet of greenish glass, the river Congo was the pressed skin of a snake, and the Lomami, a silver rope. On the beach by the river, a group of officers were enjoying a last cigarette before supper and the smoke from the club chimneys carried on it the smell of grilled fish.

III

IN YANGAMBI, IT WAS SAID THAT THE CARTRIDGES FOR THE Albini-Braendlin rifle were the most prized jewels in Africa, and that on the boats going up and down the river Congo, you were more likely to come across a diamond than a cartridge. It was also said, with less exaggeration, that King Léopold himself kept a count of the cartridges and required his representatives in Léopoldville to justify the use of each and every one, stating when, where and how it had been used. And so, after the Christmas meal, when Captain Lalande Biran named Chrysostome 'Soldier of the Year' and presented him with the prize of a box of one hundred cartridges, the seventeen white officers and ten African servants waiting on them could not suppress a sigh – of envy in some cases and astonishment in others.

'Gentlemen, I give you the Hero of the Year!' exclaimed Lalande Biran, inviting Chrysostome to take the floor.

'I started out with twelve cartridges,' said Chrysostome. 'And before coming here tonight, I had only four left. Now I have one hundred and four.'

Not a muscle in his face moved, and instead of looking

at his comrades or at the beautiful, beaming serving-woman standing next to him, he was gazing into the distance, at the river and the jungle.

Van Thiegel whispered to Lalande Biran: 'I don't know why you bother trying to please him, the man wants nothing whatever to do with us.'

Chrysostome's attitude was not, however, due to arrogance or to feelings of scorn or indifference for his colleagues. At least, not entirely. The truth is that, like many heroes, like the great Achilles himself, Chrysostome had a weak point that prevented him from enjoying his enviable position and explained the tense look on his face. Put briefly and plainly, Chrysostome harboured a terrible fear. It wasn't the fear of the Congolese rebels felt by the other officers in the Force Publique, nor a fear of lions, cheetahs, crocodiles or black mambas. Nor was he a man easily cowed by natural dangers, as he had demonstrated when they had gone to offer military aid to the post at Kisangani, where he had been seen standing at the very edge of the Stanley Falls, serenely firing at the enemy, as if God himself were whispering in his ear: 'Fire away, Chrysostome. No poisoned arrow will harm you. You will, of course, have to die some day, but not here.'

Put him near a woman, though, and all that determination and energy melted away. There lay his Achilles heel.

His fear stemmed from an incident that had occurred when he was twelve years old. One day, while playing with friends on the outskirts of the village of Britancourt, he saw a man emerge from the dark mouth of a cave. At first, Chrysostome took the figure for a resurrected corpse, and thought that the suppurating wounds on the man's face came from having been dead for some time; then, influenced by one of his companions, he thought it must be Jesus himself, in emulation of the recent apparition of the Virgin Mary at Lourdes. Before he was able to reach any conclusion, however, the man started shouting: 'I still belong to the land of the living, that is my greatest sorrow. If only God would take me to him!'

Chrysostome and his friends asked what had happened to him.

'I sinned against the sixth commandment,' answered the man. 'I was a handsome, blue-eyed man and had my pick of the women, but in the end, they proved to be my undoing.'

His words echoed in the mouth of the cave, and the pestilent stench of his body wafted to them on the breeze.

Later on, at home, he learned that the man in the cave was suffering from an illness called syphilis, and from that moment on, Chrysostome ceased to think of women as mirror images of his mother, still less of the Virgin Mary, and thought of them instead only as the creatures responsible for the unfortunate fate met by that stinking, ulcer-ridden man. The months passed, and the parish priest placed around Chrysostome's neck a blue ribbon, the very one he was wearing when he arrived in Yangambi. The ribbon represented his purity of heart, a purity as intense as his fear of women.

In normal circumstances, his fear – or his purity of heart – would have worked in his favour in Yangambi, because it saved him from having to go into the jungle in search of women, as the other officers did, and thus from contracting syphilis or some other contagious disease. That same purity should have benefited other aspects of his life, as well as the sexual, leaving him, for example, with plenty of free time; instead, it began to work against him as soon as he became 'Soldier of the Year' and the privileged recipient of one hundred cartridges – one hundred golden jewels – that he kept stored away in his hut. We are none of us safe when surrounded by the envious, by snakes, especially when, as with Achilles, we have a vulnerable heel.

Most of the officers in Yangambi felt jealous of Chrysostome's success. They suspected it would not be his last triumph, that there would be more prizes, more cartridges to be collected, and that, given the attitude of Captain Lalande Biran, who appeared to have a particularly soft spot for him, they would all end up in the hands of that novice. And this was not an alluring prospect. It was depressing having to live alongside a person who was worth more than one hundred cartridges; it was like seeing oneself in a mirror that reflected back an image of one's own military mediocrity.

Nor was this purely a matter of sentiment. There was an important practical aspect to it as well. If Chrysostome were to come across a gorilla in the jungle, for example, he could happily shoot it, whereas the other officers could not. If they were to use a cartridge to kill the gorilla, that would mean having to use the butt of their rifle or their machete as a way of subduing or breaking any uncooperative workers and, worse still, being obliged to tell a lie and report that the missing bullet – which was not theirs, but the property of King Léopold – had remained lodged in the body of the rubber-tapper in question. Fortunately, the high-ups in Léopoldville did not demand to see the whole corpse as proof, being satisfied with a hand or even a finger, small objects which, once smoked, could safely be sent in the post in an ordinary envelope. But it was exasperating having to hold back like that and to lie. It meant that not even the oldest and most experienced soldiers in the Force Publique could go hunting! Their impure hearts allowed them other pleasures – women, children, etc. – but for the officers of the Force Publique, hunting was a necessity. And they could not indulge that need, whereas Chrysostome could.

The problem grew worse with time, and this was partly Chrysostome's fault. Far from giving or even lending a cartridge to anyone who needed it, he began using them as currency, getting his colleague Lopes, for example, to hand over a gold chain bearing a medal of Our Lady in exchange for twelve cartridges. This precious, pious object immediately took its place alongside the blue ribbon. To make matters worse, he did not always treat Lieutenant Van Thiegel, Cocó, with the necessary tact.

One Sunday, when the palm wine had been flowing freely, the Lieutenant had the idea of organising a shooting match to decide who among the officers deserved the title of the William Tell of Yangambi. He would provide the cartridges, so no one need worry about that.

'And *I* will win,' he boasted to the other officers.

He sounded as if he meant it. Drink brought out the braggart in him and, to use a metaphor, it split his mind in two. On that day, the two halves were most unequal. In the first half, Chrysostome's achievements were reduced to a minimum, in the second, his own were enlarged and multiplied, especially those relating to his time as a legionnaire.

A few children were brought from a nearby *mugini*, and

the competition began with more than a dozen participants prepared to shoot at the apples that were placed on each child's head. Not wanting to disappoint the Lieutenant, Lopes and the other officers did not try very hard, but Chrysostome was incapable of pretence and he played fairly and honestly, treating the second highest-ranking officer in Yangambi as if he were just another soldier. He split open five apples with five bullets, while the Lieutenant managed only two.

At first, the Lieutenant seemed to admit defeat in the sporting spirit that often characterises soldiers, and he joked that, as a left-hander, he was somewhat handicapped when it came to shooting. He had been told this often, especially during his days as a legionnaire, but had never really understood until now just how much of a handicap it was.

At that point, Chrysostome could have humoured him, but again he chose to play fair, and to be perhaps too scrupulously honest, and before the Lieutenant had even finished speaking – using his words to dig himself a hole in which to hide his embarrassment – Chrysostome signalled to the African servants to provide him with another target, another boy with an apple on his head, and this time he fired left-handed. The boy swayed slightly, but Chrysostome still managed to split the apple in two.

'Now I've definitely run out of excuses,' said the Lieutenant.

Chrysostome then made another mistake: he missed the opportunity to remain silent. It would have been easy enough for a man like him to have said nothing, for he rarely uttered more than twenty-five words a day. Instead he chose that moment to speak:

'Don't worry, Lieutenant. You shoot pretty well for a man your age.'

Ah, the unwitting cruelty of youth! If he had at least said, 'Don't worry, *Cocó*', those words could have been interpreted as a remark made to a friend or even as a joke, but that 'Don't worry, *Lieutenant*' left no room for doubt. And then he had the impudence to judge him, saying that he shot *pretty* well!

It was a humiliation; and a feeling of resentment, a sediment of hatred, lodged in one of the two halves of the Lieutenant's mind. As for Chrysostome, it did not even occur to him that this second title – the William Tell of Yangambi – might cause him problems, and he got into the habit of swaggering around with the top three or four buttons of his shirt undone, to show off his blue ribbon and the gold chain. The other officers interpreted this as mere boastfulness, as if he were saying: 'I may be one of the smaller men in Yangambi as regards physical stature and one of the youngest too, but with my Albini-Braendlin rifle, I'm bigger than all of you.'

The resentment and hatred that now lay in Lieutenant Van Thiegel's heart began to spread throughout Yangambi.

A few weeks later, Chrysostome had turned up, carrying on his shoulders something that looked, from a distance, like a piece of timber. He passed the huts inhabited by the *askaris* and the black NCOs, crossed the firing range, walked as far as the centre of the Place du Grand Palmier, and then, instead of continuing on to his hut, he sat down on one of the white benches at the foot of the palm tree. He was clearly eager to show off what he had brought.

The officers in the square gathered round and were joined by some twenty or so *askaris*, as well as by some of the servants, male and female, who were working in the slaughterhouse or the grainstores. They saw then that the object was a hunting trophy: the horn of a black rhinoceros.

'I didn't want to shoot him straight between the eyes because I was afraid I might damage the horn,' he explained to the curious onlookers. 'That's why I had to use three cartridges.'

Everyone stared at the horn. There wasn't a mark on it. Then all eyes turned to Chrysostome. He had the top three buttons of his shirt undone, and the blue ribbon and Lopes' gold chain glittered on his chest. His firm, hairless skin gleamed with sweat.

'He's not a bad hunter for a poofter,' someone muttered, and those who heard him stored away that word 'poofter', like someone saving a sweet for later. The precise word he used in French was *pédé*.

It was only a few hours before everyone in Yangambi knew that Chrysostome had killed a rhinoceros, and Captain Lalande Biran summoned him to Government House and gave him a silver watch in exchange for the horn. Everyone was in agreement: the rhinoceros was a rare animal in that part of Upper Congo, as well as being a very difficult creature to hunt. The fact that one man had been able to do so on his own was quite extraordinary. For many days, this was the sole topic of conversation in the Club Royal.

And yet coiled beneath all these conversations, like a baby black mamba beneath the dry leaves on the jungle floor, was that word 'poofter'. It soon reached every corner of Yangambi, and not an evening passed in the Club Royal without someone mentioning it at one of the tables. One night, Van Thiegel went further, took a step forward:

'I don't know what it is with Chrysostome,' he said in the middle of a game of cards, 'but he seems to positively avoid the company of women.'

Chrysostome was not in the club at the time, and Van Thiegel did not bother to lower his voice when he made the remark. He found it strange that a man in peak physical condition should have no contact whatsoever with women, especially in a place where, as Richardson used to say, even the feeblest could find fodder for his cannon. His fellow players sniggered, but did not pursue the comment. They were more cautious than the Lieutenant. They were thinking about Chrysostome's perfect marksmanship and his large supply of cartridges and preferred to keep a low profile.

However, despite these fears and precautions, the die was cast. Like the young of the black mamba, which matures very slowly inside its egg, the word 'poofter' would need, firstly, a few months to grow and for its poison to infuse, and, secondly, the right circumstances in which to strike, for strike it would. The snake – the word – would be hurled at Chrysostome with the firm intention of destroying him.

The spring of 1904 was followed by the summer, a particularly beautiful summer that brought a round sun to the south of France, to the whole of the Riviera, to the Côte d'Azur, and, more to the point, to the small peninsula of St-Jean-Cap-Ferrat. Paradoxically, the circumstances that were about to intervene in Chrysostome's destiny and come to fruition in Africa, in the darkness of the jungle, began to take shape there, in one of the centres of the world, in one of the most luminous, glittering, marvellous places of the Belle Epoque.

IV

IN THE EARLY SUMMER OF 1904, THE TALLEST PALM TREE IN Belgium, the head of the heads of the Force Publique, King Léopold II, invited a famous dancer from Philadelphia to visit his African colonies. He issued this invitation while at his summer residence in St-Jean-Cap-Ferrat, and one could say that the monarch acted out of love or, to be more exact, out of a desire to conquer the dancer's heart and other parts of her body.

It was extravagant, a way of showing off, behaviour inappropriate in a man well advanced in the age of discretion. But the Rothschilds, the Maharajah of Kapurthala and many other tall palm trees had put down roots in that part of the Mediterranean coast, and within that select circle, the gift of an emerald and diamond brooch was as nothing; one had to come up with something more original in the battle of love. That is why, when the dancer from Philadelphia praised the King's garden, admiring the trees and the parterres, the monarch was quick not to let the opportunity slip.

'I have an even larger garden in Africa,' he said.

'I find that hard to believe, my dear,' replied the dancer.

The King looked out to sea, to the south, towards the Congo.

'It's true, my African garden measures over 900,000 square miles.'

'Really?' said the dancer.

'We could travel there together, and you could be proclaimed queen,' insisted the tallest palm tree.

'Really?' said the dancer again.

King Léopold nodded vigorously, shaking his long white beard.

'How wonderful!' exclaimed the dancer.

The King summoned Armand Saint-Foix, the Duke who was his aide in love and war, and ordered him to prepare for the journey at once. He would make an official visit to the Congo as soon as the summer season in St-Jean-Cap-Ferrat was over. He wanted to give the Congolese people a queen.

'Off you go, and don't come back until everything is ready,' he ordered. 'Quickly now.'

'Your Majesty,' replied the Duke, 'in that part of Africa, there is incessant rain until the month of December, a fact you might deem worthy of consideration. You would have to carry an umbrella at all times and travel along muddy roads.'

The King was most displeased to hear this, although not for long. He was keenly aware that, in matters of the heart, postponements were always dangerous, and that ladies like this dancer, whom he had just met in his garden, could, in the interim, have gone off with some other prince. On the other hand, December was the month of Christmas, one of the most interesting festive dates of the year. An idea came into his head: Rome would be thrilled if he could put on a solemn mass attended by the largest congregation ever seen on African soil.

'All right,' he said to the Duke, 'December it is.'

The King had a special gift for numbers. He was capable of translating any activity or event instantaneously into francs, correct to the last centime. That afternoon, in the garden of his palace in St-Jean-Cap-Ferrat, with the Mediterranean light in his eyes and a glass of Veuve Clicquot in his hand, he was less exact than usual, but exact enough. The grand Christmas mass would be celebrated in his city, Léopoldville, and would bring him 120,000,000 francs' worth of publicity in the Christian world. As for the coronation of the queen of the Congo, that would take place upriver, in some spectacular setting, the Stanley Falls, for example, preferably in the presence of Stanley himself. The explorer and the dancer would doubtless bring him more favourable publicity than the Christmas mass, for it would provide some useful counter-publicity that might silence the criticisms being directed at him by Protestant priests and journalists in America and by equally Protestant politicians in England. The operation could easily bring him a profit of 160,000,000 francs.

The tallest palm tree in Africa stroked his white beard while that number travelled through his mind. The ceremony was sure to be a great success. Like him, most people preferred dancers to priests and journalists, and explorers to politicians.

'In round numbers, the whole operation will be worth 280 million francs,' declared the King, emerging from his numerical daydream.

'Wonderful!' exclaimed the dancer.

Armand Saint-Foix looked up at her, for he was barely five foot three and she was more than five foot eleven.

'The King loves exactitude as passionately as the keenest of mathematicians,' he said.

Had these words been pronounced in more dulcet tones, they would have seemed ridiculous, but Duke Armand Saint-Foix had the loud, harsh voice of an ogre at a puppet show, and so they sounded quite sensible.

'Wonderful!' repeated the dancer. The word had clearly got stuck on her tongue.

'Armand is a poet and he can interpret my feelings better than anyone,' said the tallest palm tree. The dancer laughed, and Saint-Foix left them in order to begin preparations for the journey.

Among the many journalists who were covering the summer social scene in St-Jean-Cap-Ferrat was Ferdinand Lassalle, a professional writer who had achieved fame when he won the Prix Globe for the articles he had written about the Foreign Legion. Ever observant, Ferdinand had noticed the King's movements and gestures and suspected that something unusual was afoot. There was a definite whiff of news in the Court of St-Jean-Cap-Ferrat.

He ran hopefully after the Duke, because it was rumoured among the journalists that the Duke was far kinder to people who were less than five foot three inches tall than to those who were more. Ferdinand was among the chosen few. He was a mere five foot two. Besides, he wrote for *Le Soir*, the most widely read newspaper in Belgium.

His instincts were soon confirmed. Instead of the usual 'No comment', the Duke took his arm and led him to a summerhouse. As they sat surrounded by tulips and orchids and enjoying a cool glass of lemonade, Saint-Foix told him about the King's plans, inventing certain details to flesh out the facts a little.

'King Léopold II will be present, as will Henry Morton Stanley, the great explorer. They will be accompanying the best dancer in the world into the heart of the African jungle, like two loyal knights at the service of a queen. We're also in negotiations to see if the Pope himself might officiate at the Christmas mass.'

Saint-Foix immediately corrected what he had said to the journalist.

'Leave out that part about "like two loyal knights at the service of a queen". It's too vulgar. And add any other details you think fit: "The African continent, so far and yet so near, etc., etc."'

His voice and tone were again those of a real ogre. Ferdinand Lassalle nodded and got to his feet. 'Thank you, Armand.'

The Duke remained seated and replied only with a smile. He had put down his glass of lemonade and was holding a long, thin cigar, as yet unlit. 'By the way, congratulations on those articles of yours about the Foreign Legion. You deserved that prize.'

Deeply flattered, the journalist gave a polite bow and withdrew.

A couple of hours later, the news was already doing the rounds. The following day, it appeared on the front pages of all the most important newspapers in Brussels, Paris and Rome, and three days later, in *La Gazette de Léopoldville*.

V

THE REPORT ABOUT THE ROYAL JOURNEY, PUBLISHED IN *LA Gazette de Léopoldville*, caused a great stir in Yangambi, and, more particularly, in the mind of Captain Lalande Biran. Duke Armand Saint-Foix and he had been close friends ever since, years before, on the occasion of the publication of *Dix poètes belges*, the Captain had inveighed against the editor's failure to include the Duke's work in the anthology, crying: 'You either include both of us or neither,' adding vehemently, 'I don't know Saint-Foix personally, but I know his poems, and I wish to make it quite clear that if there are any great poets in Belgium today, he is one of them. Saint-Foix is on a par with any poet from Paris. Let there be no doubt about it, he must be included in the anthology.'

This praise was quite sincere, for, at the time, Lalande Biran had never met Saint-Foix and was unaware that he was very close to the King. The Duke was unaccustomed to receiving such sincere praise, and the incident, so to speak, touched his heart. Even better, Lalande Biran was not particularly tall, barely five foot nine in his boots. It was a pleasure to be with him and to be able to admire his eyes *d'or et d'azur*.

In the end, the anthology was entitled *Onze poètes belges*, and Saint-Foix and Lalande Biran mingled poems and blood like two adolescents. Time consolidated their friendship. This was partly because of their shared metaphysics, their poetic tastes and their love of gambling, and partly because of a shared interest in the physical world. Ever since Lalande Biran had left for Africa, they had been partners in the trafficking of mahogany and ivory, a highly profitable business that bound them ever closer.

It was a very evenly balanced relationship. Lalande Biran, who had flown higher in the fields of poetry and gambling – having published more books and suffered greater economic upsets – was the more complete artist, being a gifted draughtsman and painter as well. On the other hand, Saint-Foix was a master of the non-metaphysical world. Without his collaboration, it would have been impossible to smuggle the mahogany and ivory into Europe, and Lalande Biran would never have been able to pay off his gaming debts or been able to buy the seven houses that his wife, Christine, longed to own in France.

In his letters, Saint-Foix called Lalande Biran 'Moustachu', because, when they first met, the Captain had sported a magnificent moustache, which he had shaved off when he arrived in Africa. For his part, Lalande Biran called Saint-Foix 'Toisonet', a play on '*toiser*', to gauge someone's height, as the diminutive Duke frequently did, and '*toison d'or*', because at official receptions, the Duke made a point of wearing the sash of the Order of the Golden Fleece.

These forms of address were significant. In Yangambi,

everyone had to call the Captain by his full name, Lalande Biran, or by his rank, 'Captain'; even Van Thiegel, his second in command and his colleague in the complex business of mahogany and ivory trafficking, had to call him 'Captain' or, at most, over supper or when they swam together in the river, 'Biran'. On the other hand, anyone could call Armand Saint-Foix 'Armand', because he liked to hear his name on other people's lips; however, any member of Court who called him Toisonet in public might as well start packing his bags at once. Indeed, it was said in Brussels that certain ministers had lost their post after committing that very blunder.

Mon cher Toisonet, began Lalande Biran's letters. *Mon cher Moustachu*, said those from Saint-Foix. Month after month, year after year, the letters formed a chain, so that by 1904, the year in which King Léopold announced his visit to the Congo, they considered themselves to be more like brothers than friends.

Lalande Biran read the article in *La Gazette de Léopoldville* in the garden behind Government House. His first reaction was one of surprise – an American queen for the Belgian Congo? – his second was one of excitement. What if they were to stop off in Yangambi? If, on their way to the Stanley Falls, the King and his entourage were to pause in Yangambi, would that not be a great opportunity for him?

He gazed out at the landscape. Before him lay miles and miles of jungle bisected by a dark line, like a wound. The line – or wound – grew wider as it approached Yangambi, where it revealed its true nature: it was the Great River, the oft-mentioned River Congo.

Lalande Biran followed its course with his eyes. When it

reached Yangambi and was joined by the waters of the Lomami, the current flowed much faster on the jungle side, beyond the small mid-stream islands, and far more slowly on the village side. Over time, that quiet water had formed the beach where the first colonists in Yangambi had built the wooden platform that served as a jetty. There the *Princesse Clémentine*, the *Petit Prince*, the *Roi du Congo* and all the other steamships docked. Why shouldn't the royal boat do the same? He must put this suggestion to Toisonet as soon as possible.

Lalande Biran could already see himself standing to attention on that beach, ready to salute the King. Then he pictured the King, an erect figure at the prow of the boat, returning his salute. It was a white steamship, with five funnels, larger than the *Princesse Clémentine* and the other boats that came to Yangambi. A huge blue flag with a single yellow star fluttered on the mast. Now and then, the flag would belly out in the breeze.

Rocking back and forth in his chair, Lalande Biran imagined the full-page account of the royal expedition that would appear in all the newspapers of Europe, and he imagined, too, the large photo that would illustrate it. In the middle, Belgium's tallest palm tree; beside him, holding his arm, the dancer from Philadelphia; to her left, at the end, himself; on the other side, the explorer Stanley and Toisonet. He saw the caption as well: 'King Léopold on a lion hunt in the heart of the jungle'.

This wasn't pure imagination. Someone – possibly Toisonet – had told him that the one trophy missing from Léopold II's hunting pavilion was a lion's head, and that sometimes this gap in his collection plunged him into gloom, if not envy. And this was understandable. His cousins and other members of the family, representatives of the Spanish and English nobility, had more magnificent collections of foxes and wolves and bears than he did, but if he could bag the head of the king of the jungle, he would be the undisputed champion.

Lalande Biran was not as good at numbers as the King. He liked to say, half-joking and half-serious, that he was 'too much of a poet' for such things, and that it was his wife, Christine, who kept the accounts. Despite this, it was as clear as day that if the royal party did stop in Yangambi and the King managed to kill that other king, the king of the jungle, this would be of great personal advantage to Lalande Biran. Perhaps a position at Court, with Toisonet, or in the administration, in the Ministry of Culture. Or perhaps at the embassy in Paris, in charge of cultural affairs, a post that would help fulfil his life-long dream, to become an habitué of Paris's literary cafés.

It started to rain and he went back inside in order to continue his ponderings at his desk. The royal visit was beginning to seem like a real possibility. There were a few problems, but none were insoluble. It wouldn't be that difficult to attract a lion to Yangambi if, during the two weeks prior to the visit, bait — in the form of a couple of goats or a few monkeys — was left in an appropriate place. Naturally, it would be best if it was an older lion, or a rather sickly specimen, rather than one bursting with health, because a young, healthy lion capable of leaping thirty feet or more could prove a threat to the King's safety, which would be to no one's advantage at all.

In the evening, he got together in the Club Royal with Van

Thiegel, Richardson and various other officers. They were more excited about the prospect of seeing the dancer from Philadelphia than about King Léopold's visit. In the time it takes to drink a martini or a glass of Veuve Clicquot, they were immersed in a passionate discussion about the dancer's age. Van Thiegel reckoned she was thirty, Richardson, forty.

'She's forty if she's a day, as sure as I'm sixty!' said Richardson.

He took a piece of paper out of his pocket and spread it on the table. It was a cutting from a magazine published in Monaco and showed a photograph, a close-up of the dancer taken in St-Jean-Cap-Ferrat.

'There you are, forty if she's a day!' Richardson said for the third time.

Van Thiegel raised his martini to the photo. 'What a beauty!' he exclaimed.

Richardson turned to Lalande Biran. 'Although with all due respect, Captain, your wife, Christine, is far more beautiful,' he declared.

Van Thiegel gave him a shove that almost knocked him off his chair. 'Show some respect, Richardson!'

'That's all right,' said Lalande Biran. 'Christine is not averse to compliments.'

He started reading the accompanying article. The journalist was lavish in his praise for the dancer: 'Born in a humble shack in Missouri, she was merely the flickering flame on a match; that flame is now a great fire that can light up the world like a star, like the star that adorns the flag of the Congo.'

Lalande Biran could just imagine Toisonet dictating these words to the journalist.

That night, in his room, he lay down on his bed with the intention of continuing his thoughts about the Good that the visit might bring or the Bad that might result were the lion to eat the King. However hard he tried to focus on the matter from a pragmatic point of view, his mind insisted on responding in terms more appropriate to poetry. The words 'a duel between kings' kept slipping into his thoughts, and his literary instinct was telling him that this could be the title of a poem.

'A Duel between Kings'. The title demanded to be continued and would not leave him in peace. Finally, after nearly an hour of struggle, he saw the first lines of the poem with absolute clarity and went over to his desk to scribble them down by the light of the oil lamp: 'A duel between kings. Each in his own territory, but what territory can accommodate more than one king? I am not speaking, Calliope, of the war between white rose and red, nor of that war, years before, in which Hector faced Achilles . . .'

Feeling calmer, he went back to bed and, in his dreams, again imagined the report of the royal visit that would appear in the European press. In this new fantasy, the photo took up half the page and showed the five protagonists, each carrying a rifle: the King, the dancer from Philadelphia, Stanley, Toisonet and himself. Behind them stood another figure, a man carrying two Albini-Braendlin rifles, one resting on his shoulder and the other raised and ready to fire. He tried to identify that sixth person, but his dream grew confused at that point. This figure was a strong young man, frowning at the camera, squinting into the sun. The first three buttons of his shirt were undone. The blue ribbon and the thick gold chain bearing an image of Our Lady had got tangled up on his chest.

Then the penny dropped. His imagination had wanted Chrysostome, the best marksman in the Force Publique in the Congo, to be there in the newspaper photo. He turned over in bed. Yes, that was the solution. If Chrysostome came with them, one of the kings of that territory, the lion, would be in danger, but not King Léopold.

When he woke, it was raining, and so he rejected the idea of going down to the river and starting the day with a swim. Since he couldn't go out into the garden either, he went to his office and sat on his chaise longue to wait for Donatien to bring him his breakfast.

He picked up *La Gazette de Léopoldville*, intending to leaf through it, but couldn't concentrate. He wanted to examine the room and the state of the furniture.

The chaise longue was attractive, but, being upholstered in a pale grey fabric – pale grey with a pattern of pink roses – it looked very grubby and worn. The King couldn't possibly sit there. Nor could Toisonet. But they would have to sit somewhere when they visited the house. This was a serious problem, because the other armchairs in the office, especially those on which Van Thiegel and Richardson sat for their meetings, were in an even worse state. Otherwise, the room was light and spacious, and not without charm. With its book-filled shelves and mahogany desk, it looked like the study of a famous poet. And the round mahogany table they used for meetings was equally handsome. However, the problem remained. It would have been good, in the name of traditional values, to offer their visitors authentic African chairs, but most Africans sat on the ground. He would have to find another solution.

The walls of the office were hung with paintings and

drawings he himself had made. They couldn't possibly stay there, because most of them showed naked girls and would offend the priests travelling with the King and Toisonet, especially since the models were all black Africans. He could leave the largest of the paintings, though, depicting the porch of the Club Royal.

Lalande Biran studied the picture. A mandrill was sitting on a rocking chair. There were other mandrills on the river bank and near the storeroom. He had painted it shortly after arriving in Yangambi, and time had left its mark. The edges were blotched with mildew. Oddly enough, one of those spots resembled a monkey.

He glanced at the desk and at the photo of his wife Christine. He thought, half in jest, that her smile was wider than it had been the day before. Christine loved the Court and revelled in the friendship of people like Toisonet. She dreamed of growing richer and richer. If the royal visit did go ahead, she wouldn't just smile, she would crow with pure delight.

The rhinoceros horn he had exchanged for the watch was there in one corner. He should do something with it. In the right place, it could have a real impact. And if the King expressed an interest, he would give it to him as a gift.

He caught sight of Donatien standing in the doorway, his head almost touching the top of the door frame. He was bringing him his breakfast on a tray: baked bananas, fried eggs, the bread made from manioc flour that the Africans called *kikuanga*, and coffee.

'You'd better come and get the tray yourself, Captain,' he said. 'My boots are covered in mud and I wouldn't want to dirty the rugs. It rained a lot last night. I don't know how much longer it's going to go on like this.'

He gabbled his words – *'Ilser'teilleursiv'prenlerecipien'* – and his Adam's apple bobbed up and down.

Lalande Biran put the tray on the round table, with *La Gazette de Léopoldville* beside it.

'I think the King's visit will be a great thing for the Congo, Captain,' said Donatien from the door. He was taking off his boots. 'I haven't read about it myself, but apparently it's in the newspaper. They say it will be a happy day for everyone here.'

'We'll do our best to make it so,' said Lalande Biran.

Donatien was still lingering on the threshold, with his shoes off now. He was observing the Captain.

'I left the ring in the usual place, Captain,' he said. 'I don't know if you saw it.'

Lalande Biran found it hard to sleep with his wedding ring on his finger and used to leave it on a shelf before going to bed. Sometimes, though, he forgot and would take it off in his sleep, and it would disappear among the sheets and end up on the floor. It was a beautiful gold ring encrusted with diamonds.

Lalande Biran went over to one of the shelves. In a space between the books was a small ivory box. Donatien usually left the ring there.

'Is there anything else?' asked the Captain, turning towards his assistant, without putting on the ring.

Donatien lowered his eyes. His Adam's apple sank in his throat.

'I've sent four *askaris*,' he said.

Every Thursday, Donatien went into the jungle in search of a young girl to bring back for the Captain. In theory, this was an easy enough operation, but in practice, it proved quite difficult, for the simple reason that Lalande Biran would only accept virgins. He didn't want to take any risks. Syphilis had reached the jungle, it wasn't just something you could catch in Paris or in Antwerp.

'Whatever the weather, you have to go. It's your job. This had better not happen again.'

Donatien didn't like it when the Captain got angry with him.

'When they bring her, I'll wash her and do all the necessary tests,' he said. 'I always do that. I never leave that part of the work to the *askaris*.' '*Jamaisjélescepartd'tyravai-lauaskari.*'

'Make sure this is the last time!' said Lalande Biran.

'Yes, Captain.'

'The last time!' Lalande Biran said again.

'If I may, I'll go and tidy your room now, Captain,' said Donatien, disappearing from the door.

When the Captain had eaten the baked bananas and the fried eggs, he went over to the desk, taking a cup of coffee with him. He moved a few papers and documents to clear a space, then lit a cigarette and began the letter he had been writing in his head during breakfast:

My dear Toisonet,

Allow me to begin this message from Africa with a few words from the Master: 'When the earth has become a dank dungeon, from which Hope like a bat flits away . . .' Believe me, if he had been here, he would not have seen the bat of Hope, only its ghost. Yangambi is far more terrible than Paris, although, in some ways, it can also be more beautiful. Beauty, as you well know,

can sometimes be an aspect of the terrible. You often talk
to me of palm trees, snakes, lions, rhinoceroses and the
other inhabitants of these lands . . .

The introduction was somewhat over-long, because once
he had begun in that vein, he could go on for ever.
Nevertheless, he managed, line by line, to clarify his ideas.
He asked Toisonet to do all he could to ensure that the royal
steamship stopped in Yangambi, and not in Kisangani or in
any other place close to the Stanley Falls. He wanted to
welcome the King and the future queen of the Congo
to Government House, along with Mbula Matari and, of
course, himself, Toisonet. The problem was that there, in
that remote corner of the Congo, he lived in such utter
intellectual solitude. Not one of the eighteen officers knew
who Baudelaire was, indeed, his second in command,
Lieutenant Van Thiegel, called him Baudelaine, and thought
it was a woman's name because it sounded like 'Madelaine'.
He re-read what he had written and was pleased, especially by that mention of Mbula Matari, 'the breaker of
rocks'. This would impress Toisonet, who would know it
was Henry Morton Stanley's old African nickname, dating
from the time when the explorer had played a part in
building the railway between Matadi and Léopoldville.
Twenty-five years on, very few people remembered it, and
the few who did called him Bula Matari. And yet the name
was more exact and more meaningful with that initial 'M',
Mbula, Mbula Matari. That one little letter made it sound
far more African somehow.
He dated the letter 12 July 1904 and signed with his full
name: Philippe Marie Lalande Biran.

At the bottom of the page there was space for another ten lines or so, and he decided to fill it with a postscript:

I'm working on a new poem. It's entitled 'A Duel between Kings'. I'll send it to you as soon as it's finished. Oh, and I was going to paint a landscape for you, as you requested, but I ordered the canvases from Léopoldville over two months ago and still haven't received them. I will be having a visitor today, so, instead, I will send you a pencil sketch of the girl, in the hope that it will soften your heart and encourage you to grant the favour I'm asking you.

Lalande Biran was aware that his metaphysical superiority over Toisonet was due not only to his merits as a poet, but equally or possibly even more so to his talent for drawing and painting. That postscript would add its grain of sand when it came to tipping the scales in favour of the royal visit to Yangambi.

He put the letter in the envelope and wrote Toisonet's address: *Monsieur le Duc Armand Saint-Foix, Palais Royal, Bruxelles, Belgique.*

He consulted the calendar and made his calculations. The steamship would pass through Yangambi the next day, and so the letter would leave without delay. The letter should be in his friend's hands by the beginning of August.

Covered by the mosquito net, his bed was like a small semi-transparent hut within the room itself. Biran lay down, his eyes open.

The knotted cotton threads of the mosquito netting

formed squares or rectangles that were about the size of the canvases he used for painting. But they weren't canvases, and you couldn't paint on them. He found it very difficult to devote himself to painting in Yangambi. He had managed to finish a number of paintings during his years there, but the heat and humidity had ruined them. Even though he loved painting as much as he loved poetry and considered it a better way of passing the long hours in the jungle, he was gradually losing interest. He did pencil sketches once a week, but that was all. And he did those sketches more for sexual reasons than out of any artistic urge. When Donatien brought him a girl, he would begin by drawing her body. It was a way of postponing the pleasure.

He went over the last part of the letter in his head. 'Mbula Matari'. Toisonet would be sure to notice the African touch that the 'M' gave to Stanley's nickname. As for the poem he had promised to send, Toisonet would be sure to like that too, and he could even perhaps recite it on some occasion when the King met with Belgian poets.

His imagination gave a small leap and he began to savour in advance the image of the young girl Donatien would bring to him that day. He imagined her full lips, strong shoulders, firm breasts and thighs and, lastly, the centre of her body. Soon, that girl, or another very like her, would be his. It was wonderful to be able to allow himself such a pleasure. It was wonderful, above all, because for that young woman, he would be the first man. He couldn't risk contracting syphilis in the way that Van Thiegel, Richardson and the other officers did. Christine would never forgive him. His wife was French and Parisian to boot, and although much more open than he was when it came to sex, syphilis was quite another matter. Sometimes he was assailed by the fear that Donatien might not take enough care when it came to testing the girls or might even lie to him about them, but he had been carrying out the task for nearly six years now and there had been no mishaps yet. Donatien might be a fool, but he took the Captain's threats very seriously. He knew that one mistake would mean being sent up the Lomami River, to the place where the Congolese rebels hunted white men and flayed them alive.

He didn't want to think about disease any more and so looked instead at one of the knots in the mosquito nets. He focussed on the poem again. 'I do not speak, Calliope, of the war between white rose and red, nor of that war when, years before, Hector faced Achilles . . .' A tiny change had just occurred to him: 'I do not speak, Calliope, of the war between white rose and red, nor of that war when, as you well know, Hector faced Achilles . . .'

Sleep overwhelmed him as he was searching for the next line of the poem, and the word that had been in his mind shortly before – syphilis – stirred in his head, presenting him with the image of the Master as he had seen him in Paris once when he was very young and the Master was ill and ugly and contorted with pain. At the whim of the dream, however, the image was immediately replaced by that of another ailing man, sitting in a rocking chair at the door of Government House, staring up at the palm tree in the square. At first, he didn't realise who it was, because the man's face was all bruised, but suddenly he did: it was him, Captain Lalande Biran. He had contracted syphilis, and the monkeys were screeching at him from the dense fronds.

When he woke, he was sitting up in bed. Outside, in the

jungle, the monkeys really were screeching. And that wasn't the only true aspect of the dream, the rest of it fitted too, not the details, but the general feeling. He did not feel comfortable in Yangambi. He couldn't listen to music in Yangambi; there were no cafés in Yangambi like the ones he used to frequent in Paris, La Bonne Nuit, for example, with its white tablecloths; in Yangambi, you couldn't ever enjoy a bowl of Vichyssoise followed by *mouton à la gourmandise*. Toisonet laughed at this list of complaints. Once, he had sent Lalande Biran a photo actually taken in La Bonne Nuit, where he could be seen sitting before a platter of *mouton à la gourmandise* in the company of half a dozen Parisian poets. It should be said, though, that the same boat that brought the photo also brought a crate of Veuve Clicquot. Toisonet could be very good and very wicked at one and the same time.

The Captain noticed Donatien standing on the other side of the mosquito net, and next to him was a girl of about fifteen. She was strong, very like the girl he had imagined. She had thick lips. He could see the shape of her breasts beneath her *sariya*. And her legs were strong too. She smelled very clean, of the soap Donatien used, and an immaculately white handkerchief covered her eyes. Everything was exactly as he liked. He used to divide this Thursday play into three acts: first, the drawing, then the embraces and caresses, until the moment came to remove the handkerchief from the girl's eyes; then, the final act.

'Donatien,' he said. 'I'm going to leave a very important letter on my desk in the office. I want you to put the drawing I'm about to do in that same envelope and tomorrow take it down to the boat and place it in the hands of the man in charge of the post. Don't leave it in the pigeon-hole at the club.'

On some Thursdays, when he'd had his fill, he gave his assistant permission to take the now ex-virgin back with him to his hut. Donatien was waiting to be given this permission now. His Adam's apple moved up and down in his throat.

'Bring me my drawing things,' ordered Lalande Biran.

The Adam's apple disappeared and reappeared. There would be no prize today. The Captain wanted him to go into the jungle with the *askaris* and not leave the choice of girl to them. That was why he was being punished.

He placed a sketch pad and three pencils on the Captain's bed, then, having removed the girl's clothes, he led her to him. The girl said something, and Donatien replied in one of the few words he knew in the Lingala language: *Tsui!* Be quiet! He placed one hand on her back and was aware of the heat of her skin.

'That will be all, Donatien!' ordered the Captain.

Donatien saluted before leaving. One had to take things as they came. If he couldn't have that girl, he would have the next. The main thing was to stay in the Captain's good books and retain his position as orderly, a position that was the envy of all the officers in the garrison, because if they, so to speak, needed to satisfy their itch, they were obliged to take risks and pay for their adventures with one or even several infections.

VI

ON THE FIRST THURSDAY IN SEPTEMBER, THE STEAMSHIP *Roi du Congo* brought eight letters for Lalande Biran. Donatien collected them from the Club Royal and took them and a pot of coffee to him at Government House.

'Letters from your wife, Christine Saliat de Meilhan, and from your friend Armand Saint-Foix,' he said, placing the two letters on the desk. 'The others are official despatches from Brussels. I'll leave them here on the tray.'

Donatien poured out some coffee and waited for Lalande Biran to make room for the cup on the desk crammed with papers, most of which bore only a few lines of writing, many crossings out and the odd sketch. There were ten cigarette ends in a saucer, which Donatien hastily removed.

'Do you need anything else, Captain?' asked Donatien when he returned with the clean and empty saucer.

Lalande Biran shook his head. He had put his wife's letter on top of all the other papers and was reading it while he sipped his coffee.

Before leaving the room, Donatien picked up the crumpled sheets of paper lying on the floor and threw them into the waste basket. All bore the same title, written in capitals: 'A DUEL BETWEEN KINGS'. From the door, Donatien said: 'With your permission, sir, I'm going to do some work at the club storeroom. A lot of stuff came in on the *Roi du Congo*, and if I don't move fast, the place will fill up with mice, and I'd hate them to get their teeth into the salami before we do.'

'If you don't leave this minute, I'll banish you to the downstairs room for a whole week,' threatened Lalande Biran. The 'downstairs room' was the name given to the dungeon in Government House.

Donatien saluted before vanishing again.

As in all the previous letters, Lalande Biran's wife's overriding concern were the houses, or, more specifically, the house she wanted to buy in St-Jean-Cap-Ferrat. The letter was full of figures and, at the end, above her signature, were these words: '*Essaie, mon chéri*' – 'Do your best, my love'. They were written more boldly than the rest, as if Christine had dipped her pen deep in the inkwell before writing them.

He lit a cigarette. His wife's insistence made him nervous.

'Do you remember when we talked in the garden in Brussels, and how we chose 7 and 5 as magic numbers: 7 houses in 5 years?' she wrote. He could hear his wife's clear, crystalline voice behind the words. 'As you know, Captain, the numbers have changed. You have been in Africa now for 6 years, and in order for us to buy the house in St-Jean, we need just two more batches, 10–500 and 10–500. Do your best, Captain. I ask you this on my behalf and on that of our friend Armand. It would mean, at most, one more year and then the numbers would coincide: 7 years,

7 houses. Van Thiegel will help you. Talk to him. I'm sure he'll be prepared to put in a little extra effort.'

10–500 meant 10 elephant tusks and 500 mahogany trees. That was a lot. Lalande Biran raised his cigarette to his lips. Christine spoke of just two more batches, but that wouldn't necessarily be easy. Sometimes, several days went by without them seeing a single elephant.

The mandrills were screeching in the jungle, agitated by the torrential rain. For once, the noise did not affect him. He was too preoccupied. A troubling thought prevented him from paying attention to anything else. He was wondering about the contents of the second letter on the desk. It was quite bulky and bore two seals, the Belgian royal seal and another from the consulate in Léopoldville. Toisonet's round writing covered the whole envelope. Lalande Biran decided to open it, putting his wife's letter to one side.

'*O triste, triste était mon âme, à cause d'une femme.*' – 'Oh, sad, sad was my soul because of a woman.'

He interpreted the line of verse at the top of the letter as a bad omen, and so plunged instead into the body of the text, ignoring his friend's initial digressions. When he reached the third page, he went into his bedroom, sat down on the edge of the bed and continued reading there. When he had finished, he swore violently.

Toisonet explained in his letter that as soon as he had learned of the King's plans, he had spoken to the celebrated journalist Ferdinand Lassalle and then gone back to his own room feeling very happy. So happy, indeed, that he sat out on the terrace of his villa, smoking a cigar and laughing to himself.

'The laughter emerged from my mouth very slowly, and I had the pleasant feeling that it was pouring out of my chest like foam. It was such a gloriously absurd idea, *l'américaine* in the middle of the Congo, wearing a crown and with the blue flag with its yellow star fluttering beside her. It would seem, however, that I was staking too much on the Other, who decided to snatch that winning card from my hand.'

In Toisonet's lexicon, 'the Other' was God. The letter went on:

The thing is, the Rothschilds gave a party the following week, and the journalists all flocked to the marquee to ask *l'américaine*: 'How do you feel about becoming the future queen of the Congo?' She replied that she had absolutely no intention of going to the Congo. 'But you gave your word to King Léopold II!' said Ferdinand Lassalle reproachfully. Her delightful, memorable riposte, worthy of Parnassus's finest, was this: 'It wasn't me talking, it was Widow Clicquot.' That night, on the terrace, smoking my cigar, I laughed again, more loudly than the first time. I somehow didn't mind losing that particular game.

On the final page of his letter, Toisonet mentioned the consequences of the dancer from Philadelphia's change of heart. Obviously, the King would not now be going to the Congo either, but he, Toisonet, would come in his place. In fact, a journey was already being organised, its objective being to take a statue of the Virgin to the Stanley Falls, a statue in white marble commissioned by the King from 'a new Michelangelo'. Mbula Matari would probably travel with them, for the great explorer, aware that he would not be making many more expeditions, wanted to revisit the land that had been the scene of his greatest adventures and to say goodbye to his beloved Africa. Naturally, the boat would stop in Yangambi, not in Kisangani, and they could then hunt that lion together. 'Especially if you've given it a bit of morphine first,' said Toisonet. 'My spirit loves sleepy lions.'

Lalande Biran left the letter on the desk and, picking up his chicotte, strode out into the pouring rain and set about the trees in the garden. The rain, falling in torrents from the skies, lashed the man's face and he, in turned, lashed the trees. Some of them, especially the young palm trees, showed marks and wounds on their bark; others, like the teak and the okoume, survived without a scratch.

He heard a shrill cry and looked up. Most of the jungle was cloaked in rain and mist. The river flowed muddily on, and its islands, usually so green, were black. He could see the equally black mandrills too, three on the beach and about ten near the Club Royal.

There was a short cut from Government House down to the beach. He started running in that direction. The screeches of those vile monkeys was the worst thing about Yangambi, the worst thing about the Congo and about Africa, and he wanted to flay them with his chicotte, to whip them to the bone. He bounded down the first stretch of the path, slithering in the mud, then gradually slowed to a halt. What he was about to do was utterly absurd. He couldn't whip to death a whole troop of monkeys.

He had heard Donatien say that the monkeys, both chimpanzees and mandrills, recognised the smell of steam from the boat and the sound of its paddles, which was why they hung around on the beach and near the club storeroom, to see if they could make off with a crate or two of food. Apparently, they found the smell of salami particularly exciting. As he walked back up the path, Lalande Biran had to acknowledge that his orderly was quite right.

When he returned to Government House, it seemed to him that the garden was at peace again, and that even the young palm trees, which had borne the brunt of the beating, stood erect and serene. The rain had almost stopped. He could see the jungle again, and the mandrills' screeching sounded a long way off, as if they had crossed to the other side of the river.

He changed out of his drenched clothes and went into his study to lie on the chaise longue. Gradually, as he calmed down, the images in his head took on a more definite shape. The mandrills he had seen next to the Club Royal appeared in the first image, a scene, he realised suddenly, looking up, almost identical to the one in the picture he had painted shortly after arriving in Yangambi. The second image contained the words with which Christine had finished her letter: 'Do your best, my love.' And in the third he saw the photo he had imagined would appear in the article about the royal visit.

He closed his eyes and started correcting the photo. He erased King Léopold and the dancer from Philadelphia and put Mbula Matari in the centre. He placed himself to the right of the explorer and Toisonet to his left. Behind them, as before, stood Chrysostome with his two rifles. And in the background, the journalists. Inevitably, given the changed circumstances, there would not be ten or twelve of them, as he had first imagined, but three or four, from Brussels and the Vatican. Moreover, the mission would consist in transporting the Virgin to the Stanley Falls, and there would be no time for lion-hunts.

The image did not last long. The letter had dealt him a hard blow and, metaphorically speaking, his spirit had been badly bruised. He still couldn't quite absorb the news Toisonet had given him. And yet, however angry he got, however hard he beat the trees with his chicotte, nothing would change. Reality was what it was, and *l'américaine*'s refusal to come to the Congo condemned him to the reality of Yangambi.

'*Quand la pluie, étalent ses immense traînées, d'une vaste prison imite les barreaux . . .*' – 'When the rain, flaunting its long, long train, imitates the bars of a vast prison cell' – as the Master wrote in one of his poems. His feelings exactly. The days in Yangambi seemed very long to him, especially when the rains came. Sometimes, on Christine's advice, he tried to find new things with which to occupy himself, but to no avail. He didn't much like hunting, and drawing seemed an increasingly meaningless occupation. In his letter, Toisonet had made a joke about the Other. Wasn't he himself the victim of a cruel joke that was condemning him to experience each line of the Master's poem, word for word? 'When the earth has become a dank dungeon, from which Hope like a bat flits away . . .'

He knew that feeling all too well. On many evenings and on many nights, in his dreams, he would see bats fluttering around the palm tree in the square. Doubtless one of them was Hope.

'Do your best, my love,' Christine urged, thinking about

that house in St-Jean-Cap-Ferrat. But it wouldn't be easy to divert more mahogany and ivory. The elephants' traditional route was a long way from Yangambi, at least three days' march away. As for the mahogany, it grew abundantly near the River Lomami, but required a lot of manpower to fell and transport it, especially in the rainy season; besides, given that Cocó was in charge of the felling, he would have no option but to share the profits with him. That, however, was only part of the problem. The other part was that when he imagined himself in St-Jean-Cap-Ferrat, arm in arm with Christine, he felt no joy at all. Hope wasn't the only bat fluttering around the big palm tree.

Far off, in the jungle, the monkeys kept up their screeching. Whether they were mandrills or chimpanzees, he couldn't tell.

'The jungle swallows everything and gives back only the cries of monkeys.' That could be the beginning of a poem, he thought, except that he didn't know how to go on. Besides, it wasn't true. The jungle also gave him money. A lot of money. At least 500,000 francs a year, 100,000 through the regular channels and about 400,000 through irregular ones.

He got up from the chaise longue and sat down at the desk with Christine's letter in his hand. His wife's handwriting sloped so exaggeratedly to the right that some words looked almost like straight lines and were very hard to read. Her ideas, on the other hand, could not be clearer: '. . . in order for us to buy the house in St-Jean, we need just two more batches, 10–500 and 10–500. Do your best, Captain. I ask you this on my behalf and on that of our friend Armand. It would mean, at most, one more year and then the numbers would coincide: 7 years, 7 houses. Van Thiegel will help you. Talk to him. I'm sure he'll be prepared to put in a little extra effort.'

His wife's proposal was probably worth considering. He was stuck in Yangambi, imprisoned there. Perhaps that was why he saw so many bats. He should do more physical exercise, although not in the way Cocó did. Cocó liked to work up a sweat felling mahogany in order to control his natural tendency to put on weight. Hunting for elephants might be fun. Besides, since that whole area of the French Riviera belonged almost exclusively to Léopold II, Toisonet might be able to help them buy a villa for a bargain price. Two batches, 10–500 and 10–500, one in the rainy season and another in the dry, and that would be that. And the following year, he could bid farewell for ever to Yangambi.

VII

LIEUTENANT VAN THIEGEL WAS STARTLED TO SEE LALANDE Biran striding across the Place du Grand Palmier and hurriedly tried to disguise the chaos in his office by hiding away the piles of paper and clothes that filled the room. After life as a legionnaire and years in the desert, all he needed was a tent, nothing more, just a place to leave his weapons, another for his clothes and somewhere to sleep. He felt uncomfortable anywhere else, both in his mother's house in Antwerp and in the house he had been assigned as second in command in Yangambi, and he found it impossible to keep things in order.

Fortunately, Lalande Biran merely called to him from the door, without coming in.

'What's wrong, Captain?' Van Thiegel asked, going outside and saluting. His first thought was that it must be something to do with the rebels. Whenever some important expedition was announced, the rebels in hiding would somehow find out and prepare an attack. They must have been thrilled to learn about the visit by King Léopold and *l'américaine*.

Lalande Biran managed to startle him again. It had nothing

to do with the rebels. The royal visit had been cancelled. The King would not be visiting the Congo. And the country would have to make do without a queen. In compensation, a beautiful statue of the Virgin, the work of a great sculptor, would be placed at Stanley Falls. That was the new objective: the Virgin of the Congo. Many photographers would attend the ceremony, bearing their brand-new Kodak cameras. Not so many as would have descended on them in order to see the King, but enough to spread the image of Yangambi worldwide.

Van Thiegel had taken in only the first thing Lalande Biran had said and ignored the rest.

'You mean they're not coming,' he said. 'Bloody hell!'

He began stamping hard on the ground as if he were squashing cockroaches. His boots became spattered with mud.

'Look, Van Thiegel, we get quite enough noise from the mandrills,' Lalande Biran said, and Van Thiegel stopped his stamping.

'Bloody hell!' he said again.

'Don't be too dismissive of our visitors from Brussels,' Lalande Biran told him sternly. 'Our future lies in the hands of one of them.'

'You mean Monsieur X?' Van Thiegel's eyes grew steely beneath their puffy lids.

'This Virgin of the Congo business was probably his idea and he doubtless chose the sculptor himself. Anyway, that isn't what I came to talk to you about. I wanted to give you some good news. From now on, you are to receive twenty-five per cent of what we earn from each shipment of mahogany. The percentage you've been getting up until now was rather low.'

Van Thiegel nodded, as if he had just received an order. 'What with that and the strict rules on gambling in Yangambi, I'll be a rich man by the time I return to Europe,' he said.

They sat down under the big palm tree, on one of the white-painted benches, and Lalande Biran explained what he had in mind. His wife Christine and Monsieur X would very much like to receive another shipment of mahogany and ivory as soon as possible, before Christmas. The rains would make working in the jungle difficult, but they had to try. They could organise a more pleasant outing in the dry season.

'What do you think? Does that seem feasible? I'll take care of the ivory.'

Van Thiegel understood. The Captain was asking him to make an extra effort and that was why he had increased his percentage.

'I would have to take fifty men off the rubber-tapping.'

'That's no problem.'

Van Thiegel's mind split in two. On one side he saw the amount he would earn if he took charge of the mahogany. With the new percentage, the operation would bring in a minimum of 120,000 francs. However, on the other side of his mind – the bad side, so to speak – there was a concern. If he took away fifty rubber workers, that would mean a drop in production of 1,100 pounds over a period of three weeks. Such a fall would not go unnoticed at the palace in Brussels. It could get them into deep trouble.

Lalande Biran read the thoughts on the bad side of Van Thiegel's mind. 'I've already worked out a way of justifying the drop in production,' he said. 'I'll tell Brussels that we have to build a road on which to transport the statue of the

Virgin as far as the falls. I'll tell them that it's possible to get fairly close by boat, but that the last two miles or so has to be done on foot, which is why I need fifty sappers to do the job.'

'Good idea,' said Van Thiegel.

Boats could, in fact, get within a hundred yards of the falls, but no one in Brussels would know that.

'So get those fifty men together and prepare to leave.'

'I'll need ten *askaris* as well. The rubber-tappers have to work in small groups, but when felling mahogany they tend to spread out more, and you know what happens then.'

Lalande Biran agreed, and they walked together to the bank of the river. Lalande Biran's blue and gold eyes – *d'or et d'azur* – were shining. He was happy.

He changed the subject and started talking about the gambling situation. 'I know that a lot of the men in Yangambi resent the limit I set on how much they can bet. They would be prepared to gamble away not just ten francs or a hundred, but their own lives. And that's perfectly understandable. Any man who lives in Africa, and who might have to fight a lion today or a snake tomorrow, and the day after that a rebel, and who has to struggle on a daily basis to keep the *askari* troops disciplined and the rubber production at its highest possible level, well, one can hardly expect a man like that to behave like a spinster from Brussels in his spare time. On the other hand, Cocó, what are we doing in this damp dungeon? Why are we here?'

Pausing, Lalande Biran gazed into the distance at the point where jungle and sky merged. The cities he most loved – Paris, Antwerp and Brussels – were more than three thousand miles away.

'You mean gambling debts, don't you?' said Van Thiegel, slowing his pace, but not stopping. He wanted to get to the club.

'My wife says that it's madness to devote yourself to earning money in Yangambi only to spend it all in Yangambi as well. She's quite right, and I don't want anyone to fall into that trap. That's why I set that limit.'

'I told my mother, and she thought it was a good idea. She says I should go back to Europe and set up a business, but I'm not sure . . .' Van Thiegel shook his head. 'Anyway, I agree with you,' he went on. 'At least we have plenty of women, which is why most of us put up with being here. That's why Chrysostome's such an odd case. I just can't understand it.'

Lalande Biran ignored Van Thiegel's final comment. 'On the subject of rules,' he said, 'there's another one that my men are reluctant to accept. It seems that no one likes having to change their shoes before going into the club. But imagine what would happen if they didn't. The place would be full of mud. And that wouldn't be right. The Club Royal should be like an island in Yangambi, what the Latin poets called a *locus amoenus*.'

They had reached the river bank. The beach was completely empty. It would remain like that for another three weeks, more or less. Thereafter five hundred mahogany logs would occupy the area opposite the jetty. The elephants' tusks would be on display there too, very clean and white.

They went into the Club Royal. It wasn't really a building, but a group of four barrack huts. The first was used as a changing-room, and there you could find the officers' lockers and the pigeon-holes for their post; the second contained the bar and the gaming room; the third, right on the bank of the river, served as porch or terrace; the fourth and largest hut was set slightly apart from the others and served as the club storeroom.

'Oh, I agree with that rule too,' said Van Thiegel. He was taking off his muddy boots. 'I find the club a very restful place. It's much more pleasant than my office.'

Lalande half-closed his eyes. This was his way of smiling. 'I'm pleased to hear it, Cocó. If a garrison is to work well, the commanding officers have to be in agreement.'

'Who else will be going on the hunt?' asked Van Thiegel.

'Chrysostome. It's best to be on the safe side and take a good marksman along, don't you think?'

Van Thiegel wondered if Chrysostome would get a percentage of the profits from the ivory. If so, Lalande Biran was ranking him higher than he did Van Thiegel. Going hunting was more exciting than felling trees. A hundred times more.

'He's an excellent shot, there's no doubt about that,' he answered. 'How many men are you taking altogether?'

'Thirty porters, ten sappers and ten *askaris* as guards. It's all arranged.'

Van Thiegel crouched down to tie the laces of the clean boots he had just put on. That was a lot of men. It wasn't so very hard to find and kill five male elephants. And five *askaris* would be more than enough to guard thirty porters and ten sappers. With someone like Chrysostome on hand, you could make do with even fewer. And they would need a lot of cartridges. Knowing Lalande Biran, at least two hundred.

'That'll mean a lot of cartridges. You never can tell in the jungle,' he said.

Lalande Biran merely nodded.

That night, Van Thiegel stayed very late at the club. When

he did finally leave, a new rumour had sprung into life in Yangambi. It turned on the elephant hunt, with the number of cartridges the main motive for speculation. Various figures were bandied about, two hundred, three hundred and fifty, even the incredible figure of five hundred. A day passed, and like dough that has been left to rest, the quantity swelled and grew: it would be four hundred cartridges. Another day, and the vox populi of Yangambi announced the distribution: two hundred for Captain Lalande Biran; one hundred for Chrysostome; ten for each of the *askaris*.

On the third day, when Lalande Biran, Chrysostome, the *askaris*, the sappers and the bearers were setting off, the now poisonous rumour was circulating among the officers in Yangambi. They could understand the Captain having two hundred cartridges, and the number set aside for the *askaris* too, because they were going hunting and would need more than the customary two; but they simply couldn't stomach the one hundred cartridges allotted to Chrysostome. A sharpshooter like him would need, at most, twenty cartridges to kill five elephants.

Before the party had disappeared into the depths of the jungle, a large black mamba of a word was slithering slyly from one hut to another in Yangambi. In the end, it managed to climb not only onto Van Thiegel's table, but onto each and every table in the Club Royal. It was humiliating that such a privilege – one hundred cartridges! – should be given to that great poofter Chrysostome, the biggest *pédé* in the whole Force Publique.

VIII

THE PARTY RETURNED IN THE FIRST WEEK OF OCTOBER, a few days later than expected. When they entered the compound and marched into the European section, Lalande Biran was at their head; bringing up the rear was Chrysostome, his rifle on his shoulder; and in the middle came the *askaris*, the sappers and the porters. The latter were carrying the elephant tusks and leading along a group of live mandrills, linked together by a rope tied about their necks, as if they were a line of slaves.

Lalande Biran ordered his men to halt before they reached the Place du Grand Palmier, and the women employed in the slaughterhouses and the stores ran out to receive his commands. Five *askari* guards also approached, followed by a black NCO, and then another ten *askaris*. Striding after them came Donatien.

Half-hidden between the slaughterhouse and the store-room was the hut where weapons and munitions were kept. Van Thiegel was observing the scene from one of the hut's mean little windows and trying to understand what he was seeing. You didn't have to be particularly bright to realise that the expedition had met with problems. Apart from the delayed return, two *askaris* and four or five of the porters who had set out with the group had not come back. There was something else too. Lalande Biran looked positively haggard, as if he had suddenly lost ten or even twenty pounds in weight. In his rain-sodden uniform and with several days' growth of beard, he seemed a different person, older and almost ugly. Chrysostome, for his part, had lost the swagger with which he had strolled into Yangambi carrying that rhinoceros horn, although he still wore his shirt collar unbuttoned to show off his blue ribbon and gold chain. Beneath his hat, his hair had grown almost down to his eyes, but, thought Van Thiegel scornfully, there was still no sign of any hair on his chest.

'Poofter!' he spat out.

Lalande Biran gave an order, and the *askaris* guarding the mandrills bawled out the same words, brandishing their chicottes. Immediately, four porters came forward carrying by the legs the apparently heavy corpse of a cheetah. Lalande Biran shouted again. He was in a very bad mood indeed.

The porters carried the cheetah into the slaughterhouse, and Van Thiegel waited to see what would happen to the mandrills. Perhaps they had been captured for their meat, although none of the white officers, with the exception of Richardson, were particularly fond of it. The mandrills, however, weren't taken to the slaughterhouse, but to the firing range. The porters who had been carrying the cheetah joined those carrying the elephant tusks and, accompanied by about ten *askaris*, headed down to the river.

As they passed the hut, Van Thiegel counted twelve tusks and twenty-six porters, and as so often happened, his mind split in two. One part thought how pleased Christine would be when she learned that her husband had collected all that ivory, and how her joy would only be multiplied when she found out that he himself had amassed more than six hundred mahogany logs. The other part of his mind was more malevolent. The four missing porters, he thought gleefully, must have eluded Chrysostome's vigilance and escaped.

This second thought cheered him a little. Perhaps that was why Lalande Biran was so angry, knowing that, at the crucial moment, faced by the threatening world of the jungle, the poofter had turned out not to be such a good shot after all. As Van Thiegel always said, it was one thing to aim calmly at a target on a firing range or in the area around Yangambi, but quite another to do so when one was being watched constantly by the enemy. The rebels were not as biddable as the rubber-tappers.

Donatien ran over to the Captain, followed by an *askari* triumphantly waving a bag. Van Thiegel realised what must have happened. They had thought the bag was lost, and the soldier was pleased to have found it. This find, however, did nothing to improve Lalande Biran's mood. He made an abrupt gesture, and the *askari* raced off towards the slaughterhouse. Donatien said something to the Captain, pointing up at Government House. This, Van Thiegel knew, meant that coffee had been prepared. Whenever Donatien sensed trouble, he always made coffee. Richardson called him *le géant du café*, the coffee giant, because he was six foot five tall and made rather a good waiter. Lalande Biran ignored the offer and followed the other men down to the river.

Van Thiegel put on his hat and slipped out of the hut by the back door. Before he joined Lalande Biran, he wanted to know what was in that bag and, in passing, take a look at the cheetah.

One of the women working in the slaughterhouse showed him the creature's head. There was a bloody hole just above its left eye. A single shot; a single cartridge. Van Thiegel swore loudly.

The bag lay in one corner of the slaughterhouse, next to a clay oven. When he emptied it, three hands fell out. Just three. And yet four porters were missing, which meant that one had got away. The poofter might be a good shot, but one escapee, one out of four, meant a twenty-five per cent loss.

He left the slaughterhouse and headed for the river. Down below, near the jetty, he saw someone swimming. He assumed it must be Lalande Biran.

A black servant was coming up the hill, and Van Thiegel stopped him.

'Donatien told me to take these to Government House,' said the servant, showing him the two bottles of Martell brandy he was carrying.

'One of the bottles would be better off in my office. I drink more than the Captain,' said Van Thiegel, laughing. 'When you've done that, bring a couple of towels down to the beach and leave them on one of the mahogany logs.'

The servant looked doubtfully back at the beach.

'Oh, leave them where you like, but put them where we can see them and not underneath the logs.'

Before proceeding, Van Thiegel made a gesture with his hand as if shooing away a mosquito.

The water in the river was flowing at the ideal rate, very gently. Lalande Biran and Van Thiegel swam about a hundred yards against the current towards the pile of mahogany logs near the jetty, then turned turtle and swam back, allowing themselves to be carried almost effortlessly to their starting point, opposite the Club Royal.

The two men had very similar styles, their movements equally measured and rhythmic, heads and arms emerging simultaneously from the water. They turned at the same time too. Their thoughts, however, were very different.

Van Thiegel was wondering how the fourth porter had managed to get away, and whether it had been Chrysostome's fault. In that ever-divided mind of his, he was also concerned by the Captain's mood. He couldn't understand why he was in such a foul temper when the hunting had clearly gone so well – twelve elephant tusks *and* a cheetah – and when he, Van Thiegel, had amassed the six hundred mahogany logs that lay cleaned and placed in neat piles on the shore.

Lalande Biran could think of nothing while he was swimming upstream. The current was gentle enough, but he had little energy left after almost three weeks in the jungle, and it took all his strength to reach the jetty and the mahogany logs. When he drifted back downstream, gazing up at the sky, he was concentrating on writing the lines of a poem: 'It is not a lived-in heaven, but a desert; it is not Michelangelo's heaven, peopled by angels and saints, and with the figure of God greeting Adam . . .'

Lalande Biran felt so uninspired that he slapped the water hard. Van Thiegel glanced at him, but received no response.

As if the noise of the slap had awoken his muse, Lalande Biran suddenly knew how to continue the poem: 'This heaven is a cave, blue only in appearance, a refuge for bats.

Hanging upside down in there is the Hope of which the Master spoke; there, too, hang Love and Youth . . .'

Unhappy with the direction the poem was taking, Lalande Biran ducked under the water and stayed there for a while. Van Thiegel swam on, but very slowly, without leaving the Captain's side.

'Biran,' he said, 'if there's something worrying you, I'd like to know. I'm your friend as well as being your second in command.'

They were opposite the Club Royal now, next to the small dock for canoes. Lalande Biran stood up. The water came to his waist. 'You're also my associate,' he said. 'Allow me to congratulate you on your success with the mahogany.'

His answer to Van Thiegel's question went no further than that, but it had its continuation – its coda, one might say without stretching the metaphor too far – in Lalande Biran himself. He was feeling increasingly annoyed with Christine. She was always demanding more: more ivory, more mahogany, more effort. Not content with being the owner of six houses in France, one of them a villa in Biarritz that had once belonged to a Russian prince, she wanted another, a seventh house, in St-Jean-Cap-Ferrat, one of the most expensive places in the civilised world. And the price he paid was to spend seven years in the Congo, two more than the five they had initially agreed. Seven years beneath that deserted sky, seven years listening to the screams of the mandrills and the chimpanzees. Her demand for more would mean another hunting party, perhaps not as gruelling as the one he had just returned from, but it would certainly not be without its problems. Hunting parties were risky whether in the dry or the rainy season, and there were always unforeseen incidents. He could not help thinking, too, that he wasn't getting any younger, that he was not the man he was, and that three weeks in the jungle had left him utterly drained. His body was covered in bites and scratches, and although they hadn't encountered any tse-tse flies or red ants, he couldn't be sure he had avoided catching one of the infinite diseases lurking in the jungle. He found it very hard to understand Christine's insistence. Nor could he understand his own dejection. This was why he couldn't write any poems. Because his muse could not hear or see well in that tangle of negative feelings: disquiet, rage, the troubling sense that he was being far too indulgent with his wife.

He set aside the poem about the sky in Yangambi and started thinking about another that had been going round and round in his head during the hunt: 'When he reaches camp, the weary hunter falls, exhausted, but before he sleeps, out of his tiredness slips the truth, like a white egg from a black bird: enough, it's time to seek the company of friends . . .'

His muse's words did not convince him, but it soothed him to remember them.

'Shall we take a look at the timber?' said Van Thiegel. They were swimming again. Lalande Biran did not respond, but swam towards the shore.

Seen from the river, the piles of mahogany logs on the beach looked like the wagons of a train that had stopped there. Unfortunately, the real train, the one that Stanley – Mbula Matari – had helped build by dynamiting hundreds of rocks, only went as far as Léopoldville, and the valuable cargo from Yangambi would have to be transported there by river.

'We'll need three barges to shift this lot, but the load should reach Antwerp by the end of November,' said Van Thiegel. His eyes were flicking from pile to pile, looking for the towels the servant should have brought. He felt uncomfortable in his nakedness.

'It's a lot of wood,' said Lalande Biran.

Again, the answer inside his mind was more complex. Yes, it was a lot of wood, and he had brought back more ivory than expected, but it wouldn't be enough for Christine. Another letter would come, insisting yet again that she must buy that seventh house in France and demanding more mahogany and more ivory, forcing him to go back into the jungle in search of more elephants. And the day would come, perhaps on that hunting trip, perhaps on the next – because Christine would keep asking for more and more – when his luck would run out and he would stay in the jungle for ever, struck by a stone flung by some fleeing porter or badly wounded by a shot from a rebel rifle, and then he would be trampled underfoot by a herd of stampeding elephants, elephants weighing eight tons apiece, which would kill him, leaving only his crushed remains, remains that would become food for vermin and insects . . .

He paused to take a breath. The scent from the mahogany resin was a pleasure to the nostrils; the pinkish, reddish colour of the wood a pleasure to the eyes. Mahogany was a benign wood. It helped drive away negative thoughts.

'Ah, there they are!' exclaimed Van Thiegel. Two white towels lay neatly folded on the jetty. 'I told him to leave them on a log, but that was obviously too much to ask.'

He went over to the jetty and returned with one of the towels tied about his waist. Lalande draped the other round his neck.

'I was worried Chrysostome might be prowling around somewhere, and I didn't feel safe with my arse on view,' said Van Thiegel. His lips parted in a half-smile, but beneath his puffy lids, his gaze was like that of a snake. The blue of his irises was dark, almost black.

'Chrysostome stayed behind with the men cleaning the ivory. I get tired, but he doesn't.' Lalande Biran put his head in between two logs and inhaled deeply.

'I have some good news, Biran,' said Van Thiegel after a silence. There was a tremor of excitement in his voice. 'I've been waiting for the right moment to tell you.'

Lalande Biran removed his head from between the logs and looked at him.

'There's more than a million francs on this beach, Biran!' Van Thiegel shouted, spreading his arms wide. 'When you add in what we'll get from the ivory, that's a million and a half!'

Lalande Biran closed his eyes.

'How much did you say?' he asked, opening them again.

Van Thiegel picked up a twig from the ground and wrote the figure in the sand: 1,500,000. His eyes were once again very blue.

A light breeze from the river set the branches of the palm trees swaying. The air in Yangambi suddenly filled with good omens. On one side of the sky, the round sun was shining brightly, as if the rainy season had ended at that very moment. The mandrills were quiet. There were no bats.

'Why?' he asked, although he guessed what the answer

would be and wasn't surprised when Van Thiegel explained what had been happening on the European markets. Mahogany had tripled in value since the previous shipment, and the rise in the value of ivory had been even greater.

'When I got back from Lomami with the mahogany, I found a letter from my mother. She sends me newspaper cuttings. I have them up at the club. I'll show you.'

'That's really excellent news!' cried Lalande Biran.

'I know, Biran. A real stroke of luck.'

They started walking up the beach towards the Club Royal. They were two white men in Africa, one totally naked apart from a towel slung around his neck, the other half-naked, with a towel tied round his waist, and both were breathing in the smell of the mahogany resin, listening to the murmur of the river, and feeling all around them the presence of the endless jungle. Seen from a distance, they could have been taken for two figures in a classical painting. In reality, though, and to put it in somewhat sentimental terms, their hearts were beating like those of two adolescents. Even Van Thiegel's heart, because having that information in your head was not the same as putting it into words. When he spoke it, verbalised it – 'There's more than a million francs on this beach, Biran! When you add in what we'll get from the ivory, that's a million and a half!' – it became more real, became flesh. Especially when he saw the figure written in the sand: 1,500,000. It was so exciting that their bodies reacted. They both had goose pimples. A million and a half! 1,500,000!

It seemed so impossible that Lalande Biran wanted to hear it again.

'Have I understood you right? A million and a half just for us, without counting the part that goes to Monsieur X.'

Van Thiegel replied very precisely: '800,000 francs for you, 650,000 for me, 50,000 for expenses.'

Lalande Biran felt a deep thrill of excitement. You didn't have to be good at maths to understand what that sum of money meant. There would be no need for another expedition or another shipment. He and Toisonet would never have to discuss the sordid topic again. And, above all, Christine could buy her seventh house on the peninsula of St-Jean-Cap-Ferrat and be contented for a good long while.

They went into the changing-rooms at the Club Royal and took their clothes and boots out of their lockers. While they were getting dressed, Lalande Biran was still pondering the consequences of that unexpected bonanza. He wouldn't have to stay in Yangambi for another year. After Christmas, he would accompany Toisonet to the Stanley Falls and, once the statue of the Virgin had been put in place, he would ask one of the journalists present to take a photo of him with his Kodak camera, and thus bring to a close his contribution to the Force Publique. By spring, perhaps as early as May, he would be back in Paris. And if Christine moved quickly and bought that villa, they could spend the summer months in St-Jean-Cap-Ferrat in their seventh house.

'The grasshoppers sing all summer!' he exclaimed jubilantly, sitting down on the bench in the changing-room to put on his boots. '*Les cigales chantent tout l'été!*'

Even though he was sitting next to him, also pulling on his boots, Van Thiegel failed to notice the Captain's joyful outburst. An anxiety had taken hold not just of one part of his mind, but of both. He was shocked by Lalande Biran's response – or, rather, lack of response – to his insinuating comment about Chrysostome. 'I was worried Chrysostome might be prowling around somewhere, and I didn't feel safe with my arse on view,' he had said, and Lalande Biran had ignored his words. Was it that he respected Chrysostome as a hunter even more than he thought, and that he was prepared to forgive him everything else? Such a possibility infuriated Van Thiegel and spoiled a moment that should, in principle, have been a source of both military and economic joy.

Lalande Biran continued to sing as he tied his laces. 'The Grasshopper, having sung all summer . . .' – 'La Cigale, ayant chanté tout l'été . . .' This time, Van Thiegel understood. The Captain was very happy, indeed, he couldn't ever remember having seen him so happy. On festive days, the other officers often burst into song, inspired by the convivial atmosphere and by the palm wine, but the Captain never joined in.

Lalande Biran threw his head back and rubbed his cheeks. His beard, which had remained unshaven during the whole hunting trip, was making him itch.

'That's one good thing about Yangambi, Cocó,' he said at last. 'When we first came here, we were happy-go-lucky grasshoppers who gave no thought to winter. Now we have become ants.'

Van Thiegel opened his locker and took out a letter. He shook his head. 'It's true that I've been very good while I've been in Yangambi and sent a lot of money home to my mother,' he said, 'but I'm no ant. As soon as I get back to Europe, I'll revert to being a grasshopper. My mother knows this and squirrels away everything I send her. She says I'll have to torture her to get her to confess which bank she's put it in.'

'Are you thinking of going back then, Cocó?' asked Lalande Biran.

'I spent eleven years with the Foreign Legion, and I've been with the Force Publique for nine. That's quite enough, I reckon.'

Van Thiegel gave the letter to Lalande Biran.

'Where will you go, do you think? Antwerp?'

'I'm not sure.'

'It's my last year here too,' said Lalande Biran. 'I had my doubts, but they all melted away with the news you've just given me. I'm going back to Europe.'

'You'll find the newspaper cuttings in the envelope. They explain about the rise in value of ivory and mahogany.'

Lalande Biran read the sender's name: *Veuve Marie-Jeanne Van Thiegel* — Widow Marie-Jeanne Van Thiegel — and the address in Antwerp. Her writing leaned to the right, like Christine's.

'I imagine my wife and your mother are rather alike,' he said. 'They should go into business together.'

Lalande Biran was holding the little pile of cuttings in his hand. Van Thiegel chose one neatly folded piece of paper.

'This is the best article, from *Le Soir*. It gives a really clear explanation for the rise in value.'

The cutting, once unfolded, resembled the bellows of an accordion. 'How Ivory and Mahogany were Transformed into Gold,' said the headline.

IX

THE SECOND OF THE BARRACK HUTS THAT MADE UP the Club Royal, and where the officers had their bar and games room, was a strange sight in the middle of the African jungle. Its gable roof was covered by an insulating layer of mud and palm leaves, while inside, everything was made of hardwood — ebony, teak and mahogany — like the private clubs in Brussels and Paris. It had nine tables in all, three of which, round and covered in green baize, were intended for card games. A bar and shelving for bottles were located in one corner of the entrance hall. At the rear, beyond the tables, was the smoking-room furnished with various armchairs arranged in a circle and replete with cushions. This was also where the oddest of the club's features was to be found — a door made entirely of glass leading into another hut that served as a porch.

On the wall that ran from the bar to the smoking-room was a large photograph of Léopold II — the only picture in the entire club.

Most of the officers were seated at the three round tables, some as card-players and others as spectators. Van Thiegel immediately noticed Chrysostome's presence. He was, as usual, one of the onlookers, the worst sort, the sort who never even opens his mouth or does anything to encourage the players and liven things up a bit. The poofter obviously felt it was enough to show off his unbuttoned collar and his blue ribbon and medals. Such laxity clearly did not comply with regulations. Many *askaris* had been punished with a week or more in the guardroom for having the second button of their shirt undone. Yet Chrysostome could go around with three or even four buttons undone and no one said a thing, but then he, of course, was an officer and enjoyed the protection of Lalande Biran.

King Léopold cast a cold and disapproving eye over the scene. Van Thiegel was sure that the monarch, that highest of authorities, would agree with him. The King doubtless liked poofters as much as he did, that is, not at all.

'Would you care for a Martell, sir? Or, if you prefer, I could mix you a martini. The *Roi du Congo* brought five whole cases,' said the manager of the bar. He belonged to the Twa tribe and was now about sixty years old, having been in his day an excellent jungle guide. It was said that he had been the man to lead Stanley to Livingstone, which is where he got his nickname, although he was known as Livo for short.

'A double martini,' said Van Thiegel, before going over to the card tables. He sat down next to Chrysostome, then turned his back on him and asked to be dealt some cards.

Lalande Biran was sitting in one of the armchairs in the smoking-room, beside the glass door, reading the article from *Le Soir* and holding an unlit cigarette in his hand. The sky was heavy with dense clouds, however, and not enough light came in through the small windows or the glass door for him to be able to read easily. He went out onto the porch and sat on the edge, as near to the river as possible. His sight was getting worse and worse. Soon he would need glasses.

'Your lemonade, sir,' announced Livo, who arrived bearing a tray and set the drink down on the table. It wasn't real lemonade, but the juice from various jungle fruits. It was violet in colour and had a bitter taste.

'And what colour is your *oimbé* today? This colour?' Lalande Biran asked in friendly fashion, pointing to his drink.

Livo had told him once, on that very porch, that the Twa people could, in certain circumstances, see an aura around the body. They called this the *oimbé*, and its colour changed according to the person's state of mind. It was violet when they were sad, blue when happy, black or dark green when anxious, and red when they were afraid.

'No, not violet,' Livo said, but gave no further explanation.

He regretted ever having mentioned the *oimbé* to the Captain and always avoided responding to his questions, but Lalande Biran did not give up and often, instead of greeting him normally, would ask that same question: 'What colour is your *oimbé* today?' He had even spoken of writing a poem about it, entitled: 'The men of Twa, inhabitants of the rainbow.'

Lalande Biran put his cigarette to his lips and asked Livo for a light.

'Is Donatien in the storeroom?' he asked.

'I'll have a look, sir.'

Livo duly went to the storeroom and opened the door, telling the Captain on his return: 'No, he's not there, sir.'

'I need a shave,' said Lalande Biran.

As well as being in charge of the club, Livo was also

resident medicine man and occasional barber. However, he never shaved any of the officers for fear of cutting them.

'I wouldn't do a good enough job,' he said by way of an excuse.

'Then I'll have to wait for Donatien.'

Livo went back into the club.

Lalande Biran took a puff of his cigarette. His supply of tobacco for the hunting party had not lasted as long as expected, and he hadn't had a cigarette for a week. The smoke made him feel slightly dizzy.

The article in *Le Soir* was very thorough, and Lalande Biran read it as if it were a poem, savouring every line. He learned that the price of ivory had risen 370 per cent in eight months; that of ebony by 280 per cent, teak by 320 per cent and mahogany by 330 per cent. Knowing what these figures added up to – namely, 1,500,000 francs – filled him with pleasure. Especially when they were accompanied by confirmation that prices would continue to rise until Christmas, and that the demand for hardwood had tripled or even quadrupled.

He finished his drink and sat gazing at the water, drawing more deeply now on his cigarette. The surface of the constantly flowing river occasionally dimpled and rippled. In the little dock near the store, the canoes gently bobbed and knocked. The jungle, in contrast, was as motionless as a painting. Some lines came into his head:

"'Sisyphus', they said, "the rock you are carrying on your back has crumbled; sit down on the river bank, if you wish, and watch the water flowing. There is no weight now, there are no obligations.'"

The poem would have to continue in the same vein in

order to reflect the enormous sense of relief he was feeling. Soon, he would be following the same direction as the waters of the river, when he travelled to Léopoldville, then on by train to Matadi, and finally, by steamboat to Europe.

He considered again the numbers in the article – 370, 280, 320, 330 – and wondered if they should perhaps appear in the poem as symbols of the force that would destroy Sisyphus' heavy rock, his life in Yangambi. But it was difficult to include numbers in a poem. He had never done it before. What a shame he wasn't in Paris, where he could have debated the matter with his colleagues, the poets of La Bonne Nuit!

Donatien arrived on the porch in great haste, placed three letters on the table, then saluted.

'This one comes from the commanders of the Force Publique, this from Duke Armand Saint-Foix, and the third from your wife, Christine Saliat de Meilhan,' he told him, placing his index finger on each envelope as he spoke.

This seemed rather a scant amount of correspondence after three weeks in the jungle.

'Would you like me to shave you, sir?' asked Donatien.

'After I've read the letters.'

Donatien seemed disinclined to leave. His Adam's apple kept moving up and down. He started to say something, then stopped, stammering.

Lalande Biran looked up. 'Is something wrong?' he asked.

'Today is Thursday, sir. The girl is waiting in the grass hut,' Donatien said at last, running his words together even more than usual: '*Aujourd'e'jeuimontcatainelafielaupaillote.*'

Lalande Biran looked at him hard. Donatien was clearly having difficulty curbing his desires and, had he been made of bolder stuff, would have rushed off to join the girl in the hut. Lalande Biran felt no such urge. Those three weeks spent in the jungle, hunting for ivory, had not awoken in him the slightest desire to possess a young woman. He could not explain such apathy. Like his sight and his love of painting, his sexual desire was becoming ever feebler.

His eye was caught by a shadow flashing over the water, however, it belonged not to bats, but to some birds known as *waki*.

'Lock her away somewhere until tomorrow,' he said, stubbing out his cigarette on the sole of his boot, then placing the butt in his glass.

Donatien had a cage in his hut, which he used whenever he had to keep a girl captive for a while. He nodded; he would do as he was told. His Adam's apple was moving more slowly now, as if it were sad.

'Donatien,' Lalande Biran said. 'You saw the mandrills we brought back with us, didn't you? They're on the firing range. If you really can't control your sexual urges, I suggest you select one of the females. I'm sure you'll find one to your taste.'

For a moment, Donatien hesitated. Then he again saluted and went off to the storeroom.

The letter from the commanders of the Force Publique asked the same question they had asked every autumn for the last six years. They wanted to know if he was prepared to continue serving the company. King Léopold would, of course, be most grateful, but they were obliged to tell him that, given the huge amount of investment being poured into the Congo, an increased percentage of the profits from the sale of rubber was, at that moment, impossible.

His reply to that letter from Brussels had also been the same for the last six years, but this time it would be different: 'My sincere thanks to the King for his kind offer, but the time has come for me to retire . . .'

He put the official letter down on the table again and picked up the one from Toisonet. Before he read it, he glanced across at the river. Dozens of *waki* were flying above it, criss-crossing the air like swallows, except that they were brilliant white in colour.

Toisonet began his letter with the words '*Moustachu, mon cher ami*' rather than his usual '*Cher Moustachu*'. Lalande was taken aback by this change. Something must be wrong.

Line by line, the contents of the letter confirmed the Captain's first impression. Hardly anyone would be present on the visit to Yangambi. He, Toisonet, would not be coming, nor would Mbula Matari. The party would comprise only the sculpture of the Virgin, the bishop who would officiate at the mass and Ferdinand Lassalle, possibly the best journalist of his day, winner of the Prix Globe for his articles on the Foreign Legion.

'Moustachu, do try and make friends with Lassalle. You won't find a better companion among the delegation,' Toisonet urged him.

He also referred to the house in St-Jean-Cap-Ferrat. Christine would be sending him all the details, but he wanted him to know that the administrator of that part of the coast was fully informed and had undertaken to find them a villa in the quarter known as La Petite Afrique. Since they were rich – 'even richer now', said Toisonet, underlining the words – they would have a salon lined with mahogany.

'*Moustachu, mon cher ami,*' Toisonet said again at the end

of the letter. 'Don't break anything, don't whip the lion I'm having sent to you from Brussels. Keep your rage and your chicotte for when you come to St-Jean-Cap-Ferrat. There are as many creatures who deserve a good whipping here as in Yangambi, possibly more. Why, you need look no further than myself, for I definitely deserve to be punished. One does not treat a true friend as I have treated you, promising an embrace and then withdrawing it.'

Lalande Biran looked around him, but could not see his chicotte. He seemed to remember taking it with him when he went for a swim. He must have left it in the changing-room or on the jetty. An instant later, before he had even finished that thought, there it was in Van Thiegel's hand.

'A servant found it in the changing-room,' Van Thiegel said, coming through the glass door onto the porch. He wasn't sure where to put it.

Lalande Biran grabbed it and hurled it at one of the posts where the canoes were moored, but he threw it so hard that it reached the river's edge, where it lay like a snake that had died on leaving the water.

Van Thiegel sat down beside him, legs splayed.

'They've written to me as well,' he said, meaning the letter from the commanders of the Force Publique. 'What's that expression in Latin?'

'*Alea jacta est.*'

'That's it. It's over. For me too.'

The two men sat in silence, watching the ceaseless toing and froing of birds over the surface of the water. It was evening. The day, it seemed, was drawing to a close with not a drop of rain. There was no noise, apart from the odd word from the card-players inside that occasionally penetrated the glass door.

'Was there a lion on the steamboat?'

'On the steamboat?' Van Thiegel asked, wide-eyed.

'That's what Monsieur X says, that they've sent us a lion from Brussels. From the zoo, I suppose.'

'Not as far as I know,' Van Thiegel said. 'No lion has arrived in Yangambi on the steamboat or by any other means. And no lion has gone near the mandrills you brought back with you either.'

'Just as well. We don't need lions here. If anyone wants one, he can go and find one in the jungle and shove it up his arse,' declared Lalande Biran.

Van Thiegel laughed. He enjoyed it when the Captain got angry.

'What are we going to do with those mandrills?' he asked.

'The *askaris* will want to eat them, as will Richardson,' said Lalande Biran. 'I suppose the best thing would be to organise a shooting match. In the next couple of days. Sunday perhaps.'

Van Thiegel was taken by surprise.

'So soon?'

'It would probably be best to wait until Christmas, but that won't be possible with a bishop and a journalist hanging around. Besides, there won't be time then. We have to take the statue of the Virgin to the island of Samanga, and that will take us three or four days.'

Van Thiegel drank his martini down in one.

'Why Samanga? You've lost me, Biran. Tell me more.'

Lalande Biran gave him the necessary information. Another change of plans in Brussels meant that there would be no royal party, just a journalist and a bishop, who would celebrate mass. So there seemed little point in travelling all the way to the Stanley Falls. The idea of taking the statue to Samanga had only just occurred to him, but he was sure the little island would be the ideal place, given that it was much nearer and looked rather like a small mountain. In Europe and the Americas, statues were usually placed on some high vantage point, and Africa should be no different. The Virgin would look out over the river and over many square miles of jungle.

'So this Christmas we're going to Samanga,' he concluded. 'But first, we're going to have some fun with the shooting match.'

'Both seem like excellent ideas,' said Van Thiegel.

His mind had divided not into two this time, but three. The Captain – thought one of those three parts – had clearly reverted to his usual state of mind after that brief burst of happiness in the changing-room. According to the song, the grasshopper sang all summer, but the Captain's joy had lasted barely an hour. He was absolutely furious. The proof of this was the chicotte he had hurled away so angrily and which still lay at the river's edge.

'What news from Paris? Is your wife well?' asked the second part of his mind, but the letter from Christine Saliat de Meilhan, he realised, had not yet been opened.

'We'll find out now,' said Lalande Biran.

He read it quickly. His wife said much the same as Toisonet, that they were to be the owners of a beautiful house in St-Jean-Cap-Ferrat, and that agreement had been reached 'thanks to the mediation of Duke Armand Saint-Foix'.

'Christine is happy with her houses,' he said, putting the letter down on the table again. 'And she'll be even happier when I send her the cheetah skin. We killed it on the way back, so it hasn't started to smell yet.'

A question arose in the second part of Van Thiegel's mind. Since leave in the Force Publique was rare and only brief, even for the higher ranking officers, how did Christine cope with her solitude? Was she unfaithful to the Captain? For a moment, his mind was filled with the image of that woman, of the same Christine he had seen in a photo in his superior's office, but this time she was wearing a stole made of cheetah skin wrapped about her neck. A few golden curls spilled onto it. She was utterly adorable.

'We had no problems at all with any attempted escapees while we were in the jungle,' he said, shaking off the image of Christine and moving into the third part of his mind. 'I didn't waste a single cartridge collecting that timber.'

'I'm pleased to hear it. All the more ammunition for the monkeys,' said Lalande Biran, standing up.

A feeling of unease gripped that third part of Van Thiegel's mind. He would once again be pitted against Chrysostome in the shooting match, and if the poofter repeated his triumph, Van Thiegel's reputation as a hunter and his good name in general would reach rock bottom. His time in the Foreign Legion had taught him one thing, which he bore engraved on his mind: if an officer ever revealed a weakness, his enemies would flock to it like mosquitos to an open wound.

'How far away will the target be? A hundred yards?' he asked, picking up the chicotte from the river's edge and returning it to the Captain.

'Oh, two hundred at least,' replied Lalande Biran. 'It's not a matter of finishing off the monkeys as quickly as possible. We don't want the party to be over too soon.'

'Fine, two hundred yards it is then. By the way, Biran, what happened to the fourth porter? There were only three hands in the bag.'

'He got swept away by the current and we weren't going to hang around for the sake of a hand,' said Lalande Biran, tucking the chicotte in his belt.

Van Thiegel tried to blank out the third part of his brain, but failed. The image of Chrysostome refused to disappear.

X

THE ASKARIS IN THEIR RED FEZES HAD TIED UP THE FIRST
mandrill and placed it behind a white-painted screen, so
that only its head was visible. Richardson half-closed his
eyes. He could barely see the target.

'How many yards away is it, Captain?' he asked.

'About two hundred.'

The screen was right at the far end of the firing range.
Behind it lay the jungle.

'It's too far, Biran. And the light isn't going to help,' said
Richardson. The morning sun was just appearing behind the
screen. 'You try it.'

He handed him his rifle.

Lalande Biran couldn't really see the mandrill's head
either. It was just a dark smudge above the white screen.
Indeed, the only way he could identify Donatien – who was
in charge of the askaris dealing with the screen and the
mandrills – was by his greater height. Lalande Biran's eyes
might still be *d'azur et d'or*, but they were getting weaker
and weaker.

'Line up!' he ordered. 'Take forty paces forward!'

The officers lined up and advanced, counting the paces as they did so. 'One, two, three, four . . . !'

'That's better!' exclaimed Richardson when they reached the new position. Lalande Biran could see the target more clearly too; the smudge above the screen now bore the face of a mandrill. And the heads of Donatien and the *askaris* had ears.

'Oh, yes, much better,' repeated Richardson, after taking aim with his rifle. 'It's still not going to be easy, mind. It'll keep us busy the whole day. The trouble is, once we start shooting, the monkeys will get agitated.'

The *askaris* had been ordered to leave the upper part of the mandrill's body untethered, so that the animal could move its trunk and head freely. A moving target would make the game more of a challenge.

Lalande Biran shouted to Donatien and put his hand to his head. Donatien understood at once and ran to place a red fez on the mandrill.

'Oh, that's much better!' exclaimed Richardson. There was laughter among the officers, some even applauded.

Van Thiegel joined in the laughter and the applause, but his thoughts were elsewhere. All the officers, young and old, were enjoying the party atmosphere, with one exception: Chrysostome. He had placed himself at the far end of the line, on the outer edge of the group, just as he did at the card tables in the Club Royal. It wasn't indifference on his part, but arrogance. His very posture declared that distance mattered nothing to him and that he considered putting a red fez on a monkey to be an act of rank stupidity.

Lalande Biran noticed Van Thiegel's unease.

'A festive spirit reigns in the camp, but . . .' he thought

to himself, pursuing the first line of a poem. He looked around in search of details; he saw the cooks lighting the barbecues on which to cook the goat's meat and the smoke rising up and dispersing in the air. The blue flag with the yellow star fluttered gently in the breeze, and his men were happy because they didn't have to go into the jungle to carry out the ever-problematic task of keeping guard. The only man who wasn't happy was Van Thiegel.

He couldn't understand his lieutenant's attitude. The three huge barges that had set off downriver laden with six hundred mahogany logs and twelve elephant tusks would take less than a month to reach Léopoldville. A week later, the load would be in Matadi. Two weeks later, it would reach its final destination, Antwerp. From that moment on, Toisonet's employees would take charge of everything, and by mid-December, the money would be safe in a Swiss bank.

'A festive spirit reigns in the camp, and I am almost happy . . .' he thought to himself, going back to his poem. The sentence, with the spontaneous addition of 'I am almost happy', surprised him and he decided he would continue the poem in that personal, confiding tone. There was no time for that now, though, he had to announce the start of the contest. Richardson, Lopes and several other officers were pacing restlessly about near the firing position.

Lalande Biran went over to them and explained that the prize would be a photograph. The journalist coming at Christmas would take a picture of the winner and publish it in the European press.

'I'd better not win, then,' said Richardson.

'You know why, don't you? Because he's afraid of his wife,' explained Lopes, who had a jovial, soldierly sense of humour. 'In his last letter, he told her he was in Algeria and would be home soon. That was twenty years ago.'

Some of the officers laughed, and Richardson thrust the butt of his Albini-Braendlin into Lopes' stomach. He had an even more soldierly sense of humour than Lopes.

At a gesture from Lalande Biran, one of the black NCOs came over carrying a small bag. Each officer pulled out a number: Richardson chose seven, Van Thiegel eight, Lopes thirteen, and Chrysostome fourteen. Lalande Biran, however, did not put his hand into the bag. As commanding officer in Yangambi, he would only fire after all the others had done so.

The first mandrill did not move much when it heard the first shots, but as soon as it realised what was happening, it struggled to free itself. When Richardson fired, it was moving so frantically that the red fez fell to the ground. Richardson repeated his joke:

'The only reason I didn't hit it, of course, was because I'd really rather not win.'

Lalande Biran winked at him.

'Cocó won't miss, though, you wait.'

The Lieutenant wiped his sweaty hands on his trousers, took careful aim, then fired. The mandrill's head disappeared only to reappear a few seconds later.

'You wounded him, Lieutenant, but not fatally,' said Lopes. The monkey's head was moving frenetically back and forth above the screen. 'I think you got him in the shoulder,' Lopes added.

'And a lot of bloody good that is,' said Van Thiegel.

Lalande Biran again winked at Richardson, meaning that the more cursing there was, the better the contest.

'Calm down, Cocó, we've only just started,' said Richardson.

The officers who followed all missed: the ninth, the tenth, the eleventh, the twelfth and Lopes, the thirteenth. Then it was Chrysostome's turn.

Van Thiegel kept his eyes fixed on the screen. The wounded monkey was bleeding and moving less frenetically now. This clearly wasn't Van Thiegel's lucky day. He had achieved nothing, and succeeded only in making things easier for his biggest rival.

In one movement, Chrysostome put his rifle to his shoulder and fired. The head above the screen vanished, and Donatien waved the blue flag with the yellow star of the Force Publique. The *askaris* dragged away the dead mandrill.

They took a break for lunch, and the participants sat in four circles around four trays piled with the barbecued goat's meat. By then, Chrysostome had killed three monkeys; Lopes and Lalande one each; the other officers none.

Richardson offered Van Thiegel a jug of palm wine.

'If you want to shoot better this afternoon, have a drink, that's my advice. You were too tense this morning.'

The Lieutenant took a long draught of wine. He had already decided to get drunk and needed no encouragement from anyone. He had to change his luck. If not, he would be made to look a complete fool.

The wine, in a cask, had been left in the shade of a lean-to so that it didn't get too warm, and the servants, Livo and another five men, were hurrying from group to group to keep the officers' glasses filled. The only person striding around at his usual slow pace was Donatien, who was looking after the Captain and the two officers sharing his tray of meat, Van Thiegel and Richardson.

The sun was high and it was hot. Most of the men were eating eagerly. They were also drinking freely and unreservedly, relieved not to have to keep watch on the rubber-tappers in that dark jungle where a moment's inattention could cost them their life.

According to the programme for the day, which Lalande Biran had written out himself and pinned up in the entrance to the Club Royal, they were currently enjoying *un joyeux déjeuner sur l'herbe*, a jolly picnic. But the prevailing tension prevented the men from enjoying the party. Conversation was awkward, even acrimonious at times; the rifles had not been placed together in a neat stack as usually happened when the men were at rest; instead, each rifle lay by its owner's side; and no one had seized the opportunity to lie down on the ground and take a nap. Even Donatien, who cared nothing for the contest, was feeling increasingly nervous. He barely had time to breathe. Van Thiegel and Richardson kept calling him over and were drinking the wine as if it were water.

By the ninth or tenth summons, Van Thiegel was no longer demanding palm wine, but cognac. Donatien's Adam's apple sank beneath his collar. He had no cognac to give them.

'Don't worry, Donatien,' Lalande Biran told him. 'You have my permission to fetch the bottle of Martell from my office. That way, you won't have to go to the storeroom.'

Donatien saluted and headed for the square.

'You'll never see that fellow break into a run,' Lalande Biran said, following Donatien with his eyes. 'He's probably the laziest member of the whole Force Publique, but otherwise, he's like a good dog, faithful and obedient.'

'Faithful and obedient . . . and a bit short, wouldn't you say?' commented Richardson.

'Short?' exclaimed Van Thiegel. 'There's nothing short about him! I've seen his dick a couple of times and it's huge. The first time, I thought he had a piece of salami dangling down between his legs.'

Lalande Biran laughed out loud. He felt good, partly because of the drink, but largely because he had managed to hit one monkey. He had told his men that, regardless of whether he hit the target or not, he would make only one attempt. He was thus quite highly placed in the rankings: one cartridge, one monkey. Cocó, on the other hand, was very low down: three shots and not a single monkey. As was to be expected, Chrysostome was in the lead: three shots, three monkeys. No one was likely to beat him. They would each have six more shots that afternoon, but it would be difficult for anyone to equal his morning score, especially Cocó. As the day wore on, Cocó was growing more and more agitated. Every time Chrysostome's name cropped up in the conversation, his face darkened.

Donatien brought the bottle of Martell, and with it three brandy glasses.

'Well done, Donatien. I thought you might forget,' Lalande Biran said. He disliked drinking cognac out of a wine glass. 'You can go and have a sleep if you like. The contest won't start again for another hour.'

Donatien thanked him and went to lie down in the lean-to beside the cask of palm wine.

Van Thiegel had stood up and was watching Chrysostome. He was sitting with four other officers in the shade of a solitary teak tree, about fifteen yards away. They were toasting something, four of them holding their glasses high, while Chrysostome barely raised his at all. The great poofter was up to his usual tricks.

Van Thiegel turned to Lalande Biran.

'Before I tackle my friend Martell, I need to empty my bladder,' he said. His speech was slurred and he stumbled over his words. 'But just in case, I'm going a bit farther off,' he pointed to the solitary teak tree and added: 'That's the best place in Yangambi for a piss, but I don't want to risk him seeing my tadger.'

Richardson attempted a laugh, but his eyes were closing and he was falling asleep.

'We'll talk later,' said Van Thiegel. He walked off, trying to keep very upright, and disappeared behind a mound.

'A festive spirit reigns in the camp, and the warriors have been drinking,' thought Lalande Biran, taking up the thread of his poem. 'Some drink toasts and others sing, while the older men succumb to sleep. But there's no peace, no cama-raderie, the rivals eye each other coolly . . .'

Lalande Biran would have liked to slip in a quote at that point. He considered the story of Cain and Abel, but rejected the idea. Toisonet always said that you should never mix poetry and religion.

Van Thiegel returned to the group, walking with apparent ease, but when he bent his knees in order to sit down on the ground, he lost his balance and fell awkwardly, then struggled to his feet, cursing.

Lalande Biran poured cognac into two of the glasses and offered one to Van Thiegel.

'Come on, Cocó, tell me what's bothering you. What is all this about Chrysostome? Insinuations will get you nowhere.'

Friction among the men was not unusual, but Lalande Biran normally didn't take any action until, as Napoleon used to say, 'swords were about to be unsheathed'. There was no clash of swords as yet between Cocó and Chrysostome, but Cocó's antipathy was taking on an increasingly aggressive tone.

'He's a poofter, Biran. I don't know about you, but I doubt King Léopold would be amused to know that men like Chrysostome were in the Force Publique.'

Lalande Biran had just raised his glass to his lips and before he had even taken a sip, he gave the same spluttering laugh as Toisonet often did. Van Thiegel stared at him. It wasn't always easy to understand the Captain's reactions.

'He's obviously not interested in women, that much is clear,' said Lalande Biran, looking over at Chrysostome. Coincidentally, at that precise moment, Chrysostome turned to look at them, as if he had heard what they were saying. 'But as for him liking men, that's another matter. I myself have no reason to believe it. To be frank, having just spent three whole weeks in the jungle with him, day and night, I can assure you that I saw no sign of such a proclivity.'

Chrysostome still had his head turned towards them. He raised one hand and showed them three fingers. Three fingers, three monkeys.

Van Thiegel didn't understand; he couldn't tell whose side the Captain was on.

'Granted, as a marksman, he's second to none,' he said. 'He had a bit of an advantage with that first monkey because I'd already winged it, but not with the other two. They were leaping about like mad things, yet he still managed to hit them.'

Lalande Biran took a sip of cognac. Van Thiegel, who had already emptied his glass, picked up the bottle and poured himself some more.

'Are you tired, Cocó? Bored with life in Yangambi?' Lalande Biran asked him.

'Sometimes,' answered Van Thiegel cautiously.

'It's such a relief to know that next year I'll be back in Europe. I wouldn't want to end up like Richardson.'

Van Thiegel looked at him, intrigued. The Captain didn't often confide his thoughts to him. Then he turned to Richardson, who was sleeping with his mouth open, revealing two gold teeth. Seen from that perspective, he looked older than his years, like a real old man.

Lalande Biran again took up the conversation: 'He'll drop down dead in some corner of the jungle one day, and someone will come along and pull out his teeth for the gold.'

'That's certainly what Chrysostome would do,' said Van Thiegel. 'He loves jewellery – like all inverts. You just have to see the way he shows off his medallions.'

All the negative aspects of Chrysostome were piling up in his head. On the one hand, there was his crisp, clean appearance, with his jewellery always on display; on the other, there was the way Chrysostome had insulted him as soon as he arrived in Yangambi, by beating him in the William Tell competition, and then there were the looks he gave him now and then, which always said the same thing: 'I don't know what you were before, but I know what you are now: a second-rate marksman.' He couldn't get this out of his mind. He couldn't forgive him.

These malign thoughts rose up into his mouth like belches,

and he felt a need to spew them out. Lalande Biran, however, raised one finger to his lips and told him to be quiet.

'Calm down, Cocó. We'll talk about this another time.'

The Captain lay on the ground and placed his white hat over his eyes.

'Let's follow the example of our veteran friend here. A little rest will do us good. We still have a dozen or so monkeys to kill.'

Van Thiegel felt disappointed. He knew the Captain was not a man of hasty reactions, but he had hoped for something more from him. A few disapproving words, a promise to take steps. Instead, he had received only empty phrases, which came to nothing.

With his eyes covered by his hat, Lalande Biran returned to his poem. He was determined to pin down his muse, who, at the moment, would offer him only beginnings, but forty beginnings did not make a book. And he had published nothing for over six years.

'Some drink toasts and others sing, while the older men succumb to sleep. But there's no peace, no camaraderie, the rivals eye each other coolly . . .'

He remembered again how long it had been since he had published anything. More than six years. It didn't seem possible.

'There can be no peace because each man here harbours a secret, and secrets cause . . .'

He felt uncomfortable and changed position so that he was lying on his side. Once again, the poem refused to emerge into the light, and he thought it best just to forget about it and ponder the numbers he had seen in the article in *Le Soir*. Especially the two that represented the rise in the price of mahogany and ivory: 330 and 370.

The two numbers began to change shape in his mind. First, he saw them floating in the air and then, immediately, they were transformed into birds flying over a vast green meadow. '*Mon ami*, you see that area of flattened grass?' someone asked, someone he couldn't see, possibly Toisonet, although it didn't sound like his voice. Whoever it was, though, was quite right. The grass in the meadow was completely flattened. The voice went on: 'Well, that represents part of your life, the years spent in Yangambi, a sad, sterile time. That grass will never spring up again; the days wasted in this place will never return.' He looked at the meadow and saw the shadow of the birds flying over it. Except that they weren't birds now, but two bats. 'Yes, bats,' said the voice. 'Who are you? Toisonet?' he asked. 'No, I am the Other,' answered the voice, and the two bats flew straight at him, screaming wildly, with the clear intention, or so it seemed to him, of devouring his liver. He lay face down, hunched up, then sprang to his feet. When he opened his eyes, he realised that he was back in Yangambi. The sun was still high, and the day still hot. At the far end of the firing range, the *askaris* were dragging a monkey over to the white screen.

'Bad dreams?' asked Richardson. He was awake now and pouring himself a cognac. 'You leapt up as if the ground was burning you.'

'It's the fault of the cognac. I'm not as used to it as you are,' said the Captain.

'In that case, we'll have to punish it. We'll imprison it in here.' Richardson patted his belly and drank his glass down in one.

'I want to punish it too,' said Van Thiegel in the same

humorous tone as Richardson. He was sitting on the ground, his hat pushed back on his head, and he appeared to be sober, or was, at least, talking more coherently.

Lalande Biran studied him with some respect. Physically, Van Thiegel was his superior. And he wasn't a bad adjutant either. Certainly the best he could find in Yangambi. His strength meant that he could take charge of all the heavy work and, generally speaking, he had always got on well with the other officers and with the *askaris*. Up until now. Besides, he had that very unusual mother who dealt with all his money matters and kept him informed of those vital numbers, 370 and 330.

'I was thinking, Cocó,' he said suddenly. 'We must find Chrysostome a girlfriend.'

Richardson roared with laughter: 'That's a good idea!'

'Yes, I think so too, Biran,' said Van Thiegel, putting his hat on straight.

'If my long experience of such matters can be of any help, I am at your service,' said Richardson.

Lalande Biran spoke in a whisper: 'You're aware, I assume, that Donatien is in charge of bringing me girls from the jungle. Well, from now on, Chrysostome will go with him.'

Van Thiegel beamed, and Richardson applauded. It really was a very good idea.

'We'll meet tomorrow afternoon at Government House, gentlemen. About four o'clock. We must agree on a plan.'

Lalande Biran took his leave of his two colleagues and walked over to where the monkeys were being kept. The sky was blue, with just a few high, scattered clouds; the jungle was dark green; the teaks that grew here and there in the encampment were light green; the earth a yellowish brown.

While he walked, he diverted his thoughts back to the poem about Sisyphus that he had begun on the porch of the Club Royal after reading the article in *Le Soir*, and decided to use those two numbers – 330, 370 – as the title, but without telling anyone why, not even Toisonet. When he published his next book, he would tell the critics that they were 'cabalistic numbers' and that he preferred to leave it to his readers to interpret them.

'"Sisyphus," they said, "the rock you are carrying on your back has crumbled; sit down on the river bank, if you wish, and watch the water flowing. There is no weight now, there are no obligations." But, friends, Sisyphus cannot stop. If he does, he will be assailed by ravenous bats. He is not as brave as Prometheus, my friends. He is a child and needs to play. Pray, do not disturb him.'

As he passed by the screen where the next mandrill was already tied up, the monkey followed him with its eyes, but the Captain was too immersed in his poem to notice. He only returned to reality when he reached the enclosure where the other mandrills were being kept and the *askaris* called him over. One of the male mandrills appeared to have rabies and was uncontrollable. If they tried to muzzle it, it would bite them.

Lalande Biran peered over the wooden palisade. Most of the mandrills seemed rather weary and eyed him meekly, but the supposedly rabid male stared at him with bulging eyes, baring its teeth. The Captain raised his rifle and shot the creature in the head.

Two *askaris* beat the mandrill to see if it reacted, but it was dead.

'*Très bien! Très bien, mon capitaine!*' they shouted.

Lalande Biran walked over to the other officers, again focussing on the poem about Sisyphus. He really liked that last line: 'He is a child and needs to play. Pray, do not disturb him.' It provided a good tight ending.

He felt overjoyed. He knew himself well. If he could finish one poem, he could finish another twenty. He would write a letter to his publisher in Brussels, telling him that the new book was underway and asking him for a publication date.

Donatien came up to him and asked permission to go back to the screen and the monkeys. Five minutes later, the first of the marksmen began the afternoon session. Three hours later, the contest had ended with the following result: Chrysostome nine monkeys, Lopes four, Van Thiegel three.

Richardson patted the Lieutenant on the back. 'You were on excellent form this afternoon, but the younger men are pressing hard on your heels. You'll have to make way for them.'

'Oh, I'll be happy to help them, especially Chrysostome. Let's see if we can find him that girlfriend we talked about.'

'I'm sure Donatien will show him which of many paths to follow,' said Richardson.

And the two men laughed.

XI

DONATIEN BARELY SLEPT THE NIGHT AFTER HE HAD BEEN told that – at least until Christmas – Chrysostome would be accompanying him on his visits to the *mugini* in search of young girls. It would seem that Chrysostome was losing in the only contest that really mattered: the virility stakes. Donatien had heard Richardson say: 'He's a good shot with one of his rifles, but he can't even take aim with the other.'

These words were greeted with guffaws by Van Thiegel and Lalande Biran, and Donatien immediately suspected that something strange was going on, and that far from helping Chrysostome, as they claimed, they were probably hoping to make a fool of him. Anyway, they were completely wrong about Chrysostome. He was no pansy. Donatien knew this better than anyone, because one of his brothers had been queer, and you didn't have to be very bright to see that there wasn't the slightest resemblance between his brother's behaviour and Chrysostome's. Right up until the day of his suicide, his brother hadn't known a moment's peace. Everyone beat him: his father beat him, his brothers beat him, as did anyone else who came across him. It was quite the opposite with Chrysostome. Everyone was afraid of him. Even Cocó. Cocó was always very full of himself when he was with the other officers or with the *askaris*, but if Chrysostome happened by, Cocó, however hard he tried to disguise the fact, clearly felt afraid and his Adam's apple, like Donatien's, would start moving uneasily up and down. In Yangambi, everyone knew where they were with Chrysostome. He was easily angered and would as happily shoot a white man as a black. Donatien knew about this too, because another of his brothers was a murderer, and such people held no secrets for him.

Donatien made a decision. He would treat Chrysostome with respect, as if he were an officer of Lalande Biran's rank, but he would make no attempt to befriend him. He remembered the days spent with his murderer-brother, always fearing he might be his next victim, and he remembered, too, the sad fate of another brother, who had become close to the murderer. They were as thick as thieves and the lords and masters of the house and the neighbourhood where they lived, but one day, that same foolish brother ended up with a knife in his belly. It was always a mistake to rile a murderer, but befriending one was even worse.

Every Thursday morning, Chrysostome and Donatien would set off in a canoe, along with four *askaris*, in search of another young girl for Biran. That was the easy part of the job because the paths to the *mugini* and the procedure itself were well established. The natives knew exactly what their options were: they either handed over the girl or the village chief would receive forty lashes, and if he put up any further resistance, he would lose a finger or his whole hand, and that would be the end of the matter. He and

Chrysostome carried out this task without exchanging a single word, which was by far the best way. Respect was fine, but not friendship.

The problems began when they got back to Yangambi. Lalande Biran had made it quite clear that Chrysostome should be the one to wash the young girl and test her virginity. This order, however, proved impossible to carry out. Everything went as planned until they reached the mooring place for the canoes. Donatien would go off to fetch the soap and towel from the club storeroom, but by the time he came back, Chrysostome had always vanished, leaving only the four *askaris* and the girl. This happened every week. When the moment came, Chrysostome simply disappeared.

One Thursday, as he listened to Donatien's obligatory report, Lalande Biran was most surprised when Donatien, instead of presenting him with a simple lie as he usually did, elaborated on the falsehood, saying that Chrysostome was far better at washing the girl and testing her virginity than he was, a real professional.

'Well, that's a miracle I'd like to see,' Lalande Biran had said. 'Next Thursday, I'll come down to the club with the Lieutenant and Richardson, and we'll sit on the porch so that we can see at first hand the progress our pupil has made.'

Donatien felt trapped. He ran to Chrysostome's hut.

'Friend Liège, Lalande Biran says that . . .' he began.

'What do Lalande Biran, Van Thiegel and Richardson say?' asked Chrysostome.

'I think you'd better deal with the girl yourself next Thursday. Otherwise . . .'

He went no further, because he saw the look in Chrysostome's eyes and recognised it as identical to that in his murderous brother's eyes. He returned to his own hut feeling very frightened, his Adam's apple stuck in his throat.

That night, anxiety kept him from sleep. Lalande Biran would be very angry when he found out that he had failed to do as he was told and had lied week after week about Chrysostome's refusal to deal with the girl. 'You're a dog, Donatien, a lying dog,' the Captain would say to him, or words to that effect, and then he would smile and send him off to clean the rooms in Government House, as if it were a matter of no importance. A week or a month later, possibly longer, Donatien would find out that the matter had, in fact, been very important and he would end up being despatched by the Captain to the jungle and not just to any part of the jungle, but to the rebel-infested area near the Lomami River. There he would meet a dreadful end, because the rebels were cruel to their enemies and capable of all kinds of barbarous behaviour, burning them or skinning them alive.

When he considered the death that awaited him, Donatien felt a pulse in his Adam's apple, although the beating, in fact, came from his heart, and he told himself that Lalande Biran wouldn't inflict such a punishment for a relatively minor offence, after all, they had been together for six years, during which time he had served the Captain faithfully. This thought failed to console him though. He knew what Lalande Biran was like, because another brother of his, the eldest, was just the same, more like a crocodile than a rabid monkey. Not the sort of person who whips out a knife at the slightest provocation, but someone who knows how to wait for the moment when he can do most harm.

Donatien had to get out of bed and pace up and down in his hut in an attempt to drive away these troubling thoughts and calm the throbbing in his Adam's apple. He couldn't do it and he felt like crying. It was all his fault. The first time Chrysostome had refused to wash the girl, his initial intention had been to leave the soap and towel in the club storeroom and run directly to Government House to tell Lalande Biran what had happened. Then he saw the naked girl, standing up to her knees in the water – a sturdy girl, the sort he most liked – and he couldn't resist. He enjoyed running his hand over the girls' soapy bodies. As a boy, when he was ten or twelve, he hadn't liked it at all, and his older sisters had to pay him to 'rub them down'. With time, however, he had learned to enjoy it, and in that spot where the canoes were moored he had almost as good a time as he did in bed.

Donatien again felt like crying when he realised all that he would lose by not behaving as he should. There would be no more girls in his life, he would never again be able to surrender easily to sleep and rest. He wept a little; he was so very sorry, he would never do it again, and would always, in future, tell his Captain the truth.

His feelings of repentance were sincere, and perhaps because of that, an idea lit up his mind and he discovered a route to salvation, a path through the impenetrable jungle, a light in the darkness, to use a double metaphor. He remembered how swiftly he had acted on the day of his homosexual brother's suicide. As soon as he heard the news, he had run to search the room in the small hotel where his brother was living, and he was rewarded for his efforts. Apart from some money, he found a little mother-of-pearl box at the bottom of a trunk of clothes and inside it a pair of emerald earrings. When he returned home, his brothers managed to get some of the money off him, but not the earrings, which he had buried. They beat him, his murderer-brother even threatened him with a knife, but Donatien had played his part to perfection and kept his secret.

For as long as those emerald earrings remained buried, he had nurtured in his heart the hope that one day he would marry and that those precious stones would be his wedding gift to his bride. However, his call-up papers for the Force Publique had arrived before he could fulfil this dream, and when he left home for Africa, he had dug up the earrings and hidden them at the bottom of his kit bag. Six years later, they were still there.

Drying his tears on the sleeve of his shirt, he picked up the kit bag where it lay in one corner of the hut and took out the little mother-of-pearl box. It was slightly battered, but the emeralds shone as brightly as on the first day he found them, brilliant and intensely green. Even in the dim light of the oil-lamp, they stood apart from all the other ordinary objects and he was once again hypnotised by them.

Chrysostome might not be a poofter, but he liked jewels, adored them. Donatien knew this because he had often spied on him through a crack in the wall of his hut and seen him polishing his watch or his gold chain. In that respect, Chrysostome was like another of Donatien's brothers, who refused to sell the things he stole, taking this obsession to such extremes that when the police finally arrested him and searched his room, they found it stuffed full of booty, 'a real Aladdin's cave' as the police chief called it.

He would make a deal with Chrysostome. He would give

him the emerald earrings and, in exchange, Chrysostome would have to take charge of washing the girl on the next Thursday and on all the following Thursdays. This was not an easy decision for Donatien. His dream of marrying had endured in his mind as perfect and intact as the two emeralds set in the earrings, and it pained him to think that those precious stones would now never be the property of the long-dreamed-of *mademoiselle* whom he had hoped would become his wife.

That hope still crouched inside him. However beautiful, though, it was not enough to tip the scales in which the counterweight was the punishment Lalande Biran would mete out. He didn't want to be sent to the jungle and the Lomami River and be burned to death or skinned alive by the rebels. He didn't want to die in any other way either, but certainly not like that. He would have to give the earrings to Chrysostome.

There was a risk, of course. Chrysostome might take the box containing the earrings, then show him a cartridge, saying: 'If you tell anyone I took them off you, I'll put this bullet through your brain.' But that was unlikely. Generally speaking, murderers tended not to be thieves, and vice versa. At least, that's how it had always been in his family.

Day was breaking when he left his hut, taking with him the mother-of-pearl box. This was a very grave moment for him, and his Adam's apple rose and fell ceaselessly. Minutes later, when he met with Chrysostome and saw his eyes light up, he realised with relief that his plan would be successful.

Donatien's life changed for the better once Chrysostome had passed the test in the presence of Lalande Biran, Van

Thiegel and Richardson. Chrysostome washed the girl with great aplomb, and, as required by the Captain, checked that she was a virgin, donning a pair of rubber gloves for the purpose. Afterwards, the three officers left, convinced that their plan was being carried out to the letter. Donatien would thus escape punishment, would be spared exile to the Lomami River, and would not now run the risk, to put it bluntly, of having his balls cut off by the rebels.

However, the best was yet to come. On the following Thursday, when he joined the four *askaris* and Chrysostome by the canoes, ready to cross the river in search of another girl, Chrysostome placed his hand on Donatien's chest, stopping him from going any further.

'I would prefer to go alone,' he said.

When he heard those words, Donatien again felt that pulse in his throat, this time a pulse of sheer joy. He couldn't believe his luck.

'Are you sure?' he asked. 'You may know the paths that lead to the *mugini*, but it's easy to get lost in the jungle. I could help you, of course, but if you want to go alone, fine. I wouldn't want to stand in the way of a man from Britancourt.'

The most intelligent of his brothers had told him once that it was always a good idea to remember people's names and those of their wives, children, parents, aunts, uncles and other family members. 'The first step to getting what you want from someone is to treat them as if they were a friend or an old acquaintance,' his intelligent brother would say. He had always tried to follow this principle, although it wasn't as easy to do this in Yangambi as it was in Antwerp or Brussels, given that most officers were very tight-lipped when it came to talking about family or friends. He had, nevertheless, made some progress. Van Thiegel, for example, had been much more civil to him since Donatien had started asking after his mother: 'Any news from Marie-Jeanne?' 'What does Marie-Jeanne think of the price of rubber?' And even Lalande Biran, always so strict on matters of protocol, would occasionally allow him to ask after his wife: 'How is Christine Saliat de Meilhan, your wife?' These things were much more complicated with Chrysostome, but for lack of any other information, he always made a point, when he could, of mentioning Chrysostome's home town of Britancourt.

'We'll be back by four,' said Chrysostome, after consulting his silver pocket watch. 'I want you to be here on the dot.'

The terms of their collaboration had been agreed when they sealed the deal with the emerald earrings. If Lalande Biran or any of the other officers were around, then Chrysostome would wash the girl; otherwise, Donatien would perform his usual duties. They were helped in this by Livo and the other servants, who, in exchange for biscuits or salami, kept watch around the club so as to avoid any unpleasant surprises.

Chrysostome and the four *askaris* set off in the canoe, and Donatien sought shelter in the club storeroom. He had made a hiding place for himself out of a piece of mosquito netting and various crates containing food and drink, and there he would lie down and take his ease when he preferred not to be seen in the vicinity of Government House, particularly on Thursdays.

There was very little light in the storeroom, only what filtered in through the cracks in the roof, and usually Donatien fell asleep as soon as he lay down. On that day, though, he felt too happy to close his eyes. Things were going really well, the cards he was being dealt could not have been better. He no longer had to go into the jungle and face the ever-present threat from the girls' relatives in the *mugini*, who did not like strange men stealing their young women; he could also continue to savour the best aspects of that task, for on most Thursdays he got to wash the girl and, on every Thursday, it was he who took her up to Government House. He was, after all, still the Captain's orderly.

Lying awake in the near-darkness, he tried to work out if there was anything that should worry him about his present situation, if the current calm were merely an illusion. Everything indicated that it was not. There had only been one risky moment. While Chrysostome was testing the girl's virginity, Van Thiegel had exclaimed: 'Look at the little gloves the poofter's wearing!'

Fortunately, the insult did not reach Chrysostome's ears.

Donatien was surprised really that Lieutenant Van Thiegel was still alive. He had known men like him before, men who courted danger, and they tended not to last very long, indeed, they rarely lived beyond forty. For example, two of his brothers had been like that and had long since been buried, one before he was even twenty and the other before he was thirty. Who knows what would have happened on that Thursday if Chrysostome had learned that Van Thiegel was calling him a poofter? Especially since he wasn't. This was another thing he had noticed, how unobservant the officers were, whether it was Lalande Biran, Van Thiegel or Richardson. If they had asked him, he would have told them the truth at once: 'Things are not as they seem! He's just afraid of being infected. That's why he wears those gloves! That's why you don't see him with any women!' But they didn't ask him, and so the situation continued.

He had understood Chrysostome's fear of contagion as soon as he saw him put on those rubber gloves, precisely because one of his sisters was just the same and had always made Donatien wear such gloves before he, as a young boy, rubbed her down with soap and water. One day, he had asked her why, and she had told him: 'I don't want to catch one of those filthy diseases.' It was odd that Lalande Biran had not picked up on this, given that he himself was so concerned about contagion. The only difference was that the Captain believed that virginity was a guarantee of health and Chrysostome did not.

A faint light began to impinge on the darkness. The sun was stronger now and was shining in through the cracks in the roof. His thoughts were growing ever more agreeable. Everything was going so well and he was, in general, acting very prudently. His future looked bright too. If Van Thiegel managed to get out of Yangambi alive and kept his promise of going into business with him, he would soon find himself achieving his dream of making his fortune running a brothel in Antwerp. That would be the moment to buy his wife some emerald earrings.

It seemed to him that the rays of light coming in through the roof were rippling and undulating like snakes. He closed his eyes. There were, of course, obstacles, but, generally speaking, everything was going well.

He was woken by a siren and ran down to the jetty. It wasn't, as he had thought, one of the usual boats, but a small steamer bearing the letters AIA, the Association

Internationale Africaine. He immediately regretted his haste. On the deck, a group of men were standing around a wooden crate about nine feet high and shifting restlessly from foot to foot as if they didn't quite know what to do with it. No one else had responded to the siren, not even Livo.

One of the men beckoned to him. Donatien privately cursed himself for his lack of prudence. There had been no need for him to leave the storeroom. The people on the boat clearly needed assistance, presumably to unload their cargo.

The crate was so heavy they could barely move it. Donatien's arms ached with the effort.

'What have you got in here?' he asked the men. They were all veteran soldiers, who had doubtless spent many years in Africa. He didn't know them though.

'It's the Virgin,' said the man who had beckoned to him. He wasn't in uniform but wore the insignia of the Force Publique on his shirt collar.

Donatien said nothing, struggling to understand. Weeks before, he had overheard a conversation between Lalande Biran and Cocó about the possibility of bringing a lion from the zoo in Brussels so that the King could hunt it, and when he saw the wooden crate, his first thought had been that it must contain that lion. He wasn't expecting a Virgin.

'It's made of marble, that's why it weighs so much,' the man with the insignia explained.

'I'll go and fetch the servants from the club,' said Donatien. 'We need more help here.'

'No, we can manage fine with just you,' said the man.

'Well, if you think so,' muttered Donatien. '*Allezyvousvrrez.*'

There was no going back. Instead of sleeping peacefully in his hiding place, he would have to help them unload. And without a hat either, because he had left it behind in the storeroom. The scalding sun was beating down on his head.

'Fetch some more branches like those over there, so that we can lower the Virgin onto the beach,' said the man with the insignia, pointing to some mahogany branches scattered about the sand.

Donatien joined the crew of the AIA in picking up branches.

'How long are you staying?' asked Donatien. 'Have you got time for a drink of palm wine?'

He had just remembered that Chrysostome would be back with the girl at around four o'clock. It would be best if these strangers weren't around to see her. Lalande Biran didn't like witnesses. In that respect, he was just like Donatien's brothers.

'We'll unload the cargo onto the beach and then be off,' said the man with the insignia and started giving orders to the other men. They were to arrange the branches on the sand next to the jetty and set the crate down on top. That was the only way of dragging it along without it sinking.

The man seemed to know what he was doing. That way, they could easily drag the crate halfway up the beach.

'We'll leave it here. Tell your superior officer,' said the man with the insignia. He got back onto the boat, followed by the whole crew. They clearly had no time to lose.

'Of course,' said Donatien.

He remained standing by the crate until the boat had disappeared into the distance. Then he walked calmly over to Government House.

XII

THE CLUB STOREROOM HAD ALWAYS BEEN A PLACE OF REFUGE for Donatien, as well as the school in which he received lessons from his brothers. Sometimes, he lay down in his corner, remembering how they had behaved, what they had done or not done; at other times, he tried to get in touch mentally with the most intelligent of them and imagine what he would have advised him to do had he been by his side in Yangambi.

After the arrival of the Virgin, he made even more of an effort. In his concern not to spoil the splendid direction things had taken once Chrysostome had passed the test, he tried to be even more attentive and to assimilate more thoroughly those family lessons, in short, to study harder. He recalled one of the intelligent brother's favourite sayings: 'The fox may know a lot, but the hedgehog knows more.'

This needed no explanation. The message was clear: he should take no part in the excitement that had built up around the Virgin. Let the sirens wail, let the bugles sound, he would keep well out of the way. He would stay in the storeroom, in his school, in his refuge, like a hedgehog.

For a few days he stuck to his plan. He took Lalande Biran his breakfast, quickly cleaned his office and bedroom, then hurried back to his hiding place.

A week later, Donatien remembered his brother's exact words:

'The fox may know a lot, but the hedgehog knows more. But you're a dog, Donatien, and a dog is more like a fox than a hedgehog.'

With that, the lesson was complete. His brother was right. The hedgehog life bored him. It wasn't right to race out of the storeroom at the first blast of a siren but neither was spending most of the day dozing. It would be best to find some middle way. To have a little fun now and then, go for a stroll and see what was happening.

One day – the eleventh or twelfth day after the Virgin's arrival – he could stand it no longer. He went out onto the porch with a packet of biscuits and started eating them, sitting in the rocking chair that Lalande Biran usually sat in.

'A drop of anisette, Monsieur Donatien?' asked Livo, peering round the glass door that gave onto the porch.

'What colour is your *oimbé* today, Livo?' Donatien asked, aping Lalande Biran's usual greeting.

'Anisette? Cognac? Martini?' asked Livo, ignoring the question.

Donatien gave a laugh, which announced that he was about to make one of his jokes. 'I'll have an anisette today. My *oimbé* is thirsty.'

Livo vanished, wearing a smile whose days, one might say, were numbered.

Donatien was a little afraid of his liking for anisette. He could never forget that most of his brothers, eight or nine of them, had had serious problems with alcohol, and that they all favoured sweetish drinks. He did what he could to keep this tendency at bay: a small glass on ordinary days, two or three on Thursdays and Sundays, but never a drop more.

Livo returned with a glass of anisette.

'Livo, you must come with us when we go back to Antwerp,' Donatien said. Livo, he thought, would make the ideal waiter for the brothel that he and Cocó were planning to open there. That Twa tribesman, so small and black, with his curly, greying hair, would be the perfect emblem for the brothel. There would be nothing in Antwerp to compare.

Livo smiled and went back into the club.

'You may not want to, but if Cocó likes the idea, you'll have to come,' said Donatien, nibbling a biscuit.

He glanced over at the Virgin. She was still where they had left her, in the middle of the beach, but completely alone now. She hadn't been alone during the days immediately following her arrival, when all the inhabitants of Yangambi, white and black, had crowded round to contemplate this work by the new Michelangelo and to wonder at the expression in her eyes or the shape of her nose, or the extraordinarily lifelike folds of her dress. The flurry of excitement in those hearts, however, proved short-lived. The beach soon emptied of admirers. Now those who passed by on their way to the Club Royal gave her only a cursory glance, while they continued to think their own thoughts. Then came a storm, with high winds, and the footprints left on the sand by her admirers were erased. The place reverted to its former self. While the statue of the Virgin did not become just another feature of the landscape, like a log or a rock, it did lose its lustre and ceased to be the star of Yangambi.

Donatien ate three biscuits one after the other, then washed down the crumbs caught in his throat with a little anisette.

He looked again at the Virgin and froze as if he too were a marble statue. There on the beach, head bowed, was the Best Soldier, the new William Tell, the finest marksman in the whole of the Congo, the son of Britancourt. In a word, Chrysostome.

He wasn't usually to be seen there at that hour, for he tended to be one of the last to arrive at the club; however, the most unusual thing was his posture. Chrysostome never walked with his head bowed. On the contrary, he walked rather stiffly, with his chin lifted. He knew he was a 'magnificent' member of the Force Publique and he flaunted it.

Donatien put down the biscuits and the anisette and went to hide in the storeroom so that Chrysostome would not know he had seen him. Before going in, though, he turned and peered furtively at the beach. Chrysostome was kneeling before the Virgin.

Seated in his usual corner, Donatien began to think.

'This fact is pure gold,' he heard a voice say in his head. It was his intelligent brother again.

He was right. True, Yangambi wasn't Antwerp and Chrysostome left much to be desired as a source of information, and yet Donatien sensed that in some way what he had just seen could prove beneficial to him. There was something odd about that man kneeling at the Virgin's feet, head bowed. He needed to find out more. The following morning, as soon as he had finished his work in Government

House, he would go straight to the beach to inspect the terrain.

The tracks left by Chrysostome ran in almost straight lines along the shore of the river, but became crooked and uneven as they approached the Virgin. They seemed to contain some secret message.

'Something has happened to Chrysostome. He has a problem and is worried,' said Donatien's intelligent brother, and Donatien agreed.

He wanted to find a clear, categorical answer in those marks on the beach, such as 'Chrysostome's problem is . . .', but in that respect, the beach was silent, a blank page. When Donatien went back into the storeroom and lay down in his corner, he couldn't get to sleep. The unease provoked by the sense that something was going on, something he was unable to identify, prevented him from sleeping.

That night, the same thing happened, and he spent most of the time awake. He simply could not sleep and, when he did close his eyes, rather than the image of a girl or some other similarly soothing image, he saw the image of Chrysostome, just as he had seen him on the beach, kneeling before the Virgin, head bowed.

He felt incapable of solving this mystery, even with the aid of his intelligent brother, and decided that perhaps it would be best to refer the matter to Lalande Biran. Easier said than done. The first day, he found Lalande Biran completely absorbed in reading a book; the second, he was in a rage because he couldn't find his wedding ring; the third and the fourth, he was busy discussing the rubber crop with Van Thiegel. As Donatien waited for the right moment, time was slipping by, and the only reliable help he had were his brother's encouraging words. Often, while he sat on the porch of the club, with a glass of anisette in his hand, his brother's voice would ring out loudly in his head, always saying the same thing: 'Be patient, dog. Soon you will learn something about Chrysostome and receive your reward.'

The fifth day, he went into Government House in order to clean the Captain's office and found that Richardson and Van Thiegel were both there too. Seated on the wicker armchairs around the table, they were discussing the details of the bishop's visit with absolute military seriousness. The paths and streets in Yangambi would have to be cleaned and three new huts prepared for the visitors: a large one for the bishop, another for the priests and a third for the journalist. The blessing of the Virgin would take place, at the express wish of Brussels, on Christmas Day, which left them just two weeks to organise everything.

Donatien dusted the furniture and the various objects in the living room, the rhinoceros horn, the desk, the rocking chairs, the books on the shelves, and the photo of the Captain's wife, Christine Saliat de Meilhan, because once the rainy season was over and the mud in Yangambi had dried, dust invaded everything.

'This whole business makes me nervous,' said Lalande Biran.

'You and everyone else,' said Donatien, butting in.

Only one person noticed his remark: his intelligent brother. 'Be patient, dog,' he warned him from inside his head.

'What makes *me* nervous is that Virgin in the middle of

the beach. It will be a weight off our shoulders once we deposit her on Samanga,' added Richardson.

Donatien nodded.

'Let's move on to the next point. Let's talk about the menu,' said Lalande Biran. He got up and started pacing round the table. 'I thought we could start with a few smoked *wapose*, followed by kid soup, roast leg of goat with sweet potato sauce and, to finish, fried bananas. Oh, and a bit of chocolate to accompany the coffee. If we have any chocolate. Do we, Donatien?'

'Yes, Captain. There's a big box in the storeroom,' answered Donatien.

There was disagreement. Richardson disapproved of the smoked *wapose*. They were, of course, delicious, but they looked hideous. There was no escaping the fact that they were worms, and the bishop would be sure to find them disgusting.

Lalande Biran expressed his thoughts out loud. The bishop and the journalist, especially the journalist, would have to realise that they were in the Congo, in Africa. Kid soup and roast goat were fine, but one could find such dishes in Brussels or in Paris. They needed something distinctive, a bit of local colour. If not *wapose*, they could perhaps choose something similar.

'If we ply them with enough champagne, there won't be any problem. Our visitors will eat everything that's put before them, even grilled snake,' said Van Thiegel.

'What about smoked antelope fillets?' suggested Donatien.

This time, Lalande Biran heard what he said and looked at him with his blue-gold eyes.

'That's not a bad idea,' he said.

'Thank you, Captain.'

'How long would it take to prepare and smoke an antelope properly?' asked Lalande Biran.

'About a week, or so Livo says,' answered Donatien. '*Unesmenpepreçamdilivoquendmem.*'

Richardson clapped him on the back. He thought the antelope an excellent idea.

'And it's easy enough to hunt them at this time of year,' he said. 'The other day, when I was out with the rubber-tappers, I saw a whole herd of them.'

Lalande Biran walked up and down the room, thinking, his arms folded, his left hand cradling his chin. He stopped by the bookshelf and selected a cookery book.

'I would cook it just as I would venison,' he said as he searched for the recipe. 'We have wine, even if it is only palm wine, and nutmeg too. The trouble is,' he concluded, 'we don't have any spring onions,' and he returned the book to its place and came back to the table.

'You could use mulberries and other berries from the jungle,' suggested Donatien, who had abandoned his labours and was taking part in the conversation as an equal. 'Livo cooked it like that once. I think it was when you were off hunting elephants.'

Donatien's last sentence oozed caution.

'It would seem that you eat best when I'm away,' said Lalande Biran, but he didn't seem really bothered.

'At least let there be French champagne, made, if possible, by the Widow Clicquot. I'm sure the bishop won't object,' said Van Thiegel.

Now he was pacing the room, and when he reached the corner where the rhinoceros horn was on display, he picked it up as if testing its weight.

'The bishop won't be our most influential visitor, Cocó. I'm not drawing up the menu with him in mind. I'm thinking of the journalist and his Kodak.'

'I'll pose like this and ask him to take my photo. Then I'll have another one taken with the Widow Clicquot,' said Van Thiegel, placing the rhinoceros horn on his head.

Richardson and Donatien both laughed. Lalande Biran merely smiled.

When Van Thiegel put the rhinoceros horn back down on the floor, he inadvertently knocked over a portfolio that was leaning against the wall, and its contents spilled out. They were Lalande Biran's sketches of naked girls; one was larger than the others, and when he pulled it out, he saw something that sent a shiver down his spine. It was a photograph of Christine Saliat de Meilhan, but utterly different from the photo the Captain kept framed and on view to anyone visiting the office. According to a note in one corner, it had been taken on the beach in Biarritz. It showed Christine in a wet bathing suit, with her equally wet hair – one curl of which was stuck to her cheek – her flat stomach and her athletic thighs all the way down to her knees, where the photo ended.

He put the photo back and quickly closed the portfolio. He felt shaken. He could understand now why the Captain had those young girls brought to him. It can't have been easy to fill the space left in his bed by such a woman.

He realised that he had dust on his fingertips. Donatien only cleaned the visible surfaces, but never went further than that. The portfolio had spent weeks, possibly months, leaning unopened against the wall. It was incredible. That photograph deserved to be in some far worthier place than a dusty portfolio.

Lalande Biran was telling Richardson about Ferdinand Lassalle. He was a great journalist, the winner of the Prix Globe no less.

'He's just the man to present Europe with a favourable image of us. That's why I'm taking such care over the details of the visit.'

Richardson covered his face with both hands.

'This is how I'll be posing if he tries to take *my* photo. I gave my wife the slip years ago, but if she sees me in the newspaper, she could easily turn up in Yangambi. And I'm certainly not having that, gentlemen. Certainly not.'

This time, they all laughed, Van Thiegel loudest of all.

'Tomorrow, gentlemen, I will go and hunt that antelope with which we intend to impress our guests. I'll ask Chrysostome to come with me,' Lalande Biran announced.

'May I come too, Biran?' asked Richardson. 'As you know, we old men need our exercise.'

'I'll stay here,' said Van Thiegel, 'and start organising the clean-up. It's not going to be easy getting things spick and span, mind, especially not in the African quarter. There are too many animals there to make it entirely presentable.'

His mind had split in two again, and both halves contained the same image: Christine Saliat de Meilhan in a wet bathing suit on the beach at Biarritz.

'Excuse me, Captain, but tomorrow is Thursday,' Donatien put in.

Lalande Biran looked at him with his blue-gold eyes.

'I mean that Chrysostome has to come with me to find a girl,' he explained. '*JevedirqueCriomedoallermoipourcherunefille.*'

'You'll have to go alone,' replied Lalande Biran. 'I need Chrysostome to accompany me on the antelope hunt.'

'Of course,' said Donatien, but his Adam's apple disagreed and suddenly vanished beneath his collar.

Van Thiegel raised his arm, like someone demanding the floor at a crowded meeting.

'Speaking of Chrysostome, Biran, there's something I've been meaning to say. That poofter has been washing the young girls and so on for a while now, but I haven't seen any difference in him. We ought to change tactics.'

Donatien shook his head. They were quite wrong. Chrysostome was very different. He felt like telling them about what he had seen from the porch, but he was angry with the Captain now and disinclined to give him that information. Why didn't he invite *him* to go hunting? Why did he choose to send *him* off to find a girl without Chrysostome's help? It was partly his own fault, for talking too much. The idea of including antelope on the menu had been his, but it was also partly Livo's fault. Livo really liked antelope meat, and Donatien was tired of hearing him go on about it. Whenever Donatien took him the mice he caught in the storeroom, Livo always said: 'I'd prefer an antelope' – '*Je préférais une antilope.*'

'We have far more urgent matters to deal with at the moment,' said Lalande Biran to Van Thiegel, 'like preparing a warm welcome for our visitors and taking the Virgin to Samanga.'

'Yes, Samanga's an excellent spot for that sculpture,' said Richardson.

'I'm just worried that some rebel might have seen it on the beach,' Van Thiegel commented. He wanted to free himself of that image of Christine, which had taken root in both parts of his mind, keeping him from concentrating on the conversation. 'If they have, they'll be expecting some-thing to happen. And of course if they find out a journalist is coming, they'll probably plan an attack. It would be great publicity for them.'

'Yes, I'm nervous about that too, and getting more nervous,' said Donatien.

He hadn't been into the jungle to look for girls for weeks now and it suddenly seemed to him incredible that he once used to visit the *mugini* accompanied by only four *askaris*.

'If I may, Captain, I'll go and tidy your bedroom,' he said and left the office, forgetting to salute.

He didn't, however, go into the bedroom, but went straight out into the garden. There was no sign of smoke or drumming from the jungle, only the occasional shriek from the monkeys, nothing more. The monkeys weren't very bright and screamed at the slightest thing, whereas the rebels crouched silently in the darkness under the trees and the undergrowth, watching.

XIII

AS SOON AS THEY HAD CROSSED OVER TO THE OPPOSITE BANK, Donatien and the four *askaris* set off in the direction of the larger *mugini*, following a path that neither the undergrowth nor the trees had managed to erase completely. They had barely gone two hundred yards when the shrill cry of a monkey broke the silence and a flock of birds took noisy flight. The four *askaris* were immediately on the alert.

'Who is it?' asked Donatien.

The four *askaris* raised their rifles. Donatien stood behind them. Again they heard noises, this time the sound of voices.

'*Je crois que ce sont des enfants*,' said one *askari*, lowering his rifle slightly: 'I think they're children.' They all listened hard and agreed that he was right. They were light, young voices.

Out of the undergrowth emerged three girls of eight or nine and a very tall girl of about fifteen, so light-skinned that she didn't appear to come from that part of Africa. They were speaking gaily, as if telling each other amusing stories. The tall girl stopped abruptly, and the younger girls walked on, immersed in their conversation.

Donatien opened his eyes very wide. The tall, light-skinned girl was wearing earrings. Green earrings. They looked like emeralds. He raised his rifle and fired.

The tall girl screamed, and a monkey echoed her scream. All four girls broke into a run and vanished into the dense vegetation. Donatien roared, his throat almost bursting:

'Get that girl!'

He plunged into the jungle, along with the other men. A few yards ahead of him, the girl's head appeared above the bushes, and on that head was an ear and in that ear glittered an emerald. Donatien fired again.

The head bobbing above the bushes suddenly veered into a darker part of the jungle, and Donatien followed. Sometimes he would lose sight of her for a few seconds, then he would catch the green glint of an emerald, sometimes once, sometimes twice, and would quicken his pace, ducking now and then to avoid the lianas. The tall girl was a good runner, much faster than him. He cursed himself for being such a bad marksman. If he had even a fraction of Chrysostome's skill, those earrings would now be in his pocket.

The glints of green grew more numerous, as if he had before him twenty heads and forty earrings, and he slowed his pace. The signs continued to multiply. Soon there were fifty heads and a hundred earrings, and a moment later, a hundred heads and two hundred earrings.

He came to a complete halt, breathing hard. Before him lay thousands of glittering green lights. They were not emerald earrings, however, but the tiny round leaves of a plant. Some distance away, a monkey shrieked. He looked around him and couldn't recognise the trees. They weren't mahogany trees or teak, they weren't draped in long lianas like the rubber trees from which they extracted the sap. He was lost.

He called out to the *askaris*, but the only answer came from the monkeys. He raised his rifle to fire again, because he still had ten cartridges, but stopped. Lalande Biran would forgive him the two cartridges he had spent and even the ten still in the magazine, because he wasn't particularly strict about ammunition, but if he fired again, would the *askaris* come to his aid, or was it more likely that the rebels would make an appearance to find out what was going on? When they saw him there completely alone, they would fall on him and drag him off to their lair. Then they would chop off his limbs with a machete or beat him about the face until he was blind. Van Thiegel had told the younger officers that if ever they found themselves in that situation, it would be best to give themselves a relatively pleasant death by shooting themselves in the mouth.

Donatien peed in his trousers. His heart was beating so hard, he could feel it in his mouth. He tried to retrace his footsteps, to escape from those thousand small green leaves, but his legs felt as if they were made of wood.

A bird flew out of a tree and over his head. Someone was approaching.

Donatien's legs were like two wooden stakes stuck fast in the ground; he couldn't even run and hide behind a tree trunk. The sounds grew clearer: a twig breaking, a foot stepping into a puddle, a branch being sliced off with a machete. A figure took shape among the little green leaves. This time the pee ran down as far as Donatien's knees.

'*Monsieur Donatien, voulez-vous une anisette?*'

Before him stood Livo, a broad smile on his face. Tears sprang into Donatien's eyes and he felt an impulse to embrace his assistant from the Club Royal, but something held him back. He didn't give Livo boxes of biscuits, as Lieutenant Van Thiegel did, but he did let him into the storeroom. Had he in some way already repaid this favour? He stopped where he was.

'I was visiting my daughter in the *mugini* and I heard shots. That's why I came over,' said Livo. 'What happened?'

'Oh, nothing special,' answered Donatien.

He was still so agitated that his words were barely comprehensible: '*Rianparculie.*'

'I have to get back to the club,' said Livo. 'If you like, we can go together.'

Donatien wondered if he should promise him a box of biscuits. He was, after all, doing him a big favour and deserved some reward, but wouldn't that be setting a precedent? If you give someone one box of biscuits, they will demand another and another and another. That was what had happened with Van Thiegel. Livo was always asking him for biscuits, sometimes for his daughter, sometimes for the children in the *mugini* or for the witch doctors who supplied him with herbs, and Van Thiegel always said Yes. And that wasn't right. Van Thiegel wasn't responsible for the storeroom and so didn't care, but Donatien knew the value of those biscuits. There were many things in Yangambi, but the only sweets available were bananas and sugar cane. That's why biscuits were so highly prized.

'Have you seen the four *askaris* who came with me?' he asked.

'I saw them heading down to the river. They'll be waiting for you there,' said Livo.

'Let's go, then.'

On the way back, his heart having resumed its regular rhythm and his whole body functioning normally again, he thought once more about the tall girl with the pale skin. He had been so astonished to see her in possession of the emerald earrings that he hadn't known what to think. It was the strangest thing he'd ever seen in Yangambi. A white officer making a gift of jewellery to a native girl! And the white officer wasn't just any officer, he was Chrysostome!

The intelligent brother appeared to him as they were crossing the river. He was in laconic mood.

'It's hard enough to get information, but even harder to hold it in reserve for the right moment. Don't waste it, dog.'

It was good advice, but he didn't really have much choice. Yangambi was a garrison, and his superiors, especially Lalande Biran, were always demanding news. If he kept quiet and they later found out that there *had* been news, which he had then kept from them, he would be sent straight to the dungeon in Government House or, worse, to the rebel-infested part of the jungle. It would therefore be wisest to tell the Captain the truth. Chrysostome wasn't a poofter. He had a girlfriend on the other side of the river, a young half-white, half-black girl, as tall as a Watusi.

Lalande Biran would receive this news without a flicker of surprise, as was his way, but then he would immediately sit down on his chaise longue to ponder it.

XIV

THE IMAGE OF CHRISTINE SALIAT DE MEILHAN REMAINED
fixed in both parts of Van Thiegel's mind. He closed his
eyes, and there she was in her wet bathing suit and wet
hair, one curl stuck to her cheek, her flat stomach, her
athletic thighs. On the very morning that the Captain set
off with Chrysostome and Richardson to hunt for antelope,
an idea suddenly filled his heart. Or more accurately and
more metaphorically, a violent desire gripped his heart much
as an animal's paw pounces on a small bird. He would have
that woman. Christine would be his.

Ever since his days as a legionnaire, Van Thiegel had kept
a notebook entitled *Mon histoire sentimentale*, in which, in blunt
military manner, with no embellishments, no beating about
the bush, he kept a note of all the women he had known:
where they came from, how much he had paid for them, and
where the act had taken place. After accompanying the hunters
as far as the palisade, he returned to his office and took the
notebook from the desk drawer in which he kept it.

The last entry stated that there had been 184 women and
girls: 155 blacks and 29 whites; 159 free and 25 paid for.

Van Thiegel made some calculations. If he was thinking of spending another three or four months in Yangambi, the number of women would easily rise to 190. Then, once he had got his discharge from the Force Publique and returned to Europe, it would take him about a year to reach Christine's bed, and meanwhile, he would have another nine women, all of them prostitutes, so as not to waste time. That way, if he was man enough to meet his own calculations, Christine would be number 200.

Van Thiegel felt excited. By assigning her a round number, Christine seemed somehow more within reach. It occurred to him that she could be his in a still shorter space of time. If he went directly from Yangambi to Paris without stopping off in Antwerp, five months would be more than enough. If he lived in Paris, it would take him only a matter of weeks to meet Christine. From then on, it would be easy. A couple of outings together, three at most, and she would be his.

The NCO on duty came to the office to receive his orders. Van Thiegel reluctantly dragged himself out of the dream-state into which his calculations had plunged him and told the NCO that they must set about cleaning up Yangambi. There was no time to lose! The stables and enclosures didn't matter so much, but the area around the main street and especially around the Place du Grand Palmier should positively sparkle! They would shortly be receiving a visit from a bishop, 'a great European wizard' – 'un grand sorcier européen' – and they must give him a royal welcome.

'Get all the women together and set them to work. If necessary, use the chicotte on them.'

'Should we clean this house and the Captain's too?' asked

the NCO. '*Est-ce qu'on doit nettoyer aussi cette maison et celle du capitaine?*'

Van Thiegel said No. Donatien would be in charge of Government House, and he himself didn't want anyone coming into his house.

The NCO noticed the general disorder in the office, but said nothing.

'We also have to prepare three huts for the visitors. Choose three empty ones that are in a reasonably decent state. Inside the palisade, of course.'

He found it hard to speak. Things were changing inside his head. One part of his mind – the official part, so to speak – was reminding him that it was, in fact, his job to decide which huts the visitors should stay in, while on the other side – the rebellious side, shall we say – the image of Christine in her bathing suit was growing and coming alive.

'If you have no further orders, sir,' said the NCO.

'Are there any other officers in Yangambi at the moment, or am I the only one? I know that the Captain, Richardson and Chrysostome have gone off hunting, but what about Lopes and the others?' asked Van Thiegel.

The NCO told him that he was the only one there, that the others were with the rubber-workers.

'All except Donatien, and he's gone across the river with four *askaris*,' he added.

'Good. Well, you'd better get cleaning,' said Van Thiegel.

The NCO saluted before withdrawing.

When Van Thiegel was alone again, the two parts of his mind became embroiled in an argument. One side, the rebellious half, was trying to push him towards Government

House. The other officers were away, so there would be no witnesses. The door of the Captain's office would be open, and he would find the portfolio and the photograph of Christine in the same place as on the previous day. It would be easy enough to pick it up and take it. However, the official side was against this. He shouldn't steal the photo. Lalande Biran would never forgive him.

'Christine will be your woman number 200. The photo could be the first step in your plan of action,' urged the rebellious side.

These words proved decisive. He got up, strode across the square and entered Government House, casually saluting the *askari* on guard there. He opened the office door quite naturally, as he always did, as if expecting to find the Captain there at his desk, writing letters or poems or reclining on the chaise longue, reading a book. However, all that remained of Lalande Biran was the smell of tobacco impregnating the air.

Van Thiegel opened the portfolio and removed the photograph. Christine Saliat de Meilhan was undoubtedly a very beautiful woman, but only then did it occur to him why she was on the beach. She was probably a swimmer, which would explain her unusually athletic body.

On the chaise longue lay a copy of *La Gazette de Léopoldville*. He picked it up and slipped the photo in between the pages. The guard would assume that he had simply gone into the office to collect the newspaper.

The official side of his mind brought him up short. There was still time. He could still return the photo to its proper place and his record would remain unblemished. His time in Africa was coming to an end; an impeccable military career of more than twenty years was, fortunately, nearing its conclusion. And he would begin the European stage of his life a rich man. Was it worth risking all that? Besides, why did he need the photograph? Couldn't he just store the image in his memory?

Alas, the argument put forward by the rebellious side of his mind proved more convincing. Lalande Biran was always losing things. One of Donatien's main tasks was finding the Captain's wedding ring, which he left in all kinds of places. Therefore, if the Captain ever did realise that the photograph was missing, he would suspect nothing and blame himself. After all, you never achieved anything if you didn't take risks. When Christine became his woman number 200, he could tell her about this moment over a candle-lit supper in a romantic restaurant in Paris: 'I fell so deeply in love with you that I even stole your photograph from Government House.' What woman could resist a bold lover?

He was tempted to sit down on one of the white benches in the square and take a first quick glance at the photo, but the women in charge of the clean-up were there and he decided, instead, to go to his room. For the first time in his life, he felt something he had never felt with his previous 184 lovers: a desire to be alone. The time had not yet come when he could take Christine to a romantic restaurant or put his arms about her in person, but at least he had the photo.

There were no windows in his bedroom and so he had to light the oil lamp in order to find a place to hide the photo. This wasn't easy because, apart from the bed, the only furniture was the mahogany bedside table, with a drawer and a compartment underneath in which he stored his bottles. The drawer, however, was filled to overflowing with the letters his mother had written to him over the years.

By the light of the oil lamp, Christine's body seemed to take on a physical reality. Van Thiegel's heart filled with emotion. 'Where are you going to wait for me?' he asked the photograph. 'In bed,' he said, in answer to his own question. That is how it would be in the future. Woman number 200 would give the same answer: 'In bed.' He hid the photo under the pillow and went into the office to write a letter to his mother.

'*Chère maman: j'espère que cette lettre vous trouvera en bonne santé . . .*' – 'Dear Mama, I hope this letter finds you in good health . . .'

Van Thiegel envied Lalande Biran certain abilities. He would have liked to be able to write like him, quickly and without mistakes, whether it was a report for the Force Publique, a letter or a poem. Only then did it occur to him that his lack of writing skills could prove a disadvantage if Christine demanded not just physical strength and vigour but fine phrases, and refused to become his woman number 200 if he denied them to her. There was nothing he could do about that. It was far harder for him to put his ideas down on paper than it was to venture into the jungle.

'Aujourd'hui je vous écris pour vous dire trois choses,' he wrote in capitals, as if it were a headline. 'I am writing to you today to tell you three things.' Then he explained it all in three paragraphs. In the first, he told his mother that he was going to ask for his discharge from the Force Publique and return to Europe, having saved enough money to lead a quieter life. In the second, he explained that he wished to buy a house in Paris, and in the third, that the house should be situated in rue du Pont Vieux or a nearby street. '*C'est tout à fait nécessaire, j'aime cette rue,*' he wrote. 'It has to be there, because I like that street.' He could not tell his mother that it wasn't the street he wanted, but the woman who lived at number 2 3, Christine Saliat de Meilhan. That was the number that appeared in the return address on the letters she wrote to the Captain: *Paris, rue du Pont Vieux 23.*

The schedule of boats that stopped in Yangambi gave him a little thrill of joy. The next to arrive would be the *En Avant.* He decided that, in the future, that would be his motto, *en avant,* onward.

For the first time in years, he chose to stay in his bedroom instead of going off on patrol to inspect the work of the rubber-tappers. Shortly afterwards, his spirits slightly roused by the effects of the Martell brandy, he looked again at the photo, then closed his eyes and imagined himself strolling along the rue du Pont Vieux and engineering a chance meeting with Christine. Perhaps she wouldn't prove to be such a difficult conquest. Lalande Biran was a cold creature and didn't even seem particularly eager to see his wife again. Besides that, he spent a lot of time engrossed in thought, writing poems or reading books, usually with a gloomy expression on his face – hardly the most amusing of husbands. He, on the other hand, would offer Christine fun and a little adventure. He wasn't bad-looking, and his blue eyes usually got him a long way, as did his strong, vigorous body. And so it would be again when he returned to Paris.

XV

WHEN THE SECOND CLEAN-UP OPERATION BEGAN IN Yangambi, there was only a week to go before Christmas. A despatch from the AIA informed Lalande Biran that since the journalist Ferdinand Lassalle would be bringing the most up-to-date of cameras with him, it would be best if the older, uglier natives were removed from Yangambi and kept in an enclosure in the jungle until the visit was over.

Helped by the *askaris*, Van Thiegel and Richardson gathered together about eight hundred rubber-workers and lined them up on the firing range until Lalande Biran arrived. Then the three of them reviewed the workers, separating out those they thought would photograph badly and, at the same time, choosing the best-looking candidates, the healthiest and most handsome of the young men, whose pictures would be guaranteed to catch the eye of magazine editors in Paris, Brussels or Monaco.

Those workers deemed to be suitably photogenic, about fifteen of them, were taken to the Place du Grand Palmier, where the work of decorating the square had begun, supervised by Lalande Biran. He had found the coloured ribbons said to have been used on the day Yangambi was officially founded, and he wanted to create a kind of cupola by hanging the ribbons from the top of the palm tree. 'Ideal work for our black Adonises,' he had declared. As for the ugly or less presentable workers, about a hundred of them, they were marched off into the jungle, and Van Thiegel was charged with escorting them there.

This wasn't a particularly dangerous mission, but given that the enclosure was located in a somewhat inaccessible part of the jungle, the whole thing took all day. The outward journey lasted eight hours because of the sheer difficulty of moving such a large group of men and because one of them attempted to escape, a problem Van Thiegel managed to resolve satisfactorily. Coming back took another three hours. Not that he minded. The physical and military nature of the exercise lifted his mood, for he had been feeling uneasy ever since he stole Christine's photograph.

Back in Yangambi, he met up with Lalande Biran on the club porch. The Captain seemed very contented, and pleased with the improvements being made in Yangambi. He began singing that song again: '*La Cigale, ayant chanté tout l'été . . .*' Everything indicated that the last steamship to pass through Yangambi, the *En Avant*, had brought him good news.

'Our visitors are about to arrive,' he announced.

Two letters lay on the table. Van Thiegel looked at the return address on one of them: *Christine Saliat de Meilhan. Rue du Pont Vieux 23. Paris*. There was his woman number 200! *La femme numéro 200!*

'My wife is happy,' said Lalande Biran. 'Her ambition was to own seven houses in France, and she has just bought the last one, in St-Jean.'

'Is that where she will live? All year I mean?' asked Van Thiegel.

Lalande Biran shook his head.

'I've also had a letter from Monsieur X. The profits from the mahogany and the ivory – which were huge apparently – have been safely deposited in the bank.'

As usual, the Captain was hiding Monsieur X's letter from Van Thiegel, this time underneath the letter from Christine. Not that Van Thiegel cared who Monsieur X really was. He was about to leave Yangambi, and there would be no more of those emergency expeditions in search of mahogany and ivory.

'I've sent a letter to my mother in which I recommend that she model herself on your wife,' he said.

'As I mentioned before, they would make excellent colleagues.'

'When we get back to Europe, we could meet up in Paris, you, Christine, my mother and me.'

'Yes, why not,' said Lalande Biran.

Livo came to ask if they wanted anything to drink.

'Is there any cold champagne?' asked Lalande Biran.

'I've left a few bottles to cool in the river.'

'Bring me one, will you, Livo. The one with the best *oimbé*,' said Lalande Biran. Livo left, smiling, and returned carrying the bottle of champagne in a bucket of water.

They sat out on the porch until late in the evening, and Van Thiegel told Lalande Biran of his plans. By next spring, he hoped to be in Antwerp, where he intended opening a business with Donatien, a bar that would be simultaneously modern and old-fashioned. Donatien had some experience in the field and his family was well known in the city.

'Sounds good,' said Lalande Biran.

'Of course, I won't stay in Antwerp all year. I'll spend some time in Paris too,' added Van Thiegel.

Lalande Biran's only response was to begin softly singing that song again: '*La Cigale, ayant chanté tout l'été . . .*' Van Thiegel almost mentioned which Paris street he would like to live on, but stopped himself.

Richardson joined them, and Livo was despatched to bring another bottle of champagne.

'I have some important news for you,' Lalande Biran said when their glasses were full.

'We're all ears, Captain!' said Richardson.

Lalande Biran raised his glass to his lips. His blue-gold eyes were smiling.

'Gentlemen, Chrysostome is in love. With a girl!' he exclaimed.

'In love?'

This time Van Thiegel's look of surprise was absolutely genuine.

Richardson was pacing up and down.

'Chrysostome? In love? With a girl?' he repeated.

'Yes, with a young girl, half-black, half-white!'

Lalande Biran poured himself more champagne.

'A young girl, half-black, half-white?' Richardson repeated. He was waving his arms about like the conductor of a choir, as if urging the monkeys to scream loudly. As chance would have it, the monkeys did exactly as Richardson asked.

Lalande Biran and Van Thiegel burst out laughing.

XVI

IN THE DAYS PRIOR TO CHRISTMAS, VAN THIEGEL DRANK A
lot of cognac and a lot of palm wine, and he began to
feel that his head was dividing not into two, as was usual
with him, but into smaller segments, into eight, twelve or
sixteen compartments. In these compartments, the image
of Christine merged with that of Lalande Biran, Livo,
Donatien, Chrysostome and many other people. To make
matters still more confusing, intermingled with these images
were thoughts about his economic situation and his sentimental or sexual life and, finally, with ineffable particles
that were neither images nor thoughts and that dissolved
before they could take shape.

The images, thoughts and ineffable particles spun round
and round in his head as if driven by a roulette wheel, until
he feared he would go mad and end up, like his father, in
a straitjacket. At that point, he tried to drink less and to
pass the time playing cards, swimming in the river or going
to bed with the women who worked in the warehouses or
in the slaughterhouse. In this way, he succeeded, at least
some of the time, in slowing the speed of the roulette wheel,

but as soon as he abandoned these activities and had a few drinks, the wheel would start to spin as fast as before, so that he couldn't even follow a conversation and found it hard to pay attention to what was going on around him.

Soon, he began to see new images. They didn't belong to the roulette wheel spinning inside his head, but, so to speak, to reality, to Yangambi. He saw the *Petit Prince* moored at the jetty, and a line of priests getting off the boat, with their black cassocks hoisted up to their knees. Later – the following day or two days later, he wasn't sure – he saw one of those priests in a white chasuble blessing the statue of the Virgin and, beside him, a short man taking photographs. He saw Lalande Biran, too, wearing his white hat and with his Luger pistol at his waist.

He heard what Lalande Biran said:

'Gentlemen, kindly follow me to the Club Royal, where the finest jungle delicacies await us.'

Lalande Biran looked very elegant with his Luger at his waist. His blue-gold eyes shone as never before. Van Thiegel realised that those eyes were looking at him and ordering him to sit down.

'Have you ever eaten smoked antelope before, Bishop?' asked Lalande Biran.

Instead of the white chasuble, the bishop was now wearing a black cassock and a purple silk sash. He shook his head and smiled.

'And what about you, Lassalle, have you ever eaten it before?' Lalande Biran asked the little man who had been taking photographs of the Virgin.

The little man said No.

Van Thiegel did not feel very comfortable at the table.

He found Lalande Biran's formality irritating. He didn't like the bishop either. And he liked the little man even less. That was why he kept drinking palm wine, glass after glass, so as to forget about his companions.

He was still munching his way through his portion of antelope when something caught his ear. The others were discussing a subject he knew about. He listened more closely and heard the journalist, who was about the same size as Livo, recounting to the bishop and Lalande Biran an anecdote involving Duke Armand Saint-Foix. Although he had no desire to speak and no intention of doing so, he felt his mouth opening and closing as if it had a life of its own and exclaiming: 'Of course! Armand! Monsieur X!'

Van Thiegel was sure he was right, because as soon as he heard the name 'Armand', the roulette wheel in his head had stopped at the letter X. Encouraged by this success, his mouth started talking about the difficulties involved in felling mahogany trees and transporting such a hard, heavy wood. However, he ceased this disquisition when he saw Lalande Biran's blue-gold eyes, each of which was sending him a message:

'Why don't you shut up, Cocó!' said Lalande Biran's right eye.

'Shut up this instant or I'll put a bullet through your brain!' said the left eye.

Everyone in Yangambi knew that Lalande Biran was very quick to draw his Luger pistol and that he usually aimed for the head. Van Thiegel's mouth started speaking again, but on a different subject. It said:

'Have you ever seen a lion, *Petit Livo*?'

The journalist from Brussels said that he hadn't, and the

mouth continued talking about the king of the jungle until the roulette wheel moved on and showed him the image of another animal. It resembled a kind of flattened badger with extraordinarily powerful teeth.

'Say what you like, but the true king of the jungle isn't the lion at all,' said the mouth. 'There's another animal, which is far superior to all the others. The blacks call it *kaomo*.'

The mouth went into further explanations, sparing no detail. When a lion saw a *kaomo*, it would run away with its tail between its legs so as to protect its masculine attributes. And that was because the *kaomo* had two modes of attack. First, it crouched near its enemy's belly, then it pounced and tore off any pendulous body parts. A terrible punishment for any king, not just the king of the jungle. As someone once said, King Léopold himself would have far preferred to face the guillotine than be the victim of a *kaomo*.

The mouth formed into a half-smile and felt an enormous desire to go on giving explanations. Then Van Thiegel again caught sight of Lalande Biran's eyes:

'Why don't you shut up, Cocó!' said the right eye.

'Look who's sitting next to you!' said the left eye.

He focussed his attention on the man beside him, none other than the bishop who had blessed the statue of the Virgin. He was fairly young and had very smooth skin; doubtless another poofter. And a new topic of conversation came into his head: what would a *kaomo* make of a man like that? The question did not, however, reach his mouth. If Lalande Biran didn't want to talk about it, then they wouldn't, and that was that.

He got up to go outside and passed by the table where

the younger officers were eating. Chrysostome was among them. He was silent, concentrating on his portion of antelope, but he was wearing his shirt unbuttoned, brazenly showing off the blue ribbon and the gold chain on his flat, hairless chest.

'A soldier shouldn't go around showing his chest, especially not in the presence of a bishop,' the mouth said. 'Do those buttons up at once!'

This last sentence was followed by another, which the mouth chose not to say:

'You can do what you like when you're with Madelaine, but not here.'

Madelaine. That was the name he had given to Chrysostome's supposed half-black, half-white girlfriend. But this was not the moment to mention her. The yokel mustn't suspect that his secret had been discovered until the bishop and the journalist had gone and they – himself, Richardson and Biran – could put their plan into action. Yes, they had thought it all out. They would capture Madelaine and bring her back to Yangambi, where they would set her to work in the slaughterhouse or in the storerooms, and see how Chrysostome reacted. Richardson thought the yokel would be ashamed of his feelings and look the other way, as if he didn't care what happened to the girl. Lalande Biran, on the other hand, foresaw a strong, even disproportionate response. Chrysostome wouldn't be able to control his emotions and would make a complete fool of himself. There was nothing stronger than first love. It could turn a person's head – especially a yokel's head – more easily than ten bottles of champagne drunk one after the other.

Lopes spoke up in Chrysostome's defence:

'But sir, Chrysostome is simply following the Captain's orders, as am I. He told us not to hide our faith.'

He himself was wearing a medal of Our Lady on a silver chain.

'Is that what our religion teaches us?' bawled the mouth. 'To go around showing off our titties?'

Lopes and the other young officers roared with laughter. Chrysostome did not. He frowned and buttoned up his shirt.

'That's better,' said the mouth.

Tired of standing, Van Thiegel's legs were beginning to grow unsteady, undermining the serious tone he had wanted to give to his words. The officers' laughter grew, as did the frown on Chrysostome's brow. Somehow, Van Thiegel managed to push open the glass door and walk down to the river. Relieving himself did him good.

When he returned to the table, Lalande Biran was talking about lions. He was telling his guests that he had written a poem on the subject.

'"Each on his own territory,"' he began reciting, '"but what territory can accommodate more than one king? I do not speak, Calliope, of the struggle between white rose and red, nor of that other struggle, years before, between Hector and Achilles, but between Belgium and the Congo, between Léopold and the lion. Léopold raised his rifle, and thenceforth but one king reigned."'

The diminutive journalist from Brussels was writing down Lalande Biran's words. The bishop had his eyes closed, perhaps in prayer.

'Our King in a duel with a *kaomo*, that's what I'd like to see,' said the mouth.

No one took any notice. The bishop started telling them about a recent meeting between Léopold II and the Pope.

The roulette wheel in Van Thiegel's head began spinning faster, showing him, one after the other, images of people who were not there in the Club Royal. He saw Christine as she appeared in the photo he had hidden in his bedroom, all wet bathing suit and thighs; his mother in her house in Antwerp; his father in a room in Antwerp's insane asylum; woman number 184 in the jungle, beneath an okoume tree; the first man he had killed by hitting him over the head with a chair, lying dead in a bar in Antwerp. The wheel continued spinning, showing more and more people, until it stopped on the image of his mother. She was saying: 'The trouble with your father is that he was born too near the port.' She meant that he was an alcoholic because he had been born in an area full of bars, which is why he was always getting into fights, sometimes in the street, sometimes at home; sometimes with sailors, sometimes with his wife or his son.

'With me, you mean,' said Van Thiegel's mouth. His arm was raised, his index finger too.

The images he was seeing were closer to him now. Livo was placing on the table a dish of fried bananas and chocolates decorated with jungle fruits. Donatien was filling their glasses with champagne; the diminutive journalist was proposing a toast; the bishop's cheeks were flushed and pink.

'You look a little tipsy, bishop,' said the mouth. 'You have to be careful with champagne. But don't worry, I won't tell the Pope.'

He saw Lalande Biran's blue-gold eyes.

'Why don't you shut up?' the right eye continued to say.

'You're sullying the image of the Force Publique,' said the left eye.

Van Thiegel drank half the champagne in his glass and answered back with his own eyes.

His first eye said: 'Biran, you bore everyone stiff with your poems and your stories about kings. You're as monotonous as a mandrill. Christine can't be too happy knowing that you'll be back in Paris by the spring. But don't worry, I'll console her. She'll be my woman number 200.'

'Don't you look at me like that, Biran,' said his second eye. 'If you do, I'll bash your head in with a chair. That's how I dealt with the first man I killed.'

However, his mouth refused to translate the messages sent by his eyes.

'If you'll excuse me, I think I'll retire,' he said respectfully, and at the same time, his legs stood up and carried him outside. As he passed the table occupied by the younger officers, he saw that Chrysostome had unbuttoned two of his shirt buttons, not the usual three or four, but not just one either as he had ordered. Van Thiegel's mouth opened to repeat the order, but his feet would not stop walking and they carried him over to the glass door.

Arms spread wide and eyes fixed on the jungle, he paused to contemplate the river.

'Madelaine!' he cried.

The *askari* guards in their red fezes remained impassive. When he turned, he saw Donatien, whose Adam's apple seemed highly agitated.

'Lieutenant,' said the Adam's apple, 'I thought you might prefer to sleep in the storeroom rather than walk all the way back to your own room.'

'You're going to make a wonderful colleague, Donatien. Just you wait, we're going to be the owners of the most popular bar in Antwerp,' said the mouth. His feet followed Donatien.

In the corner of the storeroom, underneath the mosquito net, there was now a reddish carpet.

'You might find the floor a bit hard, but you'll sleep well. And, as you can see, Livo has been doing it up.'

'What a charming place!' said the mouth. Van Thiegel's eyes took in the boxes of biscuits, the wooden crates full of bottles, the salami hanging from the ceiling, the sweets, the jars of conserves. His legs gave way beneath him and collapsed onto the carpet. 'Why is everything moving?' he exclaimed. He felt as if the storeroom were spinning round as if it, too, were part of the roulette wheel. When Donatien closed the door, the darkness began to spin as well.

XVII

FOR ONCE, YANGAMBI WAS NOT THE *ROI DU CONGO*'S FINAL stopping place; instead, the boat continued upstream, heading for the little island of Samanga. On board were thirty *askaris* in their red fezes, ten young Africans who had chosen to be baptised, ten sappers, fifteen officers, a bishop, three priests and the journalist Ferdinand Lassalle. Just before the steamship set off from the jetty, Lalande Biran and Van Thiegel saluted each other, and the Kodak camera captured the moment: two white men in military uniform, one – Lieutenant Van Thiegel – with his back to the camera and his Albini-Braendlin on his shoulder and the other – Captain Lalande Biran – facing the camera, with the flag of the Force Publique fluttering behind him, and beneath the flag, the head of the Virgin with her smooth brow and her gaze turned heavenwards.

As soon as he had taken the photo, Lassalle wrote in his notebook the caption that would accompany the image. It was an imaginary dialogue between the two men:

'Keep order while I'm away, Lieutenant.'

'And you take care of Our Lady, Captain, and may She protect you and favour you with a safe return.'

Lassalle scribbled a few more sentences: 'The dangers of the jungle, the lions and the rebels', said the first. The second read: 'King Léopold will win the first duel. The Virgin's foot will trample the head of the serpent.' These would be the motifs on which his first article would be based.

The *Roi du Congo* headed slowly but surely upriver, and the figure left behind on the beach at Yangambi grew gradually smaller and smaller. Lassalle watched until the figure moved, and he saw that rather than heading for the Place du Grand Palmier, where Van Thiegel had his office, it went straight to the club. The drunken sot! That rude man who called him *Petit Livo*! Lalande Biran had told him that Van Thiegel was thinking of returning to Europe, which would doubtless be good news for the Force Publique, just as Lalande Biran's departure would be a great loss. Fortunately, Chrysostome, that extraordinary marksman, was going to stay in the Congo, and everything indicated that Lalande Biran would propose him as one of Yangambi's commanding officers. He certainly hoped so. Chrysostome, with his great devotion to the Virgin Mary, was clearly the most devout officer in Yangambi. His second article would be about him. He had already decided on the photo. He would place the young man in the foreground, with the blue ribbon, the gold chain and the medals of Our Lady about his neck; behind him, the statue of the Virgin; and in the background, as much of the landscape as he could encompass from the top of the island of Samanga.

'I hope you all drown!' cried Van Thiegel as he walked up to the club, and his eyes grew as dark as those of a black mamba. He hadn't particularly wanted to be included on the trip to the island, but it was clear that they had all wanted to be rid of him. Another officer could perfectly well have taken temporary command of the post for a few days; given his age and experience, Richardson would have been the ideal choice, and of course, as a Protestant, he had no interest in the whole Virgin rigmarole. No, Lalande Biran had wanted to punish Van Thiegel by denying him any of the advantages that might accrue from that expedition. Lalande Biran's ambition knew no limits: he wanted to appear in all the interviews and all the photos and to see his poems published in Europe. In a word, he wanted to be both rich and famous. Van Thiegel, on the other hand, would appear in only one photo, taken just before the *Roi du Congo* set off and in which he had his back to the camera. This was quite wrong, because he was, after all, the officer with most responsibility in Yangambi, the one who restored order, who went boldly into the jungle whenever the rebels surfaced, the one who organised the transport of any of those extra shipments of rubber and mahogany despatched to placate Monsieur X and Christine. But no one in Europe would know of his merits, and if the Military Academy in Brussels ever needed a teacher to give lessons about Africa, no one would think of asking him. He regretted this largely for his mother's sake, but also as a man in love. How could Christine give him his proper value if there were no photos of him and no interviews in the press? It would then be much harder for him to make her his woman number 200.

As he approached the porch of the Club Royal, he saw a group of five or six mandrills beside the storeroom, and one of them was knocking on the door. There was a scream, and they all sat there, looking at him, mouths open, teeth bared. Van Thiegel gave a laugh that sounded more like a cough. All he needed now was for the monkeys to lose respect for him as well! Perhaps they knew about King Léopold's rules on the use of cartridges and assumed that he would not, therefore, shoot. What they didn't know was that he had found a way around those rules and had spent years massaging the figures – for cartridges as well as everything else, especially the figures for rubber and mahogany.

One of the more brazen of the mandrills climbed onto a rocking chair and balanced precariously. Van Thiegel grabbed the Albini-Braendlin he was carrying over his shoulder. The mandrill on the rocking chair and the rest of the group fled into the jungle.

He opened the storeroom door and stood for a while studying the provisions piled up there. It was full to bursting. Apart from the anisette and other sweet liqueurs, there were dozens of crates of champagne and no shortage of Martell and Martini either. He saw sausages and salamis hanging from the ceiling, and on a plank, a foot or so above the ground, was a row of cheeses wrapped in cloth. Lalande Biran had obviously put in a special order before the visit of the priests and the journalist. All that was missing from the storeroom was the figure of Donatien. His usual corner was empty.

Van Thiegel walked up to the higher part of Yangambi, and when he reached the square, his eye was caught by a detail he hadn't noticed before. The coloured ribbons that Lalande Biran had ordered to be hung from the palm tree did not form a cupola, but a half-cupola, for they extended only as far as Government House, and not in the other direction, towards his house. So his marginalisation had not begun with the arrival of the journalist and the priests: it had been planned long before.

'Oh, Biran!' he cried.

He continued walking towards the firing range, and as he passed the slaughterhouse, his mind split in two. He remembered seeing the cheetah there, with a bullet hole above its left eye, and at the same time, although only in his imagination, he saw Christine walking down a Paris street, wearing a cheetah-skin stole about her neck. To these were added another two images. In the first, he saw Chrysostome strolling into the village one day, carrying the rhinoceros horn on his back. In the second, he saw Christine sitting on an armchair in her house in rue du Pont Vieux, and behind her, fixed to the wall, was that same horn. Lalande Biran would lie to Christine and tell her that he himself had hunted and killed both the cheetah and the rhinoceros. He had always been slow to acknowledge other people's qualities.

'Oh, Biran!' he cried again.

The seven hundred rubber-tappers he found gathered on the firing range seemed particularly quiet, sitting on the ground in silence, most of them eating. The NCOs greeted him with the usual words: 'Nothing to report, Lieutenant!' But there was something to report. Smoke was rising from twenty or so barbecues and there was an all-pervasive smell of roast antelope. It was a scene prepared by Lalande Biran for the journalist's Kodak camera. It seemed, however, that there had been more than enough meat, and the banquet was continuing.

At one end of the firing range, two figures appeared, one very tall and wearing a white hat and the other very short and with grey hair. Donatien was walking towards him, followed by Livo, who was carrying a basket over one arm.

'We're going to the club, Lieutenant,' said Donatien. 'We've chosen some good cuts of meat to roast on the barbecue.'

Livo lifted the lid of the reed basket and showed him the meat. They were cuts taken from near the tail, the tenderest part of the antelope, and Livo was planning to barbecue one as normal, while the other he would serve with a cheese sauce. There was more than enough cheese in the storeroom. The Captain had had it sent up from Léopoldville.

'Yes, I saw it,' said Van Thiegel. 'Our good Captain has brought many other delicacies too.'

'Sugar,' said Livo.

'Salt,' said Donatien.

They were joking, deliberately saying nothing about the champagne and the other drinks. Van Thiegel looked up past the seven hundred rubber-tappers and beyond the columns of smoke rising from the barbecues. There was a glint of pride in his eyes.

'When I was young, as a cadet at the Military Academy in Brussels, we invented a game,' he said, as if these words were written on the sky and he was reading them. 'We would pool our money and go round the bars, but we had to order a different drink in each bar. So if we drank wine in one bar, we would order beer in the next, and then gin, cognac or anisette and so on. Of course, we had them serve us the milder drinks in large glasses and the stronger ones in small glasses. And so it would go on until the weakest could no longer stand. Then for those of us with more stamina, it was time for love, and we would take whatever money was left in the pot and set off to see the ladies.'

Donatien and Livo laughed. Van Thiegel was still staring up at the sky.

'I understand that many students still keep up the tradition,' he said. 'And that pleases me.'

'Of course,' said Donatien. His Adam's apple moved up and down in his neck. He felt impatient. He hadn't had time to take off the dress uniform he had worn for the embarkation ceremony for the Virgin, and he was sweltering. And even though he was wearing a hat, he could still feel the sun beating down on his head.

'If the Captain ever claims he invented that game, don't you believe him. We invented it, the first company of fusiliers in Brussels,' Van Thiegel told them. He was no longer looking at the sky.

On their way back to the Club Royal, Van Thiegel and Donatien stopped off to change their clothes, while Livo went on ahead to prepare the meat. He was in serious mood. He didn't want the day to end without him being able to take a few boxes of biscuits to the *mugini*, along with some salami and cheese perhaps. His daughter would be pleased, and the village children even more so.

Van Thiegel took a sip of gin.

'The flag is still flying high above the palace in Brussels,' he said, and he saw Donatien and Livo smile. Behind them, ten or twelve chimpanzees appeared to be listening to his words. 'Yes, the flag is still flying high above the palace in Brussels,' he said again. 'It's still the lair of the most passionate lover the world has ever known. Oh yes.'

The images were starting to spin around in his head again as if on a roulette wheel, but his tongue could not follow them. It felt thick and clumsy in his mouth.

'There's never been another lover like Léopold II, and it will be years before anyone breaks his record. I'm no innocent myself, and with a little luck I'll soon be able to chalk up woman number 200. Beside him, though, I'm a mere babe. As for Chrysostome, well, as for Chrysostome . . .'

Donatien and Livo finally laughed. The chimpanzees did not. They remained frowning and attentive, looking at the men. Livo poured some anisette for himself, Van Thiegel and Donatien. The roulette wheel briefly stopped spinning and showed Van Thiegel the image of his father.

'My father was never a supporter of the King, and sometimes, at home, he would start saying bad things about him over supper. He said the King squandered millions on women, that he'd given a brooch worth 100,000 francs to the dancer María Montoya. This enraged him, but instead of getting angry with the King, he got angry with me and my mother and sometimes hit us. He was very free with his hands he was, sharp-tempered, sharp-eyed and sharp-eared too, and he could probably have amounted to something in the world if only he'd been able to control his drinking. There's nothing wrong with drinking, but you can't get drunk every day.'

He raised one arm and pointed his index finger.

'Anyway, my father used to hit me, I don't deny it. When I was a child, that is, but not once I'd joined the Military Academy.'

He burst out laughing.

'The day I went home on leave for the first time, my

father was in one of his rages, not with the King, but with the man in charge of the stevedores at the port. And he tried to pick a fight with me, telling me to bugger off in my fusilier's uniform, telling me to get out of his sight. I didn't move. He pushed me, almost knocked me over. After all those years spent loading and unloading ships, he was a strong man, but I was stronger, at least I was then. I grabbed him by the throat and lifted him about eight inches off the ground. He looked at me, surprised, as if it had never occurred to him that his son might be stronger than he was. I'd been lifting weights at the barracks, you see. His eyes started to go red, and his face turned scarlet too. When I let him go, it took him about ten minutes to recover, coughing and retching he was. He didn't ever try to knock me about again. And he stopped beating my mother too. He wasn't a bad man, my father, he just had a nasty habit of hitting people. Yes.'

The roulette wheel was spinning too fast now and his father's face kept passing again and again through his head. He fixed his attention on what was left on his plate. He picked up a piece of meat and tossed it onto the beach. The chimpanzees fought over it, making a terrific noise. Their cries filled the air, with those who got nothing protesting loudly.

'I knew a soldier once, a legionnaire like myself,' Van Thiegel went on. The roulette wheel had stopped unexpectedly and shown him this former colleague. 'He was the bravest fellow I've ever known. People here in Yangambi say of me that I don't know the meaning of fear, and I've heard the same said of Chrysostome, but him and me are mere chickens beside that man. He had a pretty impressive record with women too. People said he'd had every woman in the desert. Anyway, one day, he was found dead in his tent. Poisoned, they said, but I don't know. No one ever knew for sure. We did find out the secret of his bravery and his sexual vigour, though. They examined his body for a wound or a snake bite, and discovered that he didn't have two balls like most men, but *four*! Anyway, I reckon the King has probably got three. I wouldn't go so far as to say four, but three, yes. Oh yes.'

The chimpanzees had come closer again and were craning their necks. Van Thiegel threw them the plate containing the leftover meat.

'Time to change drinks, gentlemen,' said Livo when the chimpanzees' screams had abated. '*Il faut changer, messieurs.*'

He opened a bottle containing a green liquid and filled the small glasses.

'The time for love approaches,' said Donatien. 'But if we carry on like this, we'll be in no fit state for the girls.'

'I'll be all right,' retorted Van Thiegel. 'It would be the first time ever if I wasn't. I may only have two balls – because I'm perfectly normal in that respect – but I have very strong legs. Of course, you need more than that. Either it all has to work or not at all.'

He paused, trying to understand what he had just said and failing.

'How are things with Chrysostome and his girlfriend? Are they often at it?' he asked.

'It's not a question of often,' stammered Donatien. 'They d-d-don't do it at all. *Ilsnelelelefonpa.*'

Van Thiegel felt something moving in the centre of his body, but his tongue came to a dead halt. He wanted to say that the facts would prove him right in the end because, unlike Lalande Biran, he still believed Chrysostome was a poofter; but no sound came from his lips. He tried again. He wanted to ask Livo if he had ever seen this Madelaine from close to, and what kind of body she had.

Fortunately, Livo didn't need words. The look in the Lieutenant's eyes was enough.

'Bamu is an extraordinary woman,' he said. 'She's a veritable palm tree that girl.'

'A palm tree! You're the real poet of Yangambi, Livo. Better than the Captain,' Van Thiegel wanted to say, but his tongue was still stiff. On the other hand, the movement in the centre of his body grew more intense, or, rather, unstiffened.

'The palm tree is beautiful from the waist down,' Livo went on, 'and even more beautiful, if that were possible, from the waist up. Her hair isn't curly, but wavy, and her eyes . . .'

He suddenly fell silent and stood looking out at the jungle. It seemed to him that the thousands and thousands of trees had fallen silent, the river had stopped flowing, and the group of chimpanzees on the beach had turned to stone. Then the pounding of a drum traversed the silence and could clearly be heard on the porch.

'Who's that drumming?' cried Livo.

He clasped his hands to his head. Yes, the inhabitants of one of the *mugini* were holding a traditional funeral. Lalande Biran would be furious because he found the noise of drumming unbearable and had forbidden it in the area around Yangambi. Livo might have to despatch some *askaris* to silence the drummers, and he would have to be their guide, his least favourite job.

Then he breathed a sigh of relief. Of course, Lalande Biran wasn't in Yangambi, but on board the *Roi du Congo* heading for the small island of Samanga. It would take them two or three days to take the statue of the Virgin there and come back, and by then, the funeral would be over.

His *oimbé* appeared. A glow of dark green marked with black lines surrounded his body.

He understood then what was wrong. Although he had only been pretending to drink from most of the bottles, he was nevertheless a little drunk. That was why his thoughts were so slow; that was why he had spouted all that nonsense about Bamu to Van Thiegel and Donatien.

He shouldn't have told them about the young woman called Bamu, still less in the terms he had used, telling them that she was as beautiful as a palm tree. Saying such a thing to the Lieutenant was like showing a salami to a monkey.

Livo's *oimbé* changed colour. Now it was purple. A sad idea had just occurred to him. He was a monkey too and had acted as he did, playing up to Van Thiegel, in the hope of receiving a box of biscuits. He wouldn't get one though. Drunks tended to be mean, at least in Yangambi.

Donatien filled their glasses with a yellowish liquid.

'They say the girl has very round ears,' he said, 'not that I've seen them, because the first time, I caught only the briefest of glimpses, and then the Captain forbade me from going anywhere near her *mugini*. I'm obviously not going to get my reward. And I would really like to have my emeralds back. When we open our club in Antwerp, I want to see them behind the bar, adorning my wife. The customers would appreciate that. One of my sisters always used to say that nowadays people want a bit of elegance, not the seedy bars of our parents' day. And you know what, we could install Chrysostome's girlfriend there too. If she's so beautiful, she would be a real draw for the customers.'

'Why don't you just shut up?' Van Thiegel said. Gradually, the use of his tongue was returning. At least it was moving now, however clumsily. He looked at Livo. 'If they don't have sex, what do they do?' he asked.

'Observe, Lieutenant,' Donatien broke in. He took Livo's hands and gazed at him tenderly. Then he began to caress him, first one cheek, then the other, the left side of his chest, then the right. Very slowly and gently.

'So our young girl is more of a virgin than the stone one they've just carried off to Samanga!' said Van Thiegel, standing up. The chimpanzees immediately plunged off into the jungle. 'Let's go! The moment for love has arrived. Madelaine is calling me!' he bawled.

The breeze brought with it the sound of drumming.

XVIII

THE CANOE ALMOST CAPSIZED WHEN VAN THIEGEL JUMPED into the prow, landing heavily on one side of the craft; fortunately, he managed, with another jump, to reposition himself in the middle, where Livo and Donatien were rowing; soon the canoe stopped rocking violently from side to side and they could get underway.

Van Thiegel stood up, beating his chest with his fists.

'Madelaine, your monkey is here!' he shrilled. And when they reached the other shore and the path, he held out his arms to the jungle, crying: 'Madelaine! Madelaine! Madelaine!'

They could hear the drumming more clearly now, the continuous pounding of sticks on skin. Van Thiegel stopped. Where was that noise coming from? He cupped his hands round his ears so as to hear better.

He thought he could tell from which direction the sound was coming and, leaving the path, he set off into the bushes. He was walking with great determination, and when he came across a fallen tree, he leapt over it.

'That's the wrong way, Lieutenant!' Donatien warned him. '*Montenantnéspouci.*'

Livo was carrying a stick he'd picked up from the ground, and suddenly he struck Donatien roughly on the thigh with it. Donatien looked at him, surprised. Of course! He remembered perfectly now. On the day he saw the tall girl, she had fled towards the area where the larger *mugini* were to be found. The Lieutenant was mistaken. If they went in that direction, they would end up in the *mugini* where the drums were sounding and would find not the girl, but a funeral.

Livo raised one finger to his lips. Donatien obediently, but rather sulkily kept silent. It was always the same with that old Twa tribesman when he was back in the jungle; he turned arrogant and acted the big chief, quite different from the servant he was at the Club Royal.

The drumming was getting ever louder.

'Madelaine! Madelaine! Madelaine!' bawled Van Thiegel.

Livo noticed that his own *oimbé* had taken on a bluish tinge, allowing him to think much more precisely. They should let the Drunken Monkey head off towards the drumming and then, once he had realised his mistake, lead him back and forth in the jungle until his legs gave way or he sobered up.

He imagined the itinerary in some detail. The girl called Bamu lived not far from his daughter's village. He would lead the Drunken Monkey away from there, so as to avoid any chance encounters. Unfortunately, there was still Donatien to deal with. The Long-necked Dog wanted to find the girl at all costs, unaware of the consequences.

The drumming stopped.

'Madelaine! Madelaine! Madelaine!' shouted Van Thiegel. The noise from the monkeys rose to a crescendo, and a flock of startled birds flew up.

'There it is!' Livo said, pointing to a group of huts. As he had foreseen, there was no one in sight. The people attending the funeral had fled. He sat down on a tree trunk. He was in no hurry.

Van Thiegel was moving anxiously from one hut to another, while Donatien followed behind. After Van Thiegel had inspected the fifth or sixth hut, both men walked over to where a fire was still smoking. A little way beyond, he saw the dead man lying on his side. His family members had obviously tried to carry him off with them, but for lack of time or for some other reason, had been unable to.

The Drunken Monkey got angry when he saw the corpse and started kicking it. The Long-necked Dog approached him and said something. They had obviously come in the wrong direction.

Livo noticed that neither man was carrying a rifle. In their haste to find the girl, they had left them behind in the club. They didn't have their chicottes with them either, but they did have pistols.

Suddenly, the *oimbé* surrounding his body changed colour, going from blue to red. The Drunken Monkey was heading straight for him. The holster attached to his belt bumped against his thigh with every step, and Livo could see the long barrel of a Luger protruding from the bottom of the holster.

'You lied to me, you wretched pygmy!' he yelled. '*Tu m'as trompé, sale pygmée!*'

Livo had spent eight years in Yangambi and for five of them had been in charge of the Club Royal. He knew the Drunken Monkey well, but even so, he was surprised. Only a mind like Van Thiegel's could think that the drumming was actually intended for him, to facilitate his meeting with Bamu. How could he believe such a thing, even under the influence of ten different liqueurs? Now he was trying to blame Livo for their failure to find her. And how could Livo possibly tell him the truth? The Drunken Monkey had his hand raised ready to strike.

'They usually hide her away. For them, she's the princess of the jungle,' Livo said quickly. He felt as if he were talking from inside a red cloud.

'Is that poofter a better man than me, then?' roared the Drunken Monkey. Livo's eyes met his. Van Thiegel was definitely a monkey, but a monkey with the eyes of a black mamba.

'That's why they let her spend time with Chrysostome,' Livo went on, 'because the girl is in no danger from him; he even protects her in a way. The rest of the time, though, they keep her hidden away. They say she never sleeps in the same village two nights running.'

These explanations gave the Drunken Monkey much to think about. The hands he had raised to strike Livo were now grasping his own head. He was trying to concentrate.

'If you find her, I'll give you ten boxes of biscuits,' he said at last.

'And a salami too?' Livo asked. The red *oimbé* meant that he wasn't entirely master of himself and was in real anguish.

He was caught, as they say, between the sword and the wall, frightened by what was happening to him. If he refused to lead the Drunken Monkey to Bamu, he would kill him, probably with a pistol shot. On the other hand, he could all too easily imagine Chrysostome with that stern look on his face and his Albini-Braendlin rifle in his hands. If anything happened to the girl, all three of them were as good as dead. There would be no forgiveness for the Drunken Monkey, but Chrysostome wouldn't forgive him and Donatien either. He would consider them the Monkey's accomplices and put a bullet through their respective brains.

Out of the corner of his eye, Livo saw Donatien circling the corpse.

Livo was beginning to see a way out or at least the shadow of a way out. The Long-necked Dog's situation was different. He wasn't caught between the wall and the sword, in fact there was no wall, because the Drunken Monkey hadn't asked him for help and wouldn't punish him if they failed to find Bamu. There was, however, a sword hanging over Donatien. Chrysostome didn't like him; on the contrary, he despised him and called him 'a mangy dog' to his face.

The Drunken Monkey was sitting on a tree trunk, trying without success to tie the laces on one boot.

Donatien came over to them and pointed back at the corpse.

'I can't see any wound. He must have died of some illness,' he said.

'There is an illness going round, it's true,' said Livo. It occurred to him that he could have made use of this lie to start with and told them that Bamu was dying, but it was too late for that now. Besides, the Drunken Monkey wouldn't have cared.

'Is it contagious?' asked Donatien.

Livo didn't dare to say it was. 'I don't know,' he answered.

'Tie this lace for me, will you?' said the Drunken Monkey.

Donatien obeyed at once. He fumbled with the laces too, but finally managed to tie the knot.

'If the illness is contagious, that's bad news for our Captain, and for Chrysostome too. They don't like diseases,' he said, sitting down next to Livo.

'The Captain and Chrysostome will be back soon,' said Livo, nudging him. 'Another two days, three at most, and they'll be here.'

Donatien turned to him. He suddenly understood what Livo meant, and a look of fear came into his eyes. He had just realised the consequences of what they were doing.

'Let's go and find that princess!' shouted the Drunken Monkey.

'It won't be easy,' said Livo.

After a red interlude, his *oimbé* had recovered its blue tone, and his thoughts came to him clearly now.

'You said that before. I thought you were supposed to be a good guide, one of the best.'

Livo pointed to a fairly wide path that began on the other side of the *mugini*.

'It's that way.'

The Drunken Monkey thought for a moment.

'No, we'll go back to where we left the canoe and start the search again,' he said, showing unexpected good sense. 'Isn't that what you thought, Donatien, that we were heading in the wrong direction?'

'Yes, Lieutenant,' said the Long-necked Dog wanly.

Even before he heard this reply, the Drunken Monkey was off, retracing his steps. He had spent many years in Yangambi and was pretty good at finding his way among the trees and the bushes. And he wasn't stupid. He went directly to the spot where they had moored the canoe. He wasn't leaping about or shouting now; he still had enough energy left for several more hours of searching, without flagging. A few red patches began to appear in Livo's otherwise blue *oimbé*.

A large bird whistled, but Livo didn't hear it. He was searching his mind for something that would tell him what to do, which risks to take and which to avoid. He reached the conclusion he had arrived at shortly before. Chrysostome would be the best deterrent. That way, he would save Bamu. She wasn't a member of the Twa tribe, but their two tribes often helped each other.

They could hear the sound of the river now. They were reaching the point where they had first gone wrong. Livo slowed his pace and waited for Donatien to catch him up.

'You're a dead man,' he told him. 'What do you think Chrysostome, the best marksman in the Congo, will do when he finds out about this?'

Donatien's Adam's apple rose and fell.

'*We're* not going to do anything. It'll all be Cocó's fault.'

'You're wrong. Chrysostome will fell three men with his rifle. First, Van Thiegel, then you and then me.'

Donatien started to cough. He wanted to say something, but couldn't get a word out.

The Drunken Monkey stopped.

'Lead the prince to the princess!'

It was an order.

To use a universal metaphor, a Pandora's box had opened up in Donatien's head. When he heard Livo's words, all his brothers had started shouting, telling him what he should do. They all wanted to voice their opinions, and some wanted to offer him advice. The one who saw the situation most clearly was his brother the murderer. Donatien should help Lieutenant Van Thiegel achieve his objective, but when the Lieutenant lay down on top of the girl, Donatien should kill them both by bashing their brains out with a stone, then take back the emerald earrings. The risk was minimal, because a man with his trousers down and lying on top of a woman was practically defenceless, even a big strong fellow like Van Thiegel. True, the plan had its disadvantages, what with the blood from the wounds and everything, but a stone was the ideal weapon if he was to lay the blame on the natives. Who would believe him if he used his pistol? The natives didn't know how to use such weapons. 'Too difficult,' objected his intelligent brother. 'Donatien could never do it. If I were him, I'd forget about the earrings and just head back to Yangambi.' One of his sisters intervened: 'If Chrysostome is going to take his revenge on them all anyway, what does it matter?' 'You don't understand,' retorted the intelligent brother. 'It's a matter of giving yourself a reasonable chance of surviving or not. If he goes back with the emeralds in his pocket, he won't have a chance in hell.' Another sister spoke out indignantly: 'How can anyone respect a man capable of giving away some emeralds? Besides, those emeralds belong to us, not to that black girl. She has no right to them at all.'

'No, this isn't the way either. I've gone wrong again, Lieutenant,' he heard someone say. It wasn't one of his brothers, but Livo.

'You're doing it on purpose, pygmy!' yelled Van Thiegel. '*Tu le fais exprès, pygmée!*' He grabbed him by the throat with his two hands and lifted him off the ground.

Livo tried to say something, but couldn't even breathe.

Donatien looked at the trees and the bushes around him and realised that this was the place where he had got lost before. There were the same small round green leaves which, in the jungle gloom, he had mistaken for emeralds. And just as had happened then, a flock of birds flew by overhead. Nearby, a monkey screamed.

Donatien saw a path. 'It's the path that leads to the girl's *mugini*,' he heard a voice inside him say. It was his intelligent brother. 'I don't know what to do!' Donatien cried, and at that very moment, his homosexual brother, the original owner of the earrings, spoke to him in a voice from beyond the grave: 'Leave the earrings where they are. They don't belong to you or to any of my loathsome family. I would much prefer the girl to keep them, rather than one of my sisters or whatever idiot agrees to be your wife.' 'If you fall for that one, then you're a bloody fool,' chorused ten or twelve of his siblings.

Livo was lying on the ground, coughing and spluttering. Van Thiegel was kicking him.

'Lieutenant, I think I know where the girl lives,' exclaimed Donatien.

'*Alea jacta est*,' said a voice inside him. It wasn't one of his siblings this time, but Lalande Biran. The Captain often used those words. It was, according to him, one of Napoleon's favourite sayings.

Van Thiegel had already set off along the path, and Donatien ran after him.

XIX

THE JUNGLE WAS ALWAYS DARK, BUT LIVO KNEW THAT THE gloom surrounding him now was to do with his *oimbé* and doubtless, too, with the sense that he was at the gates of death. He was, after all, nearly sixty years old; he had been a member of many expeditions; he had faced grave dangers both during his time in Yangambi and before; but never had his *oimbé* been so black. He felt like curling up where he lay on the ground, but that was impossible. He could get his knees up to his chin, but couldn't lower his head. The slightest movement caused excruciating pain.

He fell asleep, and time passed. When he woke, even before he opened his eyes, he knew he was still alive. The monkeys – the monkeys, the tireless monkeys! – were screaming in the jungle; the birds – the marvellous music-making birds! – were singing and singing. Some were perched just above him.

When he opened his eyes, he noticed that the colour of his *oimbé* had changed slightly. It wasn't black now, but violet. Dark violet. He was filled with a terrible sadness. That vile creature, the Long-necked Dog, who was always putting his foot in it, who was incapable even of looking after the club storeroom, and who was the clumsiest, laziest officer in the Force Publique, had found the right path. The Drunken Monkey would, at this moment, be in Bamu's hut.

Slowly, he raised his hand to his throat. It really hurt when he touched it, but he didn't think anything was broken. Taking his weight on his arms, he managed to scramble to his feet. Through the violet *oimbé*, he saw thousands of small bright green leaves. They weren't common in that area, which is why the Long-necked Dog had noticed them and why he had recognised the place.

Then, as if Livo had summoned him with his thoughts, the Long-necked Dog appeared behind the small green leaves. He was running, crouching down so as not to bump into the branches, and he ran straight past Livo without so much as a glance. Shortly afterwards, Livo saw the Drunken Monkey. He was moving more slowly and stumbled as he passed.

'You'd better hide the girl somewhere!' he said, without stopping. On the other side of his violet *oimbé* Livo watched him as he moved away, his pistol still in its holster, his clothes dishevelled. Livo spat at him and saw on a stone his own saliva, made intensely red by his *oimbé* and by his blood. He again raised his hand to his throat and pressed harder this time. Again it hurt. He tried to say something.

'Lulago!' he muttered. That was his daughter's name and it emerged quite clearly from his lips. 'Lulago!' he said more loudly this time. Obviously no real damage had been done to his throat. This reassured him, and his *oimbé*, while still violet in tone, became more transparent. He walked over to the path.

He had gone barely a hundred paces when he saw the *mugini*. There was no one there, and it seemed as deserted as the village they had visited earlier. Looking for some sign of movement, his eyes alighted on a red-and-grey bird on the roof of the hut. It was a parrot, a *muk*.

The bird was not in its usual place, in the wooden cage that hung, with its door open, at the entrance to the hut. As he approached, the parrot hopped nervously away from him. Ever more troubled by Livo's presence, it finally began shrieking: 'Bamu! Bamu! Bamu!'

Livo went into the hut. The girl's body lay on the floor. Her hair was slightly longer than he remembered and fell in waves about her ears. The lobes of her ears were stained with blood.

'Bamu! Bamu! Bamu!' cried the parrot from its perch outside on the roof.

Livo knelt down beside the girl and closed her eyes.

He stumbled away from the *mugini*. An hour later he was with his daughter.

Lulago could not see her father's *oimbé*, but she didn't need to. He looked terrible, as if he had aged ten or fifteen years. There were dark shadows under his eyes, he had grown thinner, his neck and throat were swollen and bruised. His inner state was even worse, and Lulago only had to see her father's eyes to know what he was feeling inside: her father felt that he had reached the end of his life.

Livo went and sat down at the foot of an okoume tree, and Lulago placed a small amount of tobacco and some cigarette papers beside him. Soon, a group of children appeared, because someone had noticed the arrival of 'the old man who works for the white men', and they wanted biscuits. Lulago, however, would not let them near him. She sat down at the door of her hut and watched him while she sewed.

Her father resembled a sack that someone had left lying under a tree. He didn't move or call out to her. She waited patiently, and when she finished her sewing, she started preparing the cassava bread for supper. Only when the first shadows of evening began to fill the village and silence fell in the jungle – it was time for the monkeys to sleep, time for the birds to sleep too – only then did she notice a small cloud of smoke beneath the okoume tree. Her father was smoking and gradually returning to himself.

Livo was also watching the smoke and allowing his thoughts to organise themselves around it: where should he go, how, when? He decided that he should go first to the Twa village on the shores of the Lomami and talk to Kadissa, the medicine woman who had been caring for his people for many years now; then he would travel on as far as a narrow stretch of the river, where he would wait until the *Roi du Congo* returned from its mission in Samanga. He had to speak to Captain Lalande Biran before the steamboat reached Yangambi.

Kadissa did not belong to the Twa tribe and looked more like a Watusi, tall and strongly built like Bamu. She was very old and capable of doing effortlessly what neither Lulago nor anyone else could do: she could see a person's *oimbé*. Not only was she the best medicine woman in that part of the jungle, she was also the real chief of the Twa people in Lomami. Everyone, including hunters and warriors, came to ask her advice.

When she saw Livo, she took some ointment and rubbed it on his neck.

'That will pass,' she said, 'but as for the rest, I'm not so sure. You look exhausted, dark, anxious, frightened, filled with a desire for revenge. I know you are a man of strong spirit, but those are too many feelings to have at one time.'

Livo sat cross-legged on the ground. At that moment, he was the child, and the woman before him, Kadissa, who was almost twice as tall as him and dressed entirely in yellow, was the Mother.

'I haven't brought you anything, not even some biscuits,' said Livo.

'Kadissa can live without sweet things,' responded the Mother.

'I have come to ask you something,' said Livo. The ointment was warm on his neck.

'What has happened?'

'The white men are in the habit of stealing women from the jungle and taking their pleasure with them,' explained Livo. 'Some, like Captain Lalande Biran, only want very young girls, but most, Lieutenant Van Thiegel and others like him, don't care . . .'

Livo opened his heart and spread it out before the Mother as one might a handkerchief. There for her to see were his exhaustion, darkness, anxiety, fear, and his desire for revenge. Kadissa picked up that handkerchief and, meta-phorically speaking, tucked it away in her breast. Then, with Livo following behind, she got up and, without a word, went over to the vegetable patch next to her hut.

In a hollow in the ground, behind some reeds, stood three

baskets. Kadissa lifted the lids so that Livo could look inside. Each basket contained a black mamba.

'The largest is for the Drunken Monkey; this one for the Long-necked Dog; and this, the youngest, for the Captain. He will die more slowly, because the poison is weaker, but that is how it should be. The Captain is the commanding officer in Yangambi. He should have stopped this happening. Let him suffer then.'

The snakes were ceaselessly coiling and uncoiling.

'They're very hungry and have all their venom inside them,' Kadissa added. 'At this moment, they would be capable of attacking a lion.'

Kadissa showed him some pincers with which he could handle the snakes safely. Livo said that he didn't need them, that he had a pair the same in Yangambi.

'I'll throw one snake in on top of the Long-necked Dog when he's sleeping in the club storeroom. I'll put the Captain's snake in his bed. And as for the Drunken Monkey, I haven't yet decided.'

'Do you have mice there?'

'There are lots in the storeroom and in the granaries.'

'Now and then, put a few in the basket. The snakes need to be hungry, but not starving.'

'I must go now, Mother.'

'Go then.'

Kadissa looped the handles of the baskets onto a pole so that he could carry them easily.

It was impossible to cross to the other side of the Lomami at that point and so he continued on to the next Twa village.

'I would like to have brought you biscuits,' he told the boys standing by a canoe, 'but since I haven't, I will send some with my daughter Lulago. I need to cross to the other side.'

'What food have you got in those baskets?' asked one of the boys.

'I do not bring food, I bring death,' said Livo.

'Are you a rebel?' the same boy asked.

'No.'

'How do we know you will send us biscuits?'

'I promised Kadissa.'

They all smiled and started pushing the canoe out into the water.

The baskets carrying death did not weigh very much, and once he had gained the farther shore, Livo met with no further obstacles. By evening, he had reached the stretch of river he was looking for, and there he spent the night.

He woke the following morning and looked at his *oimbé*. He had never known it so black and shining, but it did not prevent him from thinking clearly.

He took the lids off the baskets and peered in at the snakes. They were restless and raised their heads, flicking their tongues in and out, trying to capture the smells of that new place. He wondered how best to go about things. He remembered that one day the Long-necked Dog had given a drop of cognac to a mouse he had caught in the club storeroom, and that the little creature had become completely tipsy. Perhaps it would be a good idea to leave a drunken mouse on the bodies of each of the three men condemned by Kadissa to die; he could do this while they slept, at the same time as he slipped the mambas underneath the mosquito net. The snakes would smell the mouse and move towards it. When they felt this movement, the condemned men would also stir in their sleep and then the mambas would strike.

'I'm hungry too,' Livo said to the snakes. 'But we can eat when we get to Yangambi. I'll give you some bits of salami then.'

With the pole carrying the three baskets resting on his shoulder, he walked to the shore and sat there waiting for the *Roi du Congo*.

XX

DONATIEN CAREFULLY CLEANED THE EMERALD EARRINGS
before putting them away in their mother-of-pearl box. This
was not a difficult task, far more difficult would be finding a
good place to hide his treasure. He could think of nowhere
safe enough, and yet he needed to do so quickly. The real
murderer was Lieutenant Van Thiegel, the drunkard, Cocó,
but if Chrysostome saw the earrings, he would immediately
put two and two together – 'I gave them to Bamu, and now
Donatien has them, therefore . . .' – and then, inevitably, he
would recall how beautiful the young woman was and how
well the green of the emeralds had suited her. Tormented by
this memory, he would shoot Donatien in the head before he
could even open his mouth. It could not be simpler, that was
how things were.

He sat in his hut, waiting to receive advice from his
brother and immediately heard his voice:

'Why don't you tell him the truth? Tell him exactly what
happened. Cocó forced you to go with him, threatening
you with the chicotte if you didn't, and thanks to Livo, you
easily found your way to the village. Then Cocó went inside

the girl's hut, while you stayed outside, trying to catch the parrot that kept flying about and squawking. In the end, Cocó came out of the hut and you went in to get the earrings.'

Donatien didn't know what to think. This account wasn't quite true, but it would do.

The voice went on:

'Once you've told him everything, you hand him the earrings and say: "I took the earrings, thinking of you, Chrysostome, as a souvenir." That should be enough, I think. It could save your skin.'

This advice enraged him. It was as if the emerald earrings were cursed. He had only just got them back and already he was being asked to give them away again.

'If giving him the earrings doesn't work, Donatien, don't despair,' he heard the voice in his head say. It was the same voice as before, but it didn't always sound like that of his intelligent brother. 'You go up to him, embrace him and say: "My deepest sympathies, Chrysostome." He'll be really touched by that.'

These words struck a false note, immediately putting Donatien on the alert. He heard a hollow laugh.

'And if an embrace isn't enough,' said the voice, 'kiss him full on the lips. Then he won't just forgive you, he'll return the earrings to you as well.'

Donatien recognised the voice now. It belonged not to his intelligent brother, but to the homosexual, who was imitating his other brother's way of speaking.

'You may be a mangy dog, Donatien,' the homosexual brother said, abandoning all subterfuge. 'But this time your sense of smell has let you down. The *Roi du Congo* is travelling back to Yangambi. In a day, or two at most, Chrysostome will know everything. He'll know that you and Cocó killed the girl.'

He gave a most disagreeable laugh.

Donatien rushed from his hut and, out of habit, his feet carried him to the Place du Grand Palmier. The sky was grey and the heat weighed heavily. Sweat was pouring down his back, and his head ached. Even the little mother-of-pearl box in his right trouser pocket hurt him. The edge was sticking into his thigh like a knife.

The *askari* guarding Government House saluted him, and he returned the salute. He hesitated between sitting down on one of the white benches beneath the palm tree or continuing on to the river. He decided on the latter.

The palm trees along the road would be a good hiding place, especially high up, at the growing point, but that was also where the black mambas lay coiled and asleep. No, it was no use, he couldn't risk it.

He also considered the small island in the river, or the beach itself. The mother-of-pearl box would be safe if he buried it. But how could he do that without someone seeing him? The *askaris* weren't stupid. And they were fascinated by precious stones.

The edge of the box seemed to be getting sharper and would end up cutting into his thigh. He took it out of his right pocket and put it in the left.

He reached the storeroom of the Club Royal. The corner where he slept wouldn't make a good hiding place either, because Livo tidied it up two or three times a week. And the crates of drinks weren't safe because it wasn't just Livo who helped himself, all the club servants did. The salamis might be an option, because no one took them without his consent. If he stuck the earrings inside, say, the last or the penultimate in the row, they would be safe there for a few months. Then he would take them out and put them back in his kit bag. Cocó had told him that he had definitely decided to return to Europe and that if Donatien was still interested in being his business partner, they should make the journey together. It was a good plan, and that way he could take the earrings back with him as they had come, in his soldier's kit bag, or perhaps still inside the salami.

'God, you're stupid, Donatien.'

This time, there was no doubt. It was his intelligent brother. He was quite right. He was being a fool. His thoughts made no sense at all. Hide the earrings in a salami? How ridiculous. Livo himself might make off with it without a word to anyone, as he had on other occasions, for he was in the habit of stealing provisions to take to his daughter, and then Donatien would never see the earrings again. Livo's daughter would bite on something hard and when she spat it out in disgust she would find the jewels. He had to think of something better, and quickly too. He had only a few hours in which to hide his treasure. It was midday, and the *Roi du Congo* would be back in Yangambi that evening.

He picked up a knife, chopped a salami into small chunks, put them on a plate and went out onto the porch. The river was empty, the jungle silent. That, however, was merely a first impression. The monkeys were, in fact, more silent than usual, but the drums were sounding again. A hole had opened up in the air, as if in a piece of transparent fabric, and through that hole came the call of the drums.

Donatien counted the pieces of salami on the plate. There

were fourteen in total. He put two in his mouth and the taste made him feel better. The sound of the drumming bothered him though. It was getting louder and louder, as if the hole in the air were growing wider. Besides, the hole was immediately above the village of Chrysostome's girl-friend. What bad luck, going down to the club just when they were performing her funeral rites!

He took the mother-of-pearl box out of his pocket and placed it on the table on the porch. He put three more pieces of salami in his mouth.

He felt alone, but not alarmed exactly. After all, it was perfectly logical that he should feel alone when no one else was around. Cocó had gone off into the jungle to inspect the enclosure where the less photogenic rubber-tappers had been kept, and he hadn't been back to Yangambi for two days, far too long. Perhaps he was already dead. Perhaps his arrogance had led him to enter the enclosure with only a chicotte, like a lion-tamer, and one of the rubber-workers had split open his head with a rock. In that case, Donatien would be able to hide the earrings in Van Thiegel's office and, when the corpse was brought back, he could pretend to find the earrings there and hand them over to Lalande Biran. Then no one, not even Chrysostome, would be in any doubt that Cocó had been solely responsible for what had happened.

He popped another piece of salami in his mouth.

He thought of Livo. He hadn't been seen for several days either. He was probably still in the jungle. Perhaps he had gone to the girl's funeral. Not that he was in any danger, given that he had stayed behind and seen nothing.

The hole in the air had grown smaller and the sound of

drumming fainter. On the other hand, the monkeys were making much more noise. They had emerged from the undergrowth and were sitting very close now, watching the porch. They weren't mandrills, but chimpanzees.

He put two more pieces of salami in his mouth.

Livo, of course, knew who had found the right path that led to the *mugini*, and if he told Chrysostome . . .

The thought floated in the same air that brought Donatien the sound of the drums. He sat looking at the mother-of-pearl box. He had to hide it. He got up, but, still undecided as to where to go, he stayed where he was. The chimpanzees came nearer and waited expectantly. He put the box in his pocket.

As soon as he left the porch, the chimpanzees rushed forward to grab the pieces of salami left on the plate. The hole in the air grew larger, and the urgent drumming pursued Donatien as he walked up towards the Place du Grand Palmier.

Cocó's office was in a state of utter confusion. On the desk alone, Donatien counted two pairs of trousers, a shirt, a hat, two boxes of empty cartridges, a copy of *La Gazette de Léopoldville*, five glasses, three bottles, a handful of coins, a chicotte and a machete. The shelves were in even more disarray.

The office didn't seem to him a suitable place to leave a pair of emerald earrings, and so he went into the bedroom. The contrast could not have been greater. The only furniture there was the bed and the bedside table.

He examined the bedside table and considered leaving the earrings between the bottles of cognac in the lower compartment, as if Cocó had absentmindedly put them there, but then he rejected the idea. No one would go and fetch a bottle while holding a pair of earrings. The logical thing was to put the earrings down somewhere first. Not anywhere obvious, on the bedside table, for example, but half hidden in the bed, under the mattress, beneath the pillow . . .

He saw the photo when he picked up the pillow. He didn't recognise the woman at first because the bedroom was in darkness and he couldn't quite make out her face. It was only when he lit the oil lamp that he realised who it was: Lalande Biran's wife, the exquisitely beautiful Christine Saliat de Meilhan. She was wearing only a wet bathing suit.

Donatien felt his Adam's apple pulsate violently, as if someone had struck him in the throat, and for a moment he couldn't breathe. He fell back on the bed, acting out the shock of his discovery; but the mother-of-pearl box with its sharp edges was cutting into his thigh again, and he stood up.

He took the photo and ran to his hut to examine it more closely. In one corner was a note saying that it had been taken on the beach at Biarritz.

'Donatien, you have just been handed a trump card. The Captain will never forgive Cocó for this,' he heard a voice say. It was his intelligent brother, and he was quite right. The fact that Cocó was in possession of that photo of Christine Saliat de Meilhan meant many things, how many he didn't know, but a lot.

'Seven things, perhaps eight!' he heard another voice say, and he knew at once who it was – his homosexual brother, irritated by this piece of good luck.

He knew exactly what to do with the photo. He would hand it to Lalande Biran as soon as he returned.

* * *

He waited for a moment to see if his intelligent brother would make any objection, but no voice came into his mind. He put the mother-of-pearl box away in his kit bag. Then he wrapped the earrings in a piece of rag and put them in his pocket. That way, he wouldn't even feel them.

He walked over to Government House carrying the photo and sat down on one of the rocking chairs in the garden, looking out over the river. Soon he would hear the paddles of the *Roi du Congo* and, shortly afterwards, Lalande Biran would walk through the door. Donatien would salute, hold out the photo and say: 'This was in Lieutenant Van Thiegel's bedroom, Captain.'

XXI

'THE MOST BEAUTIFUL METAPHOR WAS PROVIDED BY THE statue of the Virgin,' wrote Lassalle in his notebook. He was preparing to describe the religious ceremony on the little island of Samanga. Once he had done that, he would add the two literary portraits he had already sketched out, one of Lalande Biran and the other of Chrysostome; then his article would be complete.

He read the sentence again – 'The most beautiful metaphor was provided by the statue of the Virgin' – then looked around him, hoping to find inspiration in his surroundings. The view from the boat was, alas, dreadfully dull – *mortellement ennuyeux* – even duller than the desert patrolled by the Foreign Legion. All he could see was the murky river and, on either shore, an inextricable, almost black wall, the first line of trees. Confronted by such a landscape, he found comfort even in the sound of the paddles and the sparks that flew up from the funnel along with the steam.

He found the soldiers of Yangambi equally uninspiring. In that respect, the members of the Force Publique and those of the Foreign Legion were the same. They were brave men, capable of the most dangerous of tasks and unperturbed by potentially deadly situations, but they were also very ordinary and in no way like Achilles.

Lalande Biran had pointed this out in the interview Lassalle had made while they were travelling upriver. 'You must remember, Monsieur Lassalle, why Achilles is so famous. It is not just because of his heroism. Ajax and many other men were equally brave, but Achilles was a melancholic. He knew that death awaited him. That is what lies at the root of his melancholy and that is also why we find him so attractive. Beside him, all the other heroes are mere oafs. They are still children despite their many escapades.'

Lalande Biran was an interesting man. He may not have been a melancholic, but he was deep. More than that, he wrote poetry. Lassalle had noted down a poem of his about a duel between kings: 'Each in his own territory, but what territory can accommodate more than one king?' It wasn't a particularly remarkable piece, but it was a worthy enough effort, and the readers of *Le Soir* would enjoy it. The poem he liked best was the one dedicated to the sky of Yangambi: 'It is not a lived-in heaven, but a desert; it is not Michelangelo's heaven, peopled by angels and saints, and with the figure of God greeting Adam . . .' He would try to write a commentary on it for some literary journal.

The *Roi du Congo* was progressing so slowly that it was easy to forget that you were travelling down the River Congo. He had to make a conscious effort to think this in order to remind himself where he was: in the heart of Africa, not in Europe. This, however, was a physical truth, not a spiritual one. His spirit was still in Europe, and his greatest joy was knowing that his stay in Africa was coming to an end.

'The most beautiful metaphor was provided by the statue of the Virgin.' He returned to his notebook. He was finding it harder than usual to begin the article. Africa was utterly exhausting. It wasn't like strolling down the streets of Brussels, still less along the beaches or through the gardens of St-Jean-Cap-Ferrat. The climb to the top of Samanga had left him almost drained of energy.

'We disembarked and began our march across the island,' he wrote, having finally found a way of beginning the article. 'In the vanguard went the sappers, hacking a path through the undergrowth with their machetes, followed by the veteran officer Richardson, several other white officers and twenty or so of the irregular soldiers known here as *askaris*. Then came the bishop and two priests, Captain Lalande Biran and myself, and behind us the young native men who wanted to be baptised and who were acting as porters for the statue of the Virgin. Bringing up the rear was a second group of *askaris*, while guarding our backs was the best marksman in the Congo, the officer Chrysostome Liège.'

He raised his head and looked for Chrysostome. He was standing underneath the awning, watching the other officers playing cards. Lassalle couldn't quite make Chrysostome out. He was in part, as Lalande Biran put it, an 'Olympian' figure, like an athlete entirely focussed on his goals and who might easily win a gold medal at the next Games in London; but he was also a deeply religious fellow, who proudly wore around his neck the blue ribbon and the medal of Our Lady. He had observed him praying during the mass at the top of Samanga. And shortly afterwards, when the ceremony was over and they were setting off back to the boat, he had seen him bidding farewell to the stone Virgin, kneeling before her, head bowed. So there were two sides to him, the Olympian and the devout. And there was another less defined element to his personality. He had heard it said that Chrysostome was somewhat effeminate, and yet, when he had asked Lalande Biran about this, the Captain had dismissed the idea as mere rumour.

He went back to his notebook and continued the article.

'At first, we thought that all the dangers lurked deep in the jungle. The cries of the monkeys perhaps betrayed the presence of the rebels. The lion's roar was possibly a sign that the second monarch of these lands was angry. The faint sound of the flowing river underlined the solitude of the place, hard to bear for those of us accustomed to the parks of Brussels or the beaches of the Mediterranean. And yet the greatest danger was much closer, right above our heads, to be exact. It was none other than the mosquito. Did I say "*the* mosquito"? I should have said "whole armies of mosquitos", for there were thousands of them and they seemed to move in formation. "Try to keep awake!" joked the veteran officer Richardson, only increasing our anxiety. Because that other menace, the tse-tse fly, known as *oukammba* here, is no laughing matter. The tse-tse first sends you to sleep and then kills you. Just like that. Tse-tse, then, is a synonym for death. Fortunately, most of us had applied lion grease to face and neck, having been assured by the natives that there is no better repellent.'

He then went on to describe what had happened once they reached the top of Samanga. Before the religious cere-mony, Lalande Biran had ordered bonfires of branches and green lianas to be lit, to keep off the mosquitos, red ants and the hundreds of other insects swarming about there.

'As the smoke faded, the ceremony reached its culminating point: "*Credo in unum Deum!*" cried the bishop and every voice joined his. The officers and the *askaris* of the Force Publique, as well as the handsome Yangambi youths, all united together so that their prayer would spread, carried by faith, carried upon the air, to the whole of Upper Congo. The wizards and witches and medicine men of the jungle received our message loud and clear: "This jungle has but one king. This jungle has but one God! *Credo in unum Deum!*"'

Lassalle looked up. Chrysostome was no longer watching the card-players, but sitting in the stern with his head thrown back, taking the sun. The chain and medal around his neck glittered.

Lassalle scribbled down various basic ideas for his article: 'The statue of the Virgin is installed', 'The bishop blesses the river and the jungle', 'Baptism of the young men of Yangambi', 'Lalande Biran's words of homage to the explorer, Henry Morton Stanley', 'Surprise: Richardson asks to be baptised'. 'At the end, repeat the opening sentence: the most beautiful metaphor, etc., etc.'

He walked over to the stern, but Lalande Biran beckoned to him to come and sit with him and the bishop. Lassalle pointed to Chrysostome, indicating that he wished to interview him. Having made his excuses to the bishop, Lalande Biran joined him.

'You'll have to help me, Captain, and see if we can get anything out of the lad,' Lassalle said, although he would have much preferred to do the interview alone.

Chrysostome stood up when he saw them approach. Lalande Biran explained what Lassalle wanted.

'Why don't you tell him about the day you hunted the

rhinoceros? We could start there. I doubt that the readers of *Le Soir* realise the force with which a rhinoceros will charge when wounded,' he said.

'It wasn't really that difficult,' said Chrysostome impassively.

'Really?' asked Lassalle, surprised.

'No.'

'I've heard quite the opposite, that when a rhinoceros is angry it can disembowel a whole company of soldiers before it finally succumbs to their bullets.'

'No, to be honest, the most difficult part was cutting off the horn and carrying it back to Yangambi,' said Chrysostome.

'I have the horn in Government House,' added Lalande Biran. 'I'm going to take it back to Europe with me and display it at home.'

The blue ribbon and gold chain stood out against Chrysostome's chest, and, visible in his trouser pocket, was the silver watch chain.

'Is that what the Captain gave you in exchange for the rhinoceros horn?' asked Lassalle.

Chrysostome nodded, but gave no sign that he was going to take out the watch and show it to him.

'I'd like to ask you about that blue ribbon, if I may,' said Lassalle, drawing a line in his notebook. He had nothing worth writing down. 'How long have you had it? Why do you wear it? Do you feel safer with it round your neck? Safe from the dangers of the jungle?'

'No, not safer,' answered Chrysostome, taking three cartridges from another smaller pocket in his trousers. 'This is what makes me feel safer. The more cartridges you have, the safer you are.'

'The blue ribbon was given to him by the parish priest in Britancourt, the village where he was born,' Lalande Biran explained. 'He came elephant-hunting with me a few months ago and told me a little about his life. His years in Britancourt were a vital influence on him.'

'Is Britancourt pretty?' asked Lassalle.

'I think so, yes.'

Chrysostome's character and that of the landscape visible from the *Roi du Congo* chimed perfectly. His way of speaking was as inexpressive as the noise of the steamboat's paddles. '*Stupide?*' That was the adjective that popped into Lassalle's mind, but at that very moment, he caught the look in Chrysostome's eyes, as if Chrysostome had read his thoughts. It was a hard, frightening look. Lassalle immediately swallowed the adjective and saw, in its place, the caption he would give to the photo he would take: '*L'énigme de Chrysostome Liège*' – 'The enigma of Chrysostome Liège'.

The boat slowed. Lalande Biran stood up.

'What's going on?' he said, leaning over the side. Then he cried out in surprise: 'Why, it's Livo! What's he doing here?'

When he joined the Captain, Lassalle saw a small man with very black skin standing on the shore. He was carrying a pole over his shoulder from which hung three baskets. When the boat stopped, he recognised him as the servant in charge of the Club Royal. He couldn't help smiling. Livo was even smaller than he was, and even smaller than Toisonet. Lalande Biran could offer him to his friend the Duke as a valet. He had also heard it said that Livo was an intelligent man.

All the passengers had now joined the Captain on the

shore side of the boat, until the helmsman shouted at them to go back because the boat was beginning to list. Livo passed the three reed baskets one by one to an *askari*. Then, with some difficulty, he climbed on board.

Chrysostome had clambered onto the roof of the boat and was watching, his Albini-Braendlin in his hand.

'See anything?' asked Richardson from below.

Chrysostome was scanning the jungle. He shook his head. Richardson explained to the journalist:

'It could be a trap set by the rebels.'

The boat got underway again, and Chrysostome came down from the roof.

'As you know,' Lassalle said to Richardson, having abandoned the idea of interviewing Chrysostome, 'I'm writing a chronicle of the journey, and I will, of course, mention your baptism. Why that sudden decision to abandon Protestantism and convert to Catholicism? Why now and not before? You've had plenty of time in which to convert. You're a veteran soldier, after all.'

Richardson burst out laughing and then led the journalist to a place where no one else could hear them.

'I'll tell you what happened, but you must tell no one else. You know Lopes, don't you? He's the young officer who was stationed in Angola before. Well, I don't know if you've noticed, but he's a real practical joker. He's always playing tricks on people. Anyway, when we were up there, hearing mass, he positioned himself behind me. And when the bishop asked those who had not yet been baptised to step forward, Lopes gave me such a shove that I took not one but two steps forward. There was the bishop beaming away at me. What was I supposed to do? Take a step back? Disappoint him?'

Richardson laughed again, wagging his finger.

'This story must go no further, mind.'

Lalande Biran was sitting in the prow of the boat, alone with Livo, and Lassalle's journalistic instincts impelled him to join them. The two men stopped talking when they saw him approach.

'You should definitely dedicate a few lines to Livo,' Lalande Biran said. 'Sometimes he thinks he has a brightness or a kind of vapour around him. Not like the steam coming out of the funnel on the boat, which is always white, but one that changes colour all the time. His *oimbé* – that's what they call it – takes on a different colour depending on his mood.'

'How interesting.'

And he wasn't lying, because, as a journalist, he found everything interesting, but he knew that what really mattered was the thing they weren't telling him.

'Livo and I have something we need to talk about, Ferdinand,' Lalande Biran said, thus confirming Lassalle's suspicions. 'We'll be back in Yangambi soon and, if you like, you can ask him about that luminous vapour then.'

'Of course. I'll interview you later, Livo, if I may.'

Livo had scratches on his face and would not meet his gaze. It seemed to Lassalle that Livo could not even see him, as if the *oimbé* to which Lalande Biran had referred stood between them. He gave no reply.

'Livo has some family problems, that's why he's looking so downcast,' Lalande Biran explained. 'The Twa are like that. If there's anything worrying them, they lose all heart. He's come to ask my advice.'

For the first time since he arrived, Lassalle felt like staying on in the Congo. His journalistic nose was telling him that there was some juicy bit of news there. What he had written so far wasn't bad, and he was sure that European readers would find his article interesting, but it lacked that special something, the pinch of salt that would lift the story off the page and into after-dinner conversations. In his article about the Foreign Legion, the story about the 'well-endowed soldier' with four balls had served that purpose, and was doubtless the 'pinch of salt' that had led to him winning the prize.

'I'd like to interview you in the Club Royal,' he said to Livo.

'It's probably best if I tell you about it, Ferdinand,' said Lalande Biran. 'As you can see, our man here is not feeling too well. I'll tell you tonight over supper, if you like.'

'Or some other day. I've decided to stay on in Yangambi. I'll leave on next week's boat.'

He himself was surprised by what he had just said, but it was done now.

'If you don't mind, that is,' he added.

The Captain's blue-gold eyes took on a special intensity.

'No,' he said, 'that's an excellent idea.'

Lassalle gave a discreet bow and returned to the stern of the boat. He sat down where Chrysostome had been sitting. There was no sun now. Thick clouds covered most of the sky.

'The most beautiful metaphor was provided by the statue of the Virgin,' he read in his notebook. Then he re-read his other notes and crossed out the sentence saying: 'Surprise: Richardson asks to be baptised.'

The words flowed easily from his pencil now, and he

reckoned that he would finish the description of the ceremony on Samanga before they reached Yangambi. However, just then, the boat started to sway and rock, and when he looked up, he realised that they were already at the point where the two rivers met, and were manoeuvring into shore.

The *Roi du Congo* left the main part of the river and, after passing between two islets, advanced in the direction of the Club Royal and turned towards the jetty. Ten *askaris* were standing on the beach and some raised their rifles in salute.

Lalande Biran waited for the bishop so that they could disembark together, and the other members of the expedition followed one by one. The beach filled up with people, as always happened when a boat arrived. On that occasion, though, the excitement was more muted. The officers, the *askaris*, the newly baptised youths, all seemed exhausted. Besides, the *Roi du Congo* was not bringing with it, as it usually did, boxes of biscuits or salami, still less alcoholic drinks. Its cargo was, so to speak, a spiritual one. They had managed to install the Virgin in her place.

Livo was among the first off the boat. He stepped down with the help of an *askari* and walked very slowly towards the Club Royal, as if he barely had the strength to put one foot in front of the other. On his shoulder, hanging from the pole, were the three reed baskets.

The last to disembark was Chrysostome. Holding his rifle in one hand, he jumped onto the beach without even getting his boots wet.

L'énigme de Chrysostome Liège. There was definitely something strange about him. If what everyone said was true, how was it that such a vigorous young man had remained as virginal as the statue they had left on Samanga? He thought of a good opening sentence: 'He's like a cheetah, yet he moves through the world as shyly as a hedgehog.' Not bad. However, as with all such enigmas, what mattered was its resolution.

XXII

CHRYSOSTOME HAD NEVER FORGOTTEN THE WORDS HE heard as a child from the parish priest in Britancourt.

'Cleanliness is the greatest of the virtues,' the priest told the children after their chance meeting with a syphilitic man who lived in one of the caves near the village. 'If a Christian keeps himself clean inside and out, he will develop an iron exterior that no enemy sword can penetrate.'

The priest was a lean man who, for many years, had worked as an army chaplain, and his forthright words made a great impression on them all. While the priest was speaking, it seemed to Chrysostome that he was looking at him in particular, as if addressing him directly. He felt proud of this, and that feeling of satisfaction only increased when the priest asked him to stay on after the talk.

'I am not a prophet like Daniel, but I believe that one day you will be a soldier,' the priest said. 'Listen, Chrysostome, if you keep yourself clean, abstain from drink and tobacco, you will be an astonishing marksman, a rifleman comparable to those in Napoleon's guard. You have amazed everyone with your extraordinarily sure aim with the sling, but if you want to be a real David and defeat the giant Goliath, then you must nurture that gift and encourage it to grow.'

The priest's words found a sweet, warm, snug corner in Chrysostome's heart, comparable, metaphorically speaking, to that found by birds' eggs in their nest. Up until then, there had been nothing remarkable about his life apart from being poor and having no mother, for she had died shortly after he was born, and he felt like a nobody. Then suddenly, there was the priest predicting that he would be a rifleman as good as those in Napoleon's guard!

A few days later, when the priest tied the blue ribbon of the Virgin around his neck, he promised himself that, one day, he would, indeed, be a soldier and become an excellent shot with a steady hand and a prodigious eye. He would always keep himself clean, and he would never fall ill with syphilis or any similar infection.

The blue ribbon sealed his promise.

Chrysostome worked on a farm in Britancourt from morning to night, and his arms and legs had grown strong from driving the oxen and the plough. At twelve, he had the muscles of a fifteen-year-old, and at fifteen, the muscles of an eighteen-year-old. When the other village boys quarrelled with him and punched him, they would immediately back off when their fists met with flesh as hard as iron, just as the priest had foretold. Chrysostome could even defeat the fittest of wrestlers. On one occasion, a soldier from a neighbouring village yelled an insult that had been doing the rounds among certain people in Britancourt, namely, that there was a reason the priest gave *him* such special attention. Chrysostome picked up first a stone and then his sling, and left the slanderer lying flat on his back on the ground, unconscious. No one dared provoke his anger after that, not even if they were the size of a Goliath, and people generally spoke well of him and took care to do so loudly.

Then one day, something changed. Chrysostome seemed depressed and cast down. As he walked from the fields to the farm and from the farm to the fields, he never once raised his eyes from the ground. The priest pondered what could be wrong. The boy was fifteen, and would soon turn sixteen. On the other hand, he had not been to confession for a month, whereas, normally, he never let a week pass without confessing. He knew then that Chrysostome was under serious attack, not from the other boys in Britancourt or anyone else who, so to speak, walked the same roads, but from the enemy within. He went to fetch his pupil and brought him back to the church.

First, they prayed, kneeling before the Virgin. Then they went through the main sacristy behind the altar into a second, older sacristy that served as a storeroom and where they kept the images of saints for which there was no room in the church.

In the old sacristy, the smell of damp mingled with that of faded flowers. Any other smells, the wild pinks growing along the edges of the fields, the mimosas in the orchards, the roses in the gardens, along with the scents of all the other flowers in the world, remained, as did the world itself, outside the church walls. The priest and Chrysostome were alone, surrounded by wooden saints.

The priest indicated the two saints nearest to them.

'This one here is St Luis Gonzaga. That one is St Sebastian,' he said.

The two saints had a tender look in their eye, but, unlike

Chrysostome, they were gazing heavenwards, not down at the ground.

Sebastian was tied to a tree and had arrows stuck in his body, which streamed with blood.

'You, too, can feel the pain caused by the sharp points of arrows, isn't that right, Chrysostome?'

Chrysostome kept his head bowed.

'Except, of course, your arrows come from within.'

The parish priest began pacing up and down between the two saints, his eyes half-closed, his breathing agitated. With each step he took, his cassock rustled, and every time he turned, it created a faint breeze.

Finally, he stopped, his clasped hands pressed to his chest. This was the same posture as St Luis Gonzaga, but the expression on the priest's face was quite different. His face was made of flesh, for a start, and much thinner than the saint's, and one could see the veins on his forehead and the lines on his cheeks. At last, he recovered his composure and was able to ask the question he needed to ask:

'Tell me the truth, now, do you masturbate?'

Chrysostome's head sank still lower, and the priest remained in that St Luis Gonzaga pose, waiting for his answer.

The answer was inaudible, but to the point. Chrysostome nodded. The priest sat down. He, too, had his head bowed.

'Sometimes the Lord's ways are very strange, Chrysostome. He gives us vigour, but the consequences of that vigour are not always pleasing to him and he punishes them. It was vigour that impelled Michel to go with women and, as you saw, the poor wretch ended his days as a prisoner to madness.'

Chrysostome was looking at him, uncomprehending.

'Michel was the man you saw in the cave, the one who was ill with syphilis,' explained the priest. 'He was a member of this parish and often received the Sacred Host from my hand. Then he became a soldier, and vigour drove him to visit unclean establishments, houses of ill repute. And, as you see, the Lord sent him a terrible punishment. As I imagine you know, shortly after you saw him in the cave, he was found drowned in a pool in the river. Now he will be in Hell.'

The smell of damp in the sacristy grew more intense, as did the silence. Had it not been for his eyes, Chrysostome could have been mistaken for another wooden saint, but his eyes had an ardour in them that wood never has. Indeed, at that moment they were like molten iron.

'Wait one moment,' the priest said, getting up.

He started rummaging around in a corner full of various bits and pieces, until he found a musket wrapped in a military cape.

'It's an 1867 Mauser, but it's in good condition. I tried it out myself not long ago. Ask your father to show you how to use it.'

Chrysostome stared at the weapon apprehensively, not daring to take it.

'You guessed correctly. It belonged to that poor unfortunate, Michel,' said the priest. 'But don't worry, you won't catch syphilis from it. On the contrary, it will protect you from the disease. Owning this weapon will remind you of what happened to him and of the beauty of keeping oneself pure.'

The bell began to toll, calling people to prayer. The priest handed the musket to Chrysostome, indicating that it was time for him to leave. The women of Britancourt always arrived very punctually at church, and he liked to be there at the altar, waiting for them.

'Yes, the Lord moves in mysterious ways. He gives us vigour and then punishes us for having it,' he said, as if still pondering the matter. A mischievous smile appeared on his face. 'However, I think in our case, there is a solution, and I'll tell you what it is, Chrysostome. The solution lies in . . . *pollutio*. Continue along that path. I wouldn't dare to say so in front of the Virgin, but both these saints, Luis Gonzaga and Sebastian, were soldiers and they won't be shocked by such manly talk.'

Like the two saints, Chrysostome now had his head raised. He wanted to know more.

'A minor or venial sin is always preferable to a grave one. Far better a daily *pollutio* than visiting a house of ill repute. And it's safer, too, Chrysostome. Don't forget that. Much safer. Are we in agreement?'

Chrysostome nodded and stored away that word *pollutio* like another small egg. Then, with the musket underneath his arm, he followed the priest out of the old sacristy, leaving St Sebastian, St Luis Gonzaga and the other wooden saints alone.

The priest did not use the word *pollutio* again until the time came for Chrysostome to say goodbye to Britancourt. He was twenty by then and setting off to Antwerp to do his military training and join the Force Publique. After six months in the barracks, he would leave for Africa.

They were standing outside the church, waiting for the

coach and talking about the Mauser, which Chrysostome was now handing back to the priest since he clearly wouldn't need it at the barracks.

'The partridges we Britancourt priests have eaten thanks to you and this Mauser!' said the priest. 'I've certainly never regretted giving it to you!'

Then, when he heard the jingle of bells announcing the arrival of the coach in the main street of the village, the priest spoke in a different tone:

'Do you have the blue ribbon with you, Chrysostome?' he asked.

Chrysostome undid the top buttons of his shirt to reveal his chest and the blue ribbon. The priest's face lit up with joy.

'Yes, wear it like that, Chrysostome, in full view! Let the other soldiers see that symbol of your purity! And at difficult times, remember, Our Lady is with you. And I will be praying for you too!'

The coach stopped in front of them. The priest embraced Chrysostome. He was not his son, but he loved him as if he were.

During his first year in Yangambi, Chrysostome did not lack for letters from the priest. Once a month, he would look in his pigeon-hole at the Club Royal and find an envelope with just one word on the return address: Britancourt. In a very firm, upright hand, the priest would bring him up to date on the village news, on the births and deaths, on how things were with his father – 'he's had a good crop of beet this year'; he would also summarise the sermons he had given and sometimes, along with comments about the weather, he would speak to him of flowers – 'there are a lot of poppies this year, some meadows are completely red with them'. The letters were quite long, and Chrysostome read them a little at a time. And with each reading, the words from his childhood nestled deeper down inside his heart. 'Cleanliness is the greatest of the virtues. If a Christian keeps himself clean inside and out, he will develop an iron exterior that no enemy sword can penetrate.' He also remembered the priest's other advice: 'The solution lies in . . . *pollutio*. Continue along that path.'

Thanks to *pollutio*, he kept himself healthy, pure, and maintained an iron exterior, quite unlike the other officers of the Force Publique stationed in Yangambi. Most of them were infected with some vile disease or other and had to turn to Livo, who gave them a plant called *olamuriaki*, which helped relieve the pain and discomfort. The worst afflicted were, as always, Richardson and Van Thiegel. On one occasion, after drinking heavily, Richardson had shown them his male member, exclaiming like a madman: 'What do you think of that, eh?' Chrysostome thought it disgusting, covered as it was in scabs and ulcers. And the Lieutenant, that loudmouth Cocó, was in an even worse state. His hands shook now, although it was hard to say in his case if this was due to excessive drinking or because he overdid the *olamuriaki*. And the fool thought himself a good marksman! Didn't he realise that the other officers let him win in the shooting competitions? Until, that is, Chrysostome came along, because he never played games and would never have allowed anyone to beat him, not even the King himself. If a man wanted to win, then he should improve his aim. He should live in purity and prudence. He should wear a blue ribbon around his neck.

Captain Lalande Biran was better than the other officers.

He avoided infection by having only virgins brought to
him, thus ensuring Donatien's health as well, because in
that respect, too, his assistant followed him as faithfully
as a dog. In other ways, though, Lalande Biran was a
strange man. Chrysostome would have liked to talk to
the priest about him, but when he tried to put his thoughts
down on paper, he couldn't. He found it hard to explain
exactly what the Captain was like. Livo said he was a
muano, a servant of the Devil, which is why he could be
two or three different men at any one time; it was why
his *oimbé* was always so murky. Perhaps Livo was right.
The Captain didn't drink much, but he smoked a lot; he
enjoyed swimming, drawing and writing poetry, and was
generous enough to be able to recognise other men's good
qualities. He had often told Chrysostome how much he
admired him as a marksman and said that when he returned
to Brussels, he would place him at the service of a duke
who held a high position at Court and was in need of
protection. Believing that the Captain respected him,
Chrysostome had felt profoundly disappointed when
Lalande Biran gave in to Van Thiegel's cajolings and sent
him off into the jungle in search of girls, as if he were
some twopenny-halfpenny officer, on a par with Donatien.
That order had been a hard blow to Chrysostome. He
went from thinking himself the best soldier in Yangambi
to feeling that he was the lowliest of servants. He would
have liked to talk to the priest about it, but found having
to acknowledge the degradation so shameful that he could
not write a single line. In the end, he told Livo, who gave
his usual response:

'The Captain is a *muano*. A great enemy.'

Livo put his fingers to his eyes to remind Chrysostome of Lalande Biran's blue-gold eyes, the eyes of a *muano*.

Life went on for Chrysostome with no great upsets, as long as he kept safely stored away, like eggs in a nest, the words engraved on his heart. Suddenly, though, the enemy's sword launched a fierce attack on him.

First, with one powerful blow, it snatched the priest from him. He received the priest's last letter shortly after winning the contest for shooting the most mandrills. 'The Lord is calling me,' the priest wrote in a hand that was no longer upright or firm. 'I will protect you from above. Goodbye, my child.' For the first time, Chrysostome thought about his life, about the twenty or so years he had been in the world, and a shudder ran through him. At night, clutching the gold medal of Our Lady in his hands, he would pray himself to sleep.

A few weeks later, the enemy's sword struck again. This was a far gentler attack, or so it seemed, but that only made it all the more dangerous, very dangerous indeed.

One day, on an expedition in search of another virgin for the Captain, Chrysostome came across Bamu. He noticed her at once. Her skin was cinnamon-coloured rather than the deep black of the tribes living near Yangambi, and she had green eyes. And her hair, although short, wasn't stiff and curly. The most surprising thing, from his point of view as a soldier, was her attitude. When cornered, she did not meekly bow her head, but grabbed a spear with her two hands and forced the *askaris* accompanying him to take a step back. A grey-and-red parrot flew out of its open cage onto the roof of the hut and started shrieking: 'Bamu! Bamu! Bamu!'

Chrysostome ordered the *askaris* to march on and leave the place as quickly as they could, but it was too late. The arrow, just one arrow, but far more lethal than all the arrows fired at St Sebastian, had pierced his heart. And its poison left him feeling confused, intoxicated, incapable of seeing what lay before him, incapable of hearing what the *askaris* were saying; he was, in short, in love. In his mind he heard the parrot shrieking: 'Bamu! Bamu! Bamu!'

When he returned to Yangambi, he tried to remove the arrow, but the poison was already flowing in his veins, and nothing could now stop the transformation that had begun in the jungle. He found Livo and asked if he knew a tall girl with light skin and green eyes.

'Bamu,' said Livo.

'Is she clean?' he asked.

'She is a child.'

Chrysostome gave a sigh of relief.

Livo had travelled, he had known many white men, and this question did not surprise him. The only thing that shocked him was Chrysostome asking him to act as intermediary, because he wanted to make a formal visit to Bamu and needed the consent of her parents to do this. Unbeknown to Livo, Chrysostome was following the customs of Britancourt peasants, not those of the soldiers of Yangambi.

'Are you going to send her a present?' Livo asked. He, in turn, was following African customs.

'I'd like to, but I don't know what to give her.'

'Send her a box of biscuits. I'll tell you which are my daughter's favourites. Bamu is sure to like them too.'

As the best marksman in Yangambi, Chrysostome did not have to go every day to keep watch over the rubber-tappers, because he needed time to check the other officers' rifles and keep them in tip-top condition. Taking advantage of these free moments, he started visiting Bamu, always taking with him a box of biscuits, and what was bound to happen happened; first, there were kisses and then caresses. So powerful was the effect of the sweet poison that he forgot the blue ribbon around his neck and the old words about purity, which had now been relegated to the remotest corner of his heart.

The number of his *pollutio* increased. Despite that, the danger continued to grow. On one such visit, Chrysostome gave Bamu some emerald earrings and she hurled herself at him, embracing him with arms and legs. This put Chrysostome in a terrible predicament, and only his condition as *commençant* saved him from plunging into sin.

Naturally, the Virgin was not about to give up the struggle, and that very day, as if fallen from Heaven, she appeared on the beach at Yangambi. Chrysostome saw her from the canoe, on his way back from visiting Bamu, and being utterly oblivious to everything apart from Bamu's existence, he did not even recognise her. He forgot that it was nearly Christmas and that they were expecting a delegation from Brussels. The canoe travelled a few yards downriver, closer to the beach, and then he understood. It was the Virgin, the statue they were going to place on the island of Samanga.

He saw in that apparition the hand of his parish priest. He had obviously wanted to keep the promise he made in his last letter – 'I will protect you from above' – and had placed that symbol of purity there on the beach, where she could best be seen.

When he reached her side, he knelt down and prayed.

However, even at that moment of devotion, the image of Bamu was still in his mind, and it was clear that *she* would never surrender either. Britancourt would fight its corner and so would the jungle. The priest would give him good advice, and so would Livo.

In the struggle that began inside him, sometimes it was the Virgin and all he had learned in Britancourt and from the priest that predominated, but at others, it was Bamu, the jungle and Livo who came out on top. When they set off upriver, for example, and placed the statue on Samanga and celebrated mass, it seemed that victory would go to the First Team, but as soon as the boat set off back to Yangambi, the Second Team – Bamu, the jungle, Livo – returned to the attack. And then, unexpectedly, Livo himself appeared. The *Roi du Congo* had to pick him up on the river bank, shortly before they reached the mouth of the Lomami.

By the time they reached Yangambi, the competing armies within were at stalemate, but he was troubled by the thought of Bamu waiting for his visit on the farther shore. When he saw Livo walking up to the Club Royal, carrying three baskets on a long pole, he considered talking to him about his dilemma. In the end, though, he didn't. Livo looked ill, and Chrysostome preferred not to risk infection.

XXIII

THE WORDS OF LALANDE BIRAN AND THE BISHOP MARKED
the end of the farewell meal held in the Club Royal
before the *Roi du Congo* made its return journey to
Léopoldville. The bishop declared that the statue of the
Virgin, the work of a new Michelangelo, was now safely
installed on top of Samanga, from where she would, in
future, protect all those who travelled the River Congo.
Lalande Biran emphasised how very pleased the Force
Publique were. It had taken them almost three whole days
to get there and back and they had seen not a sign of the
rebels. The Catholics of Europe and Léopold II's subjects
could rest easy. The kingdom was at peace.

Lalande Biran asked if anyone else would like to speak,
and Lassalle got to his feet to say that, as a journalist, he,
too, felt satisfied with his work, but that in his case, credit
was due, above all, to his assistant, Monsieur Kodak. If the
text was not up to much – and here he smiled – the photographs would ensure that readers in Europe and America
got a clear idea of what Africa was like.

'We journalists may occasionally tell fibs, but Monsieur

Kodak does not,' he concluded, smiling again. There was a ripple of applause.

Generally speaking, though, the banquet was a joyless affair. Despite the speeches and the toasts, despite the exquisite grilled fish that Livo and the other servants brought to the table, and despite the pains Donatien took to ensure that the champagne glasses were never empty, the atmosphere – the atmosphere's *oimbé* – remained a constant purple. Most of the visitors from Europe were impatient to get back on the boat and leave Yangambi; and the residents of Yangambi and the officers of the Force Publique could not wait to be left alone to resume their normal lives. At the top table, however, the *oimbé* was more black than purple due to the absence of Lieutenant Van Thiegel. His chair was empty. No one in Yangambi knew where he was.

'He's in the jungle on a routine patrol,' said Biran to the bishop. 'He has to make sure the surrounding area is free of rebels. The Lieutenant may tend to drink too much, but he's a responsible soldier.'

The bishop nodded.

'Are you sure he'll come back?' Lassalle whispered to the Captain. Richardson and he both knew what had happened with Bamu, and Lassalle had tried to interview Livo and corroborate what the Captain had told him, but without success.

'Who knows what that pig will do,' Lalande Biran whispered back as he removed the bones from his fish. '*Je ne sais pas ce que fera ce cochon.*'

'Let's eat this difficult but delicious fish in peace,' said the bishop, and his fellow guests at table agreed.

After the meal, and once the *Roi du Congo* had set off for

Léopoldville, Lalande Biran, Richardson and Lassalle walked up to Government House at such a brisk pace that Lassalle almost had to break into a run to keep up. Donatien followed behind with the coffee.

When they reached the Place du Grand Palmier, Lalande Biran paused to give instructions to the black NCO on guard. Then he took the tray from Donatien and went to join Lassalle and Richardson, who were waiting for him in Government House.

The three men drank their first cup of coffee in silence. When they were on their second cup, the black NCO reappeared at the door. Behind him came Chrysostome, flanked by two *askaris*, rifles at the ready.

After the usual exchange of salutes, Lalande Biran said very calmly to Chrysostome: 'I am obliged to lock you up in the dungeon. I ask you, please, to go down into the cellar.'

Chrysostome hesitated, and the *askaris* levelled their rifles at him.

'Please, don't put up a struggle,' Lalande Biran said, indicating the stone steps.

In the dim light of the cellar, which was lit by only one small window in the upper part of the dungeon wall, the *askaris* were struggling to get the key in the lock. Lalande Biran told them to leave, and he himself locked the door.

'I have to give you some bad news,' he told Chrysostome when they were alone. 'Your friend, young Bamu, is dead. Van Thiegel killed her while attempting to rape her.'

If Chrysostome made a gesture or a movement, however slight, Lalande Biran did not see it. The dust motes, visible in the ray of light coming in through that one window, continued calmly floating. A long way off, a monkey screamed.

Lalande Biran had prepared a speech inspired by the words Napoleon had spoken at the funeral of one of his soldiers. Apparently, the sorrows of love had driven the young man to commit suicide, and the Emperor wished to warn his comrades that hard battles were not only fought on the fields of Borodino or Marengo; emotional battlefields could, at times, be even more dangerous.

'I know full well, Chrysostome, that your beliefs would not allow you to kill yourself, and that you would be incapable of doing such a thing,' he was thinking of saying at the end of his speech. 'But I was afraid that when you heard the news, you would go straight out and kill Van Thiegel. And, as commanding officer of this military post, that is something I have to avoid. There are certain rules that all soldiers must obey. If you feel your honour has been compromised, then you can challenge Van Thiegel to a duel. The journalist from Brussels, Monsieur Ferdinand Lassalle, has agreed to be your second.'

But Chrysostome said nothing, thus depriving Lalande Biran of the chance even to begin his speech.

'Lieutenant Van Thiegel is at present in the jungle. He will return tomorrow or the day after,' Lalande Biran said.

In the dungeon, Chrysostome's breathing sounded a little louder than normal, but there were no other sounds. Silence also reigned in the living room of Government House, where Richardson and Lassalle were awaiting events.

'The Lord's ways are strange indeed,' Chrysostome said at last. 'Who would have thought that he would seek the help of that filthy drunk to save my purity?'

Lalande Biran was somewhat disconcerted.

'The Lord's ways may be strange, but not as strange as you,' he said after a pause. He forgot about Napoleon and his soldiers and suggested to Chrysostome the possibility of a duel. 'If you feel that your honour has been besmirched, then the best thing you can do is challenge Lieutenant Van Thiegel to a duel. The journalist from Brussels, Monsieur Ferdinand Lassalle, has agreed to be your second.'

'Fine,' said Chrysostome. 'It can be at two hundred yards or twenty, as he wishes. And if he prefers a machete to a rifle, that's fine with me too.'

'The seconds will sort out the details.'

Lalande Biran had already spoken to Richardson and to Lassalle about this. The duel would be with rifles, on the beach, and not on the firing range. The only other thing to be decided was the distance, although it would doubtless be the same as during the mandrill-shooting contest.

'You agree then. You're not going to go running off to find the Lieutenant,' he said, opening the dungeon door.

'I would like the duel to take place at the earliest opportunity,' said Chrysostome.

'It will take place as soon as the Lieutenant returns to Yangambi. On Sunday morning if possible.'

Richardson and Lassalle were surprised to see them come back up the steps together and they kept their eyes trained on Chrysostome until he had gone out through the door. Lalande Biran continued to watch him as he crossed the Place du Grand Palmier. He wanted to see how he behaved when he passed Van Thiegel's house. Chrysostome did not stop or look up or spit; he carried straight on to his own hut.

Lassalle wanted to know what had gone on in the dungeon.

'I thought he'd go mad when he heard the news and race off to find Van Thiegel,' Lalande Biran explained. 'That's why I decided to put him in the dungeon, so that he wouldn't do anything against army regulations. But, as you see, he remained perfectly calm.'

'The man is an enigma,' declared the journalist.

'What distance shall we put them at, Captain?' asked Richardson.

'What was it when we shot the mandrills?'

Richardson sighed. 'I think, in the end, it was one hundred and eighty yards, more or less, but as Cocó's second, I would ask for a shorter distance. Otherwise, Chrysostome will be at an advantage.'

Lalande Biran shook his head. 'No, one hundred and eighty is the minimum. Given that they will each have twelve cartridges, I imagine that at some point, they'll manage to hit the target.'

'As Cocó's second, I would prefer one hundred and twenty-five yards,' Richardson insisted.

He had just realised that the Captain was wearing his wedding ring, something he rarely did. Perhaps what Donatien had told him was true, that Cocó really had stolen an intimate photograph of the Captain's wife from his office. That would explain the Captain's stubbornness over the duel. It was a way of holding a firing squad, the only way. You couldn't shoot someone, still less a lieutenant, over a photograph.

Lalande Biran addressed the journalist.

'What do you think? I've given my opinion, but it's up to you really. You are his second, after all.'

'What about something in between, say, one hundred and fifty yards?' Lassalle suggested. 'But do you really think there will be a duel? Will Lieutenant Van Thiegel come back to Yangambi?'

'He's not a coward. He'll come back,' said Richardson.

'And if he doesn't, we'll go into the jungle to find him, then bring him back here and shoot him,' said Lalande Biran.

Richardson raised his coffee cup to his lips, but it was empty.

'All right,' he said, getting up. 'One hundred and fifty yards it is. And on the beach, right?'

'Yes. Speaking both as Chrysostome's second and as a journalist, I prefer the beach,' said Lassalle.

'I'll go and measure up,' said Richardson, and left.

XXIV

ON HIS WAY TO FETCH THE RUBBER-TAPPERS WHO HAD BEEN
left corralled in the jungle, Van Thiegel was barely in
control of himself because the two parts of his mind were
constantly arguing and he could do nothing to stop them. They
were quarrelling about Madelaine. One part insisted that
the girl was conquest 185, while the other kept impatiently
repeating 'No, no, no, no!' Then the disagreement between
the two parts grew more acrimonious.

'So that's 156 black women and 29 white women,' said
the first.

'No, 155 blacks and 30 whites,' the other retorted.
'Madelaine was more white than black.'

'No, you're wrong. It's 156 blacks and 29 whites!'

'No, 155 blacks and 30 whites!'

The *askaris* with Van Thiegel stared in amazement as he
slashed a path through the densest parts of the bush like a
true sapper, chopping down any lianas, brambles and roots
that got in his way. Such physical effort would have rendered
anyone else incapable of thought, but in his case the two
parties in dispute refused to surrender. Just when they

seemed about to reach agreement, they would start again, always at the same point:

'So that's 156 black women and 29 white women,' the first would say.

'No, 155 blacks and 30 whites,' the other would riposte.

The *askaris* eyed him warily. Van Thiegel kept shouting out, not like someone trying to urge on his men, but like a rabid monkey.

When the patrol finally reached the enclosure, they found the terrified captives all huddled together at one end. The black NCOs had to threaten them with the chicotte to get them to line up.

It turned out that the supply lines had failed, and no one had thought to bring provisions for the captives, leaving them both terrified and starving. When Van Thiegel saw the state they were in, a new discussion broke out inside his head. The first half argued that it wasn't worth wasting time looking for food when it would be far easier simply to abandon any rubber-tappers too weak to survive the march back to Yangambi; the second half replied that they couldn't just get rid of a group of men employed in the service of Léopold II, and, besides, it wasn't so very hard to find food in that part of the jungle. It would be better to take a couple of days longer, kill a few monkeys to feed the men, and then return with the group intact. Lalande Biran might be angry with him for leaving responsibility for the garrison at Yangambi in the hands of someone like Donatien and for taking four or five days to sort out a matter that could have been resolved in two, but the fault lay with Lalande Biran himself for having locked up a hundred or so rubber-tappers in the middle of the jungle without making any arrangements to keep them fed.

The hunt for monkeys brought Van Thiegel some rest, because it required all his concentration and left him so physically exhausted that he could at least manage to sleep. On the third day, however, the images inside his head began to proliferate, just as they did when he got drunk. Chrysostome, Lalande Biran, Donatien, Livo, his mother, his father, King Léopold, the legionnaire with the four balls, all of them and many more were there, visible, so to speak, to his inner eye. He feared that, as had happened on other occasions, the images would start to spin around on the roulette wheel, but this didn't happen, because the image of Chrysostome imposed itself on all the others: Chrysostome with the top three buttons of his shirt undone; Chrysostome with his blue ribbon and the gold chain he had received from Lopes in exchange for the cartridges; Chrysostome checking the time on the silver watch that Lalande Biran had given him for the rhinoceros horn.

At first, it seemed preferable and far less demanding to have a single image rather than an endlessly spinning roulette wheel of them. However, as the hours passed, he began to see its negative side. The image was telling him the truth, namely, that he was worried and afraid of Chrysostome. That's why he had fled Yangambi. That's why he'd persuaded himself that he really should go with the *askaris* to bring back the captive rubber-tappers, when the *askaris* could easily have done the job under the command of a black NCO.

There were no two ways about it. He was very frightened.

Chrysostome might not find out what had happened to his 'Madelaine' at once, but it would be, at most, a matter of a week before he did. Chrysostome would go to her village to visit her, the people there would tell him what had happened; then, naturally, the yokel would come after him to put a bullet through his head. If only he was a bad shot! But even he could not deny that Chrysostome was an exceptionally fine marksman. The man who had felled a cheetah and who, at a distance of nearly two hundred yards, had shot a mandrill through the head, would have no trouble killing him.

This was painful to acknowledge. He, Cocó Van Thiegel, who in his youth had served in the Belgian army, been a sergeant in the Foreign Legion, a lieutenant in the Force Publique, always ready to plunge into battle or join a party hunting for rebels, who, to put it bluntly, had never known fear, that same man now quailed before a mere yokel. He feared him. And this was not a new feeling, it had been there since the very first day.

His mind again split in two.

'You're shitting yourself over this,' said one half.

'I'm going to tell you what to do,' said the other half. 'Go back to Yangambi at night, creep over to Chrysostome's hut and cut his throat with a machete. End of problem.'

'And what if he's awake?' asked the first half.

The second half did not reply.

Van Thiegel gave the order for the black NCO to set off with the captives. They had to get back to Yangambi, they could wait no longer, and if any of the captives were still too weak, then it would be best to leave them where they were. When the NCO informed him that this would not be the case, that they could have started their return journey the day before, once the men had eaten their fill of monkey meat, Van Thiegel realised even more acutely what lay behind his behaviour. He resolved that he would not be made to look like a coward in front of Richardson, Lopes and the other officers. He must go back and kill Chrysostome as soon as possible.

For a moment, the mere thought of this made the rage he felt at his humiliation far stronger than his fear, and he clung to that feeling on the march back to Yangambi. His intense rage also meant that the image of Chrysostome faded somewhat and was replaced by an analysis of all the possible ways of killing him. How should he do it? The machete was, of course, an option. Another would be to go straight to Chrysostome's hut as soon as he reached Yangambi and make some mocking remark about his lack of manliness. Chrysostome, enraged by this insult, would immediately reach for his rifle, and Van Thiegel would shoot him, later alleging self-defence. He could also, of course, turn to Lalande Biran for help and make a clean breast of what had happened. 'Madelaine' had fought like a tigress, her parrot had kept screaming in the most irritating manner, and while he and Bamu were struggling, he had underestimated his own strength and inadvertently killed her.

'I know I was wrong, Biran, and I take full responsibility,' he would say, 'but if Chrysostome tries to exact his revenge, that will only make matters worse. Regardless of whether he succeeds or not, it will be a bad thing. We are both, after all, members of the Force Publique. Summon him, please, and tell him the punishment laid down in the military code for anyone who kills a colleague.'

The punishment was the firing squad. If Lalande Biran reminded him of this, Chrysostome would immediately understand the rules of the game.

They reached Yangambi that evening, and, having left the rubber-tappers in the hands of the *askaris*, Van Thiegel had supper with the black NCOs. Then, after dark, he walked over to his residence. No officer was to be seen in the main street or in the Place du Grand Palmier. They were probably all in the Club Royal.

He went into his bedroom, sat down on the bed and poured himself a glass of cognac. Of the various options, turning to Lalande Biran for help seemed the best one. It was the most sensible and the most militarily correct. Lalande Biran was his superior officer and, as such, was obliged to defend him. On the other hand, however cool a customer that yokel Chrysostome was, he would not want to die in front of a firing squad.

The thought of Lalande Biran brought with it the memory of Christine, and he picked up the pillow under which he had hidden her photo. It wasn't there. He put down his glass and looked underneath the bed. Nothing, only his boots and socks. He went into his office, knowing full well that he would not find the photograph there either. In a flash, he understood. Donatien had spent several days completely alone in Yangambi! *He* had taken the photo, there was no doubt about it. The dog was always poking his nose in where it wasn't wanted! The traitor!

He sat down at his desk. The photo would now be in Lalande Biran's hands. Matters, he realised, were getting complicated.

He sat waiting for Lalande Biran to arrive. He was

absolutely sure he would come. His only doubt was how the Captain would react. Would he mention the photograph straight away or launch into one of his speeches, talking about this and that, without coming to the point or giving any clue as to what form his revenge would take? If he did that, thought Van Thiegel, picking up the rifle on the desk to check that it was loaded, he would have no compunction about shooting him because the man had not yet been born who could play cat-and-mouse with him. Then, as Lalande Biran himself never tired of repeating, *alea jacta est*, the die would be cast. He would kill the Captain, he would kill Donatien, he would kill Chrysostome, and then he would hide in the jungle until things calmed down. He wouldn't be the first man to desert from the Force Publique. The only snag was that he would have to give up Christine and his dream of making her his woman number 200, but everything had its price.

He saw Richardson standing at the door of his office, as still and timid as a beggar come to ask for alms, his eyes fixed on Van Thiegel's rifle.

'What are you staring at?' Van Thiegel asked. Richardson's presence displeased him. He wanted to see Lalande Biran. And shoot him.

'We have to talk, Cocó,' said Richardson. 'Legionnaire to legionnaire.'

'You mean ex-legionnaire to ex-legionnaire.'

'As you wish, but we have to talk. Chrysostome wants to challenge you to a duel.'

Still keeping hold of his rifle, Van Thiegel gestured to Richardson to take a seat, then he took two glasses and poured them each a cognac.

'Let's have a drink,' he said. Richardson was still standing, and Van Thiegel asked him again to sit down. 'Now tell me everything – from the beginning,' he said, when Richardson finally did as he was asked. For once, Van Thiegel's mind was perfectly calm. It didn't feel as if it was about to split, even if only into two, and this gave him confidence.

'When Chrysostome found out what had happened to his girlfriend, it was as if he'd been bitten by a black mamba,' Richardson told him. 'It was as if he'd stopped breathing, as if he couldn't move his lips, as if the poison had entered his internal organs and was destroying them one by one and as if, at any moment, his skin would become covered in . . .'

Richardson paused, looking for the right word.

'Make it short, please,' Van Thiegel said. What Richardson was saying cheered him, but the way in which he was speaking reminded him of Lalande Biran.

'Then, suddenly, he regained the power of movement and started screaming like a madman. I mean it, Cocó, you've really hurt him. I've rarely seen a man so wounded. The Captain says the girl was his first love, which is why it's hit him so hard.'

Richardson paused again. He was holding his glass in both hands.

'You have to understand, Cocó. There was no alternative. The Captain tried to persuade him that there was no point getting upset over a native girl, but he wasn't having it. He wanted to come after you and kill you. Then the Captain proposed the duel, and he accepted.'

'Drink up,' said Van Thiegel.

Richardson drank his cognac down in one, then said, 'I'll

be your second, if that's all right with you. The journalist, Lassalle, will be Chrysostome's.'

'What form will the duel take? You haven't told me yet.'

'On the beach, with rifles. At one hundred and fifty yards. Tomorrow morning.'

'Tomorrow.'

'Yes, tomorrow.'

Van Thiegel filled their glasses again.

'One hundred and fifty yards. That's too far for me. As my second, you should never have agreed to that. Twenty yards would have suited me better. At least I would stand a chance of hitting him. That's what I'm going to find most annoying, that he'll manage to hit me, but I won't hit him.'

'I've asked that we stand at the Club Royal end of the beach, which would be best for you. That way, on Sunday at midday, you won't have the sun in your eyes. Chrysostome will.'

'What does that matter if he's wearing a hat!'

'I'll try to make sure he isn't, Cocó.'

Van Thiegel finished the cognac left in his glass, then yawned and stretched, saying: 'I'm going to bed. It was hard work bringing those blacks back from the jungle.'

'Just one more thing, Cocó,' Richardson said, standing up. 'In accordance with tradition, tonight, on the eve of the duel, a special supper is being held at the Club Royal. I'll be going, as will Lopes and the other officers on your side, about ten or twelve of us. I've spoken to Livo and it's all arranged.'

'What about the others?' Van Thiegel asked, grabbing the bottle of Martell again and drinking straight from it.

'Chrysostome didn't want any celebrations. You know what he's like.'

'Don't I just. A village yokel who doesn't even know what to do with a woman. Well, if he doesn't want to celebrate, neither do I. I'll get some rest so that I have a steady hand tomorrow.'

'As you wish. I'll gladly eat your supper for you,' said Richardson.

Van Thiegel went into his bedroom. When he undressed and got into bed under the mosquito net, he raised the bottle as if he were giving a toast, which was his way of saying goodbye to Richardson.

In his dreams, Van Thiegel thought he was back in the jungle and that a black NCO was stroking his chest. He tried to slap him, but the NCO dodged the blow and started touching his belly instead, moving his hand in circles as if to relieve a stomach ache, but he didn't have a stomach ache and the hand wasn't warm like his mother's. Again he tried to slap the man, harder this time, but the NCO was very quick and the blow struck empty air. For a few moments, the cold hand stroked his thighs and knees, then returned to his belly. This time, he attempted to punch the man, three times, each time in vain, because the NCO had excellent reflexes. Cursing, he felt behind him for his rifle, but it wasn't there. It occurred to him that the black NCO had stolen his rifle, which is why the bastard had the nerve to stroke his body with that cold hand of his. He knew the NCO, but had no idea he was a queer. Perhaps he was Chrysostome's partner.

When he woke, the morning light was coming into the bedroom. Before him, with half its body raised up, was a black mamba. It was a very strong specimen and its tongue kept nervously, ceaselessly, flicking in and out.

Van Thiegel felt a need to move his legs, but as soon as he bent his knees, the snake slithered down to his belly. Its skin wasn't just cold, it was rough.

He closed his eyes and very slowly lowered his legs. When he looked again, the mamba seemed even more nervous, its tongue moving frenetically.

Something crawled over his neck, something with tiny feet that tickled his skin. When it reached his arm, he saw that it was a mouse. The snake's mouth was wide open now and its head was swaying back and forth, as if the creature were making careful calculations before it attacked. The attack did not happen, though, and the snake continued to sniff the air with its tongue. What was it that smelled so strongly? Van Thiegel felt a glass object next to his right side, and his skin told him what it was before his nose did. It was the bottle of Martell, empty now, having spilled its contents. Now he understood. The snake was nervous because it could smell both the mouse and the cognac and found the unfamiliar smell of cognac confusing.

Van Thiegel could see his machete next to the bed, still in its case, hanging from the belt on his trousers. It was within reach, but making use of it would not be easy. He would have to lift the mosquito net, grab the machete and then strike.

The mouse was crawling back up his chest towards his neck. It seemed to be moving rather slowly and uncertainly, as if bemused by the snake's presence. Van Thiegel snatched it up in his hand and threw it to the snake as he might have thrown it to a dog. Then he raised his legs sharply and the mamba was hurled against the mosquito net.

When he grabbed the machete and cut off the snake's head, the mamba still had the mouse in its mouth, in the act of swallowing it. Van Thiegel gave a joyful whoop. It was his finest victory in a long time. Death had come looking for him, but now there it was lying on the floor of his room. Its tail continued to swish furiously in a last attempt either to propel itself forward or, perhaps, to swallow the mouse. But, as Lalande Biran might have said, there would be no more jungle for him, or for the mouse.

The swishing gradually slowed and when it finally stopped, Van Thiegel got dressed very slowly, laughing to himself. His mind never ceased to surprise him. That Sunday morning, a few hours before he was due to face Chrysostome, it was calmer than ever. It had not divided in two, there was no roulette wheel, nor did it insist on assailing him with painful memories.

He scooped up the snake on the blade of his machete and held it at waist height. The head dangled by a slender strip of skin. It was quite heavy. It must have had enough venom in its fangs to kill an elephant.

Richardson was sitting on one of the benches in the Place du Grand Palmier with two rifles by his side. He was asleep, and Van Thiegel approached very slowly. Twice the snake slid off the machete blade, and twice he patiently picked it up again.

'Watch out, Richardson!' he shouted.

When Richardson opened his eyes, Van Thiegel hurled the snake at his face and roared with laughter when he saw his colleague leap up from the bench and roll a few yards on the ground.

'You're too old to be on guard duty!' Van Thiegel told him.

Richardson had taken off his hat and was wiping his cheeks and forehead with the sleeve of his shirt. Beside the bench, the snake looked like the limp end of a whip. Its head had come off, the thread of skin that had kept it attached to its body finally broken.

'I haven't seen a mamba in years,' Richardson said, holding the snake's head between index finger and thumb. 'God, it's ugly! As ugly as you, Cocó!'

Van Thiegel was still laughing, and he laughed even louder when Richardson threw the snake's head at him, hitting him on the chest.

'I'm glad to see you so cheerful, Cocó! You look marvellous!'

'I have a feeling I'm going to give that poofter a surprise today.'

'What do you want to do, Cocó? We've got five hours before the duel.'

Van Thiegel picked up the snake, this time with his hand.

'I'm going to treat myself to a good breakfast,' he said. 'Do you like grilled snake?'

'I haven't eaten it for years, not since my days as a legionnaire. I can't even remember the taste,' said Richardson.

'Well, today, among other things, we will eat a little snake. Let's go and see if Livo can fire up the barbecue for us.'

Time, that morning, passed neither very quickly nor very slowly. It was as if the world had started turning to a regular beat – *au fur et à mesure* – and was imposing that rhythm on all beings, on the monkeys and the birds in the jungle, on the fish in the river, and – at a more elevated level – on the wind, the currents, the clouds and the sun.

Now and then, the mandrills and the chimpanzees screamed, neither very far nor very near; the *waki* flew tranquilly past, neither very high nor very low; the fish swam easily by, neither very deep nor very near the surface. The wind was stirring the leaves, but not the branches of the okoume, the teak and the palm trees. And the current in the river, although strong, was not dragging whole tree trunks with it, as it did in the rainy season. As for the clouds, to use a rather bolder figure of speech, they resembled leisurely steamboats, and the sun shone gently out of that same sky.

The inhabitants of Yangambi were the only beings not keeping to the general rhythm of that Sunday morning. Those in the village – Lalande Biran, Ferdinand Lassalle, Donatien, Chrysostome and the other officers, the black NCOs, and the *askaris* with their red fezes – were more silent than usual, and were nowhere to be seen; on the other hand, those in the Club Royal – Van Thiegel, Richardson, Livo and the other servants – were notable for the ruckus they were making.

On the club porch, Livo barbecued the snake lightly at first, to remove its skin, and then grilled it on a higher flame until its flesh was nicely golden. When he judged it to be done, he picked up a piece on his knife and offered it to Van Thiegel.

The other servants on the porch laughed when they saw Livo wrinkle his nose, because the snake had the same rank odour as chicken giblets.

Van Thiegel took a deep breath in, as if savouring the aroma, and there was more laughter. When he put the meat in his mouth, everyone fell silent. For a few moments, all action was suspended. Then Van Thiegel raced down to the river and spat the meat out, before returning to the porch, swearing and cursing, but laughing too.

'Livo, bring me some salami and biscuits. And coffee. And bring me any other tasty titbits you see in the storeroom,' said Richardson.

While they were eating, the rhythm of the world slowed still further. The mandrills and the chimpanzees fell silent, the *waki* vanished from the air, the fish swam down to the river bed, the clouds stopped moving, and the sun lost its strength.

'This is what I call eating,' said Richardson with a calm he did not feel in his heart. He had noticed the sun growing dimmer. Its rays would be no obstacle to Chrysostome. Cocó would have no advantage.

'Like kings, Richardson. I've heard it said that King Léopold II is mad for salami,' said Livo.

There was even less calm in his heart than in Richardson's. His *oimbé* was completely black. He was furious. He couldn't understand what had happened. The snake he had left on Van Thiegel's bed hadn't eaten for days, and the mouse was tipsy on the little drop of cognac he'd forced it to drink. Why had the snake not pounced on the mouse? Why had it not bitten the Drunken Monkey?

'Livo, bring me a bottle of cognac. It's time for a little drink,' Richardson said.

Livo went into the storeroom. He had hidden the baskets behind the boxes of biscuits. He spoke to the two remaining mambas.

'Your comrade was too stupid. The Drunken Monkey cut off its head with a machete.'

His *oimbé* grew still blacker. He picked up a bottle of Martell and returned to the porch.

'This is what saved me,' said Van Thiegel, snatching the bottle from him. 'The mamba was put off by the smell of cognac, and so I seized the moment.'

'We don't like his flesh, and he doesn't like our cognac,' said Livo.

The Drunken Monkey's words were showing him the way. He shouldn't have given the mouse any cognac. Or perhaps, he should simply not bother with a mouse at all and just empty the contents of the basket straight onto the victim's sleeping body. That's what he would do with Donatien and with the Captain. They might wake up and see the snake, but it was worth the risk.

Van Thiegel refilled his glass.

'Cocó, don't drink so quickly. I speak as your second!' Richardson said.

Livo had taken the charred snake skin and was rolling it up into two small balls.

'Livo, give me those,' Van Thiegel said. 'Say something to me, *légionnaire!*' he told Richardson, after putting the two balls in his ears. He had spoken more loudly than he intended.

'There's not much time. We need to try out the rifle,' Richardson said.

'Excellent! I didn't hear a word,' said Van Thiegel. 'I don't intend taking these out until our Captain has finished his speech. That, I'm sure, will be the most painful part of the duel.'

Richardson stood up.

'Come on, Cocó, let's go and try out the rifle.'

'The Lieutenant doesn't need any practice,' said Livo.

'Not in shooting, no, but there are three movements he has to perform before getting into position to fire, and the faster he can do them the better.'

'One last drink, Richardson,' said Van Thiegel, filling his glass again. He felt good; his mind was calm. The yokel was in for a surprise. He wasn't going to make those three movements. He would stand up, take one step back and fire, just like that, straight at Chrysostome's chest. Neither his blue ribbon nor any of his other fripperies would help him then. And if Lalande Biran tried to lecture him about fair play, for the benefit of that dwarfish journalist, he would shoot him too. And then, well, who knows.

Van Thiegel still had the snake-skin plugs in his ears when they walked onto the beach, and Richardson guided him to the centre. Chrysostome arrived almost at the same moment, accompanied by the journalist Lassalle. They stopped ten paces from each other.

Unable to hear, Van Thiegel could only see. Everyone in Yangambi was gathered on the upper part of the beach. In the first row stood his comrades – Lopes at one end, Donatien at the other, and Lalande Biran in the middle, standing slightly forward of them. Behind, in the second, third and fourth rows were the *askaris* and their respective NCOs. At the back, in some disorder, were the natives. The blue flag with the yellow star of the Force Publique seemed to hang heavy on the flag-pole. There was no movement, not a breath of air.

Lopes opened his mouth, and all the soldiers, the *askaris* with more brio than anyone, stood first to attention and then at ease. Afterwards, Lalande Biran began to speak, opening and closing his mouth vigorously and fluently. How the cuckold loved to talk! There he was on the banks of the River Congo, giving speeches, and there was Christine alone in Paris, hopping from one bed to the next, from one lover to the next. In the end, though, that woman would be his, because she had been born to be his woman number 200. Of that there was no doubt.

He turned towards Chrysostome, but his eyes alighted instead on the journalist, who was taking a photo with his Kodak. That Lassalle fellow was another poofter.

Van Thiegel stroked the barrel of his rifle and lifted it an inch or so from the ground. He felt its weight and felt, too, the weight of the twelve cartridges. The magazine was full. This was unusual. Usually in duels, each man had just one bullet, and if both men missed, then the matter was closed, and there was no loser. The magazines had clearly been filled on the orders of Lalande Biran. Both Van Thiegel and the yokel would have twelve shots. The cuckold obviously wanted to get rid of him. Well, he was going to be disappointed.

Richardson went over to him and touched his arm. Lalande Biran's mouth was closed. Chrysostome and the journalist were walking to the other end of the beach.

When Van Thiegel removed the plugs from his ears, he was surprised at how quiet it was, far less noisy than when he'd had them in.

'You're as good as dead, you poofter, you yokel!' he yelled.

Chrysostome, however, was too far away to hear all the foul words pouring from Van Thiegel's mouth. Cocó addressed Lalande Biran:

'Biran, if your champion misses, then you'd better start running!'

Finally, he spoke to the white officers, to Donatien in particular.

'And if he kills me, bury me with a bottle of cognac!'

'The sun is a little brighter now,' Richardson told him as he led him to his position.

XXV

VAN THIEGEL'S DEATH DID NOT CHANGE LIFE IN YANGAMBI.
The sole consequence was an argument that broke out
among various officers after he died. Some said that the
bottle of cognac that was to accompany him to the grave
should be empty, others that it should be full. In the end,
they buried him with the bottle he had been holding
shortly before the duel.

Ferdinand Lassalle was sitting writing on the porch of the
Club Royal, while he awaited the arrival of the *Princesse
Clémentine*. Richardson kept coming in and out of the storeroom, followed at all times by two servants. On the beach,
the *askaris* stood guard.

Lassalle raised his eyes from his notebook and looked
down at the river. The *waki* were flying very high now,
but he dismissed the idea of including them in his report.
They would not do as a symbol of the situation. If they
symbolised anything, it was his state of mind, because,
from where he sat on that porch, he was imagining his
destination, Brussels, as if Europe were a huge mountain

and Brussels were perched on top, and he found it hard to believe that he could set out from Yangambi on a steamboat and travel entirely on the flat, without soaring up into the sky.

He glanced across at Richardson. It was odd that he didn't realise he was stuck in a hole, neither he nor the other officers, nor the *askaris* in their red fezes or indeed anyone. It reminded him of the horses he had read about in a book by Zola. When visiting a very deep mine, the writer asked the miners how they managed to get the Percheron horses they used for transportation out of the mine, given that the animals were so large and the entrance to the galleries so narrow. One of the miners told him: 'Oh, we don't take them out. They're brought down here when they're only a few months old and then they stay here for good.' According to him, there was no reason to pity the poor beasts. The horses knew nothing else and had adapted to the world they inhabited.

Lassalle continued to write in his notebook:

After burying Van Thiegel, everyone wanted to know about the wound Chrysostome had sustained less than two inches from his heart. Livo explained that the bullet had only grazed his shoulder, and that he would be fine in a week, thanks to the ointment supplied by his tribal medicine woman. Young Chrysostome seemed saddened by the duel, because — and he said this two or three times — it was no way to resolve disputes between Christians. The Captain tried to reassure him. He had to bear in mind that the Lieutenant had changed, been poisoned, metamorphosed into a black mamba.

Completing this train of thought in his own way, Chrysostome showed us the medal on its blue ribbon and declared: 'Yes, it was a duel between the Virgin and the serpent, and, as always, the Virgin won.' His words brought a great feeling of peace to the hut in which we were gathered, giving us all a sense of breathing pure air. Then came the most moving moment of all. Lalande Biran took a small mother-of-pearl box out of his pocket and gave it to the wounded man. Since Chrysostome could not open it singlehandedly, the Captain himself offered to help. It contained two beautiful emerald earrings. 'I was aware how desperate you were to know where these earrings were, Chrysostome, because they were your engagement present to poor Bamu,' said the Captain. 'I feared that the serpent had snatched them from her when he committed his crime, and so I ordered Donatien to search for them. My assistant is very good at finding things, and here they are.' At last, after spending whole days plunged in gloom, Chrysostome smiled. And we smiled too. Donatien could not contain his feelings and, going over to Chrysostome, he clasped his hand.

Richardson came out onto the porch and sat down beside Lassalle. He sighed.

'It was Livo,' he said, his eyes fixed on the jungle before them. 'I've just found the proof in the storeroom. Three stinking baskets. He brought the snakes here in them. And there are ten boxes of biscuits missing, as well as loads of salami. It was obviously him.'

'I remember now,' said Lassalle, after an initial start of

surprise. 'When we were coming back from Samanga, he got onto the boat shortly before we reached the Lomami, and he had three reed baskets with him.'

'Yes, that sounds like them.'

'What are you going to do?'

'I don't know. Donatien knew where Livo's village was, but I don't. We'll see. But now I'm going to ask you a favour. I need you to help me write two letters. I'm not much good at writing.'

'Of course, with pleasure. Bring me some paper and envelopes, and we'll have it done in no time.'

'And a little coffee. The boat won't be here for another hour.'

Not wanting to leave his report half-finished, Lassalle returned to his notebook.

In the wounded man's hut, we all thought that the serpent had been crushed. We believed that the words repeated by young Chrysostome had come true, about the Virgin crushing the serpent. It was evening, the end of a difficult day, and we were all weary. After a light supper, we retired for the night. And lying in my bed, I was filled by the same peace I had felt earlier, in Chrysostome's hut. When dawn broke, however, that peace was shattered. The serpent had not been crushed and was intent on spreading its poison.

That noble soldier Richardson came to my hut to tell me that Lalande Biran was dying and would I please go to his side. On the way, I learned that Donatien had also died. Both had been attacked by black mambas. 'First, it was Van Thiegel and now it's the Captain and Donatien.

It's like a plague,' Richardson said to me as we entered Government House.

I found Lalande Biran close to death. His breathing was laboured and he kept trying to raise his hand to his throat, where he had been bitten. 'Say something, Captain,' I begged. It seemed important to me to capture his final words, the words of a great poet and a great soldier. He turned his aristocratic eyes to me. Grimacing and making a superhuman effort, the following unforgettable words sprang from his soul: 'I am going to the eighth house.' Now this would be an enigma to most people, but not to those familiar with the secrets of the Cabbala, because in astrology, the eighth house is the house of death.

Richardson had returned. He poured them both some coffee and set before Lassalle three envelopes and three sheets of paper.

'I actually need you to write three letters. My writing is terrible, which is why I'm asking you this favour,' he said. 'But first, let's drink our coffee.'

'Why not do both things at once,' said Lassalle, closing his notebook and taking up one of the sheets of paper.

'The first is to the Captain's widow, Christine Saliat de Meilhan,' said Richardson. 'The second is to a close friend of the Captain's, Duke Armand Saint-Foix. And the third is to the authorities in charge of the Force Publique, to tell them that I, Eric Richardson, am now in command at Yangambi, but that they should send a captain and a lieutenant as soon as possible. I'm far too old for this sort of thing. Besides, something tells me that the rebels could attack any day. Livo was probably one of them. Anyway, let's just hope Chrysostome gets better soon.'

The more he listened to Richardson, the more Lassalle wanted to leave Yangambi.

'Shouldn't you write to Donatien's family?' he asked.

'He seemed to have hundreds of brothers and sisters, but he wasn't in touch with any of them. Even at Christmas, the only letter he got was from the Force Publique. So that's one less job to do.'

By the time they had written the letters, the hulking shape of the *Princesse Clémentine* was filling the beach, and they were walking down to the wooden jetty together, Lassalle carrying a suitcase and Richardson his three letters. In the prow of the boat was a huge metal cage, like those used in zoos.

'Just what we need, a request for a lion,' said Richardson. 'Well, I have no intention of going hunting. Let them ask the company at Kisangani.'

When they reached the boat, Richardson flung his arms wide.

'What *are* they playing at!' he exclaimed.

The cage on the boat was not empty. Inside was a lion.

'I have no idea,' said Lassalle, although he preferred not to give the matter any further thought. He had quite enough material without having to open a whole new chapter devoted to lions.

A man wearing the insignia of the Force Publique came over to them. He, too, was carrying a letter. Lassalle realised then that Richardson's problem wasn't his writing, but his eyes. Unable to read the letter, Richardson passed it to Lassalle.

'What does it say?' he asked, in a voice that was more like a sigh.

Inside the envelope bearing the seal of the Royal Zoological Gardens of Brussels was a note explaining that they were sending them their oldest lion. They were doing this at the express wish of Léopold II's secretary, Duke Armand Saint-Foix, so that the lion could die a dignified death in the jungle as befitted the king of the beasts.

The cage was lowered onto the beach, and Richardson and Lassalle stood studying the lion. It tried to get up, but its back legs buckled beneath it.

'He wasn't so bad when we reached Matadi,' said the man wearing the insignia of the Force Publique, 'but this last part of the journey has pretty much finished him off.'

'It wouldn't even be any use as part of a shooting contest,' said Richardson. 'I can't imagine what Lalande Biran would have wanted with an old lion.'

'You know what poets are like,' said Lassalle. 'I imagine you're aware that Saint-Foix and Lalande Biran both figure in several Belgian poetry anthologies.'

'Well, I don't,' said Richardson angrily. 'And as soon as you leave, I'll finish the beast off.'

The lion did not move a muscle. It remained lying down, watching the men unloading the cargo.

Near the beach, a monkey screamed. The lion appeared completely oblivious. It seemed to be deaf.